The *Bounty* Sped Through Warp Space.

"Estimating planet earth, one point six hours, present speed," Sulu said.

"Continue on course," Admiral Kirk replied.

"Admiral, I'm getting something very strange," Uhura said. "And very active. Overlapping multiphasic transmissions . . . It's nothing I can translate. It's gibberish."

"Can you separate them?"

"I've been trying, sir. . . . Captain! They're distress calls. Maydays from starships, and—"

"Let's hear them!" Kirk said. "Have you got any visuals? Put them on screen."

The Maydays flicked onto the holographic viewing area: starships overtaken and drained by a huge spacegoing object that blasted their power supplies and sailed past at high warp, without answering their greetings or their supplications.

The blurry image of the president of the Federation Council formed before them. His message broke and dissolved, but Uhura had captured enough that its meaning could not be mistaken.

"This is . . . president of . . . grave warning: Do not approach planet earth. . . . To all starships, repeat: Do not approach!"

Look for STAR TREK Fiction from Pocket Books

STAR TREK: The Original Series

STAR TREK: The Next Generation

STAR TREK® IV

THE VOYAGE HOME

A NOVEL BY
VONDA N. McINTYRE

BASED ON PARAMOUNT PICTURES
SUPREME SPACE ADVENTURE!

Screenplay by
STEVE MEERSON & PETER KRIKES
and
HARVE BENNETT
&
NICHOLAS MEYER
Story by
LEONARD NIMOY
& HARVE BENNETT

POCKET BOOKS

New York   London   Toronto   Sydney   Tokyo   Singapore

An *Original* Publication of POCKET BOOKS

POCKET BOOKS, a division of Simon & Schuster Inc.
1230 Avenue of the Americas, New York, NY 10020

This book is published by Pocket Books, a division of
Simon & Schuster Inc., under exclusive license from
Paramount Pictures.

ISBN: 0-671-70283-1

First Pocket Books printing December 1986

16   15   14   13   12   11   10   9   8   7

POCKET and colophon are registered trademarks of
Simon & Schuster Inc.

Printed in the U.S.A.

STAR TREK® IV
THE VOYAGE HOME

Prologue

THE TRAVELER SANG.

Amid its complexities and its delicate, immensely long memories, it sang. In the complete cold of deep space, the song began at one extremity, spun in circles of superconducting power and speed, and evolved. It culminated in the traveler's heart, after a time counted not in micromeasures, but on the galactic scale of the formation of planets.

The traveler sent each finished song into the vacuum. In return it received new songs from other beings. Thus it wove a network of communication across the galaxy. Oblivious to the distances, it connected many species of sentient creatures one with the other.

From time to time it discovered a newly evolved intelligence to add to its delicate fabric. On those rare occasions, it rejoiced.

On much rarer occasions, it grieved.

The traveler followed a long curve, spiraling inward

from the perimeter of the galaxy to the center, then spiraling outward again. It traveled through eons, embroidering its course with the music of intelligences.

The touch of the songs gave it a joy that held its single vulnerability. It was immune to the radiation of exploding stars. It could protect itself against any damage by mere matter. But if any of its threads of communication parted, grief and agony possessed it.

When the song of one of its entities changed from delight and discovery to distress and confusion, pain and fear, the traveler listened, it decided, and it gathered up the tremendous energy it needed to change its course.

Singing reassurance, the traveler turned toward the other side of the galaxy, toward a small blue planet circling an ordinary yellow sun.

Admiral James T. Kirk paced back and forth in a vaulted stone chamber, ignoring the spectacular, sere view spanning one entire wall. Vulcan's red sun blazed outside, but the retreat of the students—adept of the discipline of ancient thought—remained cool, shielded by the mountain from which it was carved.

"Relax, Jim," Leonard McCoy said. "You won't get to see T'Lar any faster by running in place. You're making me tired."

"I don't care if I see T'Lar or not," Jim said. "But they've had Spock practically incommunicado for three days. I want to be sure he's all right before we leave."

"Whether he is or not, there isn't much you can do about it now." The doctor managed a wan smile. "Or me, either, I suppose."

"No," Jim said gently. "You did your part. You saved his life." Jim worried about McCoy almost as

2

much as he worried about Spock. The doctor's exhaustion troubled him. Even a quick flash of McCoy's usual wit, a snap of irony, would ease Jim's concern.

"Are we leaving?" McCoy asked. "You've had word from Starfleet?"

"No. But we've got to return to earth. At least, I do. I have to answer for my actions. For disobeying orders. For losing the *Enterprise*."

"You won't be alone," McCoy said.

"I don't want anybody to try to be a hero for my sake!" Jim said. "I bear the responsibility—"

"Who's talking about taking responsibility?" McCoy said. "I'm talking about getting off Vulcan. Jim, this damned gravity is squashing me. If I have to live in it much longer, I'll turn into a puddle of protoplasm."

Jim laughed. "That's more like it, Bones."

"Kirk. McCoy."

A young Vulcan stood in the doorway.

Jim stopped laughing. "Yes? Do you have news of Spock?"

"I am T'Mei. I will take you to T'Lar."

She turned, her long dark robe brushing softly against the stone floor. She wore the deep blue of a student of the discipline. Only once, many years ago, had Jim met any other Vulcan as fair as she, with blond hair and blue eyes and a golden-green cast to the skin.

"I'll just wait here and you can tell me all about T'Lar afterward," McCoy said.

T'Mei glanced back. "McCoy, it is you, not Kirk, that I am requested to guide."

"What does she want?"

"I am her student, not her interpreter."

"Come on, Bones," Jim said. "I'm sure T'Lar will satisfy your curiosity."

3

"I've had about as much curiosity as I can take right now, thanks just the same." But he pushed himself from his chair. Grumbling under his breath, he followed T'Mei down the long corridor. Jim accompanied them.

The Vulcan student ushered them to a chamber, then silently departed. Jim and McCoy entered the presence of the discipline's high adept.

Though T'Lar had divested herself of the ceremonial garments of the rite of *fal-tor-pan*, neither the effect of her personality nor her power depended on the trappings of her rank. Even in a plain green robe, her white hair arranged severely, the elderly Vulcan emanated dignity and authority.

"We have examined Spock," she said without preliminaries. She spoke to McCoy. "The transfer of his *katra*, his spirit, is complete."

"Then he's all right," Jim said. "He's well again, he can—"

When she glanced at him, he fell silent. She returned her attention to McCoy.

"But you, McCoy, were not properly prepared to accept the transfer. I have determined that he retains certain elements of your psyche, and certain elements of his personality and his mind remain in your keeping—"

"What!" McCoy exclaimed.

"I will continue to facilitate the transfer between you, until it is complete." She rose. "Please come with me."

Beside Jim, McCoy stiffened.

"What are you saying?" Jim said. "That Bones has to go through *fal-tor-pan* again? How much do you think he can take?"

"This has nothing to do with you, Kirk," T'Lar said.

"Anything concerning my officers has something to do with me!"

"Why must you humans involve yourselves in matters you cannot affect?" T'Lar said. "I will create a simple mind-meld. In time, the process will permit Spock and McCoy to separate themselves."

"In time?" McCoy said. "How long is 'in time'?"

"We cannot know," T'Lar said. "The refusion of the *katra* with the physical body has not been attempted within historical memory, and even in legend the transfer proceeded from Vulcan to Vulcan."

"What if I prefer not to undergo another mind-meld?"

"You will cripple Spock."

"What about McCoy?" Jim said.

"I think it likely that the force of Spock's psychological energy will once again possess McCoy, as it did when he held Spock's *katra*."

McCoy grimaced. "I don't have much choice, do I?"

"No," T'Lar said. "You do not." She gestured toward a curtained entrance. "The facilitation room. Come."

McCoy hesitated. Jim moved to his side.

"Kirk," T'Lar said, "you must stay behind."

"But—"

"You cannot help. You can only hinder."

"What's to prevent me from following?"

"Your concern for the well-being of Spock and McCoy."

"It's all right, Jim," McCoy said. T'Lar led him into the facilitation room. They disappeared into the darkness beyond the curtain. Nothing but a drape of heavy fabric held him back.

Jim paced the anteroom, fuming.

McCoy followed T'Lar into the facilitation room.

5

Spock waited, his expression dispassionate. He wore a long white Vulcan robe, so different from the uniform in which McCoy was used to seeing him. Otherwise he looked the same, black hair immaculately combed, short bangs cut straight across his forehead. His deep-set brown eyes revealed nothing.

"Spock?"

McCoy had known the Vulcan, who was also half-human, for a long time. But Spock neither spoke to him nor acknowledged his existence. He did not even quirk one upswept eyebrow. His human side seemed more deeply suppressed than it had for many years.

T'Lar beckoned to McCoy. Neither power nor accomplishment had endowed her with patience. Spock lay down on a long slab of granite. Its crystalline matrix sparkled in the dim light. McCoy paused beside an identical slab, glaring at it with antipathy.

"Haven't you people ever heard of featherbeds?" he said.

Neither T'Lar nor Spock responded. McCoy hitched himself onto his slab and lay on the hard stone.

T'Lar placed one hand at McCoy's temple and the other at Spock's. An intense connection entwined all three people. McCoy flinched and closed his eyes.

"Separate yourselves," T'Lar whispered hoarsely, "one from the other. Become whole again . . ."

Jim waited impatiently. He was used to being in control. He was used to acting. He was not used to cooling his heels and having his questions put off.

Intellectually he understood what T'Lar had told him. He, and they, and most of all Spock and McCoy, were involved in a unique occurrence. Only in legend had a dying Vulcan given up his *katra*, his spirit, yet lived to reclaim it. Spock's death and regeneration in the Genesis wave gave the Vulcans a challenge they had not faced within their history.

Both McCoy, who unknowingly accepted Spock's *katra*, and Spock, who must reintegrate his memories and his personality with his physical self, had been in extreme danger.

"Admiral Kirk?"

Jim started, rising to his feet.

"Admiral Cartwright!"

The new Commander of Starfleet entered the anteroom. Cartwright offered his hand. Jim shook it warily.

"What are you doing on Vulcan?" Jim said.

"I came to talk to you, of course. I want to know what happened straight from you, not from reports or gossip or even from Harry Morrow. You left him one hell of a mess to end his tenure."

"And to begin yours."

"It comes with the job. But I've got to know what happened, and you're going to have to tell the story to the Federation Council."

"I know."

"How soon can you leave Vulcan?"

"That I don't know."

"I don't mean this as a polite request. You've already disobeyed enough orders to hold you for the rest of your career."

"I didn't have any choice. I asked for Harry Morrow's help and he refused it. Sarek's request—"

"Sarek should have made his request through regular channels."

"There was no time! Leonard McCoy was going mad, and Spock would have died."

"I didn't come here to argue with you," Cartwright said. "You and your people have caused an enormous amount of trouble. I can't vaporize the charges

7

against you. Much as I might like to deal with this within Starfleet, it's gone too far for that. The Federation Council demands your presence. So far, all anyone is talking about is an inquiry. If you come immediately, an explanation may suffice. If not, you'll face a criminal trial."

"On what charge?" Jim said, shocked.

"The murder of Commander Kruge, among other things."

"Murder! That's preposterous. I tried to get him off Genesis and he tried to pull me into a pit of molten lava! Kruge invaded Federation space, he destroyed a merchant ship, he instigated espionage, he destroyed the *Grissom* and everyone on board! He killed David Marcus—" Jim's voice faltered.

"I know." Cartwright's voice softened. "I know you're grieving. I'm very sorry. But you must return to earth and tell your side of the story. If you refuse, the assumption will be that you've no answer to the Klingon Empire's claims."

"I can't leave Vulcan. Not yet."

"Why not? When *can* you leave?"

"Because McCoy—and Spock—are still in danger. I can't leave Vulcan until I know they're all right."

"It's hardly abandoning them to leave them in the hands of the Vulcans. They'll be in the care of the finest medical technologists in the Federation. What more do you think you can do?"

"For Spock, I don't know. But McCoy—it isn't medical technology he needs. He needs support. He needs a friend."

"Leonard McCoy has many friends," Cartwright said. "I'm sure he has one who can stay with him who isn't under indictment."

"I'll come to earth as soon as I can," Jim said.

"Then I have to give you this." Cartwright drew out a folded paper and handed it to Jim.

"What is it?" It was thick, ragged-edged paper, heavy with a Federation seal. The Federation only used paper for the most formal of purposes.

"A copy of the inquiry order."

Jim broke the seal and scanned it. "I'm still not coming."

"You're disobeying a direct order, Admiral Kirk." Cartwright's brown eyes narrowed and his dark face flushed with anger.

"Yes," Jim said, equally angry. "And it's easier the second time."

"I've done all I can for you," said Starfleet Commander Cartwright.

His second's hesitation gave Jim Kirk one last chance to concede. Jim said nothing. Scowling, Cartwright turned and stalked from the anteroom.

Jim cursed under his breath. He shoved the order into his pocket and paced impatiently. In one more minute he was going to rip down that curtain—

The drape rustled. Haunted and drained, McCoy stood in the entryway.

"Bones?"

"It's over . . . for the moment."

"Haven't they completed the process?"

McCoy shrugged.

"Is something wrong?"

"Vulcans jump up and walk away after a mind-meld," the doctor said. "I shouldn't be any different, right?"

Jim smiled. "Right."

McCoy fainted.

McCoy slept. Jim sat at the foot of the bed, rubbing the bridge of his nose. McCoy suffered merely from exhaustion, the Vulcans said. The doctor would recover in time for the next facilitation session. When that might be, or how many more sessions might be required, they could not answer.

Jim rose, silently left McCoy's room, and returned to his own. He sat down at the communications terminal, made a request, and waited with both impatience and dread for a reply. Even the technology of the twenty-third century took a few moments to route a call from Vulcan to earth.

The "please wait" pattern on the screen of the comm unit flicked out, replaced by the pattern of Carol Marcus's household computer concierge.

"Dr. Marcus cannot reply at this time," the concierge said. "Please leave identification and location so she may return your call."

Jim took a deep breath. "This is Jim Kirk again."

He had been trying to call Carol Marcus since the morning after his arrival on Vulcan. Every time, he had failed to reach her. By now she must know of the death of her son David. It both relieved and distressed Jim that he would not be the one to tell her. But he had to talk to her.

"It's extremely urgent that I speak with Carol," he said. "Please have her call me as soon as possible."

"She will receive your message." The pattern faded.

Jim rubbed his eyes with the heels of his hands. He had barely known the young man, yet David's death affected him as if a piece of his heart had been ripped away and burned to ashes. It would almost have been easier—

Easier! he thought. No, nothing could make it easier. But if I'd known him, I'd have at least the comfort of memories of Carol's son. My son.

* * *

Carol Marcus sat cross-legged on the observation deck of the courier *Zenith,* staring down at a glittering green planet.

"Dr. Marcus." The ship's computer voice glided easily over the intercom. "Dr. Marcus. Please prepare to beam down."

Carol rose reluctantly.

It would be so easy, she thought, so easy just to stay on board and keep traveling from world to world and never have to talk to anyone, never risk getting close to anyone again, never have to tell anyone that a person they love has died . . .

She left the observation platform and headed for the transporter room.

Carol Marcus felt it her duty to speak to the families of her friends and co-workers on the Genesis project. And so she found herself orbiting a world known familiarly as Delta, the home world of Zinaida Chitirih-Ra-Payjh and Jedda Adzhin-dall, two mathematicians, two friends who had died.

The casket bearing Zinaida's body stood on the transporter platform. Jedda had died by phaser, and nothing at all remained of him.

Carol stepped onto the platform. She did not know what she would say to the people waiting below. She had not known what to say to the parents of Vance Madison or the families of the others. She only knew she had to control her own grief so she would not add it to the grief of others.

"Energize," she said.

The beam took her to the surface of Delta. A rosette of light surrounded her. A dazzling stained-glass window cast colors across the reception room's pale slate floor.

Two Deltans waited for her, a woman and a man, Verai Dva-Payjh and Kirim Dreii-dall. *Partners* was the closest word in Standard to describe the relationship of these two people to Zinaida and Jedda. They had formed a professional and economic and sexual partnership that should have lasted for decades.

They approached her. Like most Deltans, they were supernaturally beautiful. Verai, heavyset and elegant, had mahogany skin, pale eyelashes, and fair eyebrows like the most delicate brush strokes of a Chinese painting. Unlike Deltan women, who grew no hair on their heads, Kirim had fine, rose-colored hair. He wore it long and free, spilling in great waves over his shoulders and down his back nearly to his knees. The red mark of mourning on the forehead of each did nothing to detract from their beauty.

Carol blushed. Human beings could not help their response to Deltans; nevertheless the powerful sexual reaction embarrassed her. Deltans never took advantage of humans, always holding themselves aloof. But Verai and Kirim approached her more closely than Zinaida or Jedda ever had. Verai offered Carol her hand. Carol stepped back in confusion.

"You have not been in contact with earth," Verai said.

"No. Not since I left."

The stained-glass window cast patterns over them. Verai and Kirim grasped her hands. She had never been touched by a Deltan before. Both grief and comfort flowed into her.

"I'm sorry," she said. Tears sprang to her eyes. "Your partners—"

"We know," Verai said. "And we are grateful that you came to us. We will speak of them, and remember them. But we must speak of someone else as well."

Holding Carol's hands, Verai and Kirim told her of the death of her son.

Shocked speechless with grief and horror, Carol sank to the floor and stared at the window's light. The pattern crept across the floor with the motion of the sun. In the warmth of the hall she started to shiver.

"Come with us, Carol," Verai said. "We will grieve for our partners, and we will grieve for your son."

In a visitors' chamber of the habitation, Lieutenant Saavik of Starfleet also failed to reach Carol Marcus.

Perhaps, thought the young Vulcan, Dr. Marcus will never speak to me or to anyone else who participated in the Genesis expedition. She must know of David's death by now. It is possible that she has no wish to be reminded of it by those who witnessed it.

She rose from the terminal, left her room, and stepped onto a balcony that overlooked the plain at the foot of Mt. Seleya. After so many years and so much hope, she finally found herself on Vulcan, beneath its great scarlet sun. She hoped that the Vulcans would permit her, a half-Romulan, to remain long enough to walk in their world's deserts and explore its cities.

She returned to the cool shadows of the habitat. Loud footsteps approached. One of her human shipmates, no doubt; Vulcans moved more quietly.

"Fleet commander!" she said, surprised.

Blinking, the new commander of Starfleet brought his attention back from somewhere else. The tall, black-skinned officer carried a compact travel case. He looked both angry and in a hurry. Yet now he stopped.

"You are Lieutenant Saavik, are you not?"

"Yes, sir."

"Do you know where the transporter is? My ship's about to warp out of orbit."

"Certainly, sir. I will show you."

He followed her deeper into the maze of stone corridors.

"You handled yourself well on Genesis, lieutenant," he said. "You won't be named in the indictment."

"The indictment, sir? Surely Admiral Kirk and his shipmates aren't to be punished for saving Spock's life!"

"I hope not. Despite everything, I hope not."

"I, too, am alive because of the admiral's actions. Had Admiral Morrow permitted him to depart for the Genesis world without delay, the science vessel *Grissom* and all hands might have been saved as well."

"It isn't your place to second-guess the Commander of Starfleet," Cartwright said. "The Genesis project was a disaster, but your part in it was fully admirable. That won't be forgotten, I promise you."

"I do not look for credit from these events," she said. "Too many people lost their lives. A survivor should not gain benefit." Especially, she thought, a Starfleet officer who survived because of the death of a civilian.

They reached the transporter room. Cartwright programmed in a set of coordinates and climbed onto the platform.

"Nobody will get much benefit out of Genesis," Cartwright said grimly. "But that isn't your concern. I'll trust you to comport yourself as well during your Vulcan assignment as you did on Genesis. Good-bye, lieutenant. Energize."

"What Vulcan assignment?"

But the computer responded to his command; the transporter beam swept Cartwright away before he could hear her question, before he could reply.

Perhaps Cartwright simply meant her time on Vulcan until new orders arrived from Starfleet. But he had sounded like he meant something more.

Surely Admiral Kirk would know. Perhaps he would have a moment to explain.

She knocked at the entrance of the admiral's chamber.

"Come."

She pushed aside the curtain.

James Kirk stared disconsolately at the comm terminal's disconnect pattern. It occurred to Saavik that he, too, must have been attempting to contact Carol Marcus. He, too, must have failed.

She hesitated. The question of her assignment seemed trivial now. She saw the indictment order lying crumpled on the desk. At least she did not have to tell him that news.

"Yes, lieutenant?" He glanced at her. His expression held the pain of loss and uncertainty, the kind of pain that could only be eased with knowledge.

"Sir," she said hesitantly. "May I speak with you?"

"Certainly, lieutenant." He rose.

"It is about . . . about David."

He flinched. "Tell me."

She wanted to say, I should have died in his place. I am a member of Starfleet, and he was a civilian, and I should have protected him. I could have protected him, had he not acted when he should have restrained himself.

But for all Saavik's uncertainty about human beings and their often incomprehensible emotions, she knew as surely as she knew anything that she could not help James Kirk accept his son's death by saying he should not have died.

"David died most bravely, sir," Saavik said. "He saved Spock. He saved us all . . . I thought you should know." She also wanted to say, I loved your son. He taught me that I am capable of love. But that was not something a junior lieutenant could say to a flag officer of Starfleet, nor was it something someone trying to be a Vulcan should ever admit to anyone. She kept her silence.

James Kirk did not reply in words. His hazel eyes glistened. He gripped her shoulders, held tight for a moment, then dropped his hands.

Saavik slipped past the curtain and left him alone. She could do nothing more for his grief.

Captain Hikaru Sulu climbed into the Klingon fighting ship. The sharp, acrid smell of seared plastic and fused electronic circuits permeated the air. He entered the command chamber. He had managed to nurse the bird all the way to Vulcan, but it would never take off again without repairs. Maybe it would never take off again at all. He settled into the command chair, tied a universal translator to the computer, and requested a complete set of damage reports.

Salvaging the fighter is worth a try, he thought. And if I succeed, I'll have a ship. A ship of my own.

Amanda Grayson listened to Spock reading out loud from a fragile bound volume of ancient Vulcan poetry. She wanted to touch him, to reassure herself that he was alive.

He paused. "Reading out loud is very slow, mother. And the words of this piece are archaic."

"Try to hear the beauty in them, my dear," she said. "No one on Vulcan writes poetry anymore. Those lines are a thousand years old."

"If no one writes poetry, why must I read it?"

"Because I didn't read it to you when you were a child. We have another chance, and I won't make the same mistake twice. I want you to be able to enjoy beauty and poetry and laughter."

He cocked his eyebrow, a heartbreakingly familiar gesture. Moment by moment he crept back toward himself. But Amanda wanted to take this second chance to help him release his other half, the half of himself that he had always held in check.

"Beauty and poetry and laughter are not logical," Spock said.

"I agree," she said. "They are not."

He frowned, puzzled. He read another stanza, stopped, and closed the book.

"I am tired, mother," he said. "I will meditate. I will consider what you have said."

Chapter One

THE TRAVELER ACCELERATED to a tremendous speed, but the galaxy spanned an enormous distance. The traveler perceived that its journey had lasted for only an instant. But in that instant—the mere time of a half-life of the minor isotope of the eighteenth element, the brief interval in which a small blue planet would revolve around its ordinary yellow sun three hundred times—the troubled music from that blue world ripped apart into incoherence. The songs faded, and finally they died. Now the traveler hurtled toward the silence, its own song a cry. As the stars sped past and it received no response, it gradually transmuted its music into a dirge.

The Romulans might come raiding out of the Neutral Zone at any time.

Captain Alexander stared at *Saratoga*'s viewscreen and into the silent Neutral Zone. Three months on yellow alert was bad for anyone's nerves. She was as jumpy as the rest of her crew, but she could not admit it.

It had been like this ever since the Genesis disaster. Diplomats, Starfleet, the Federation, the shadowy oligarchy of the Klingons, even the mysterious Romulan Empire reacted to Genesis by exciting themselves like electrons in a plasma of mutual suspicion.

Subspace communications brought each day's proceedings of the Genesis inquiry to every ship and starbase. Everyone had an opinion about Admiral James T. Kirk's actions, his motives, his ethics.

When the inquiry returned its findings, the Klingons might disagree with the conclusions. They might go to war. If that happened, Alexander must be prepared, for the Romulans, their allies, to join them. So far, though, the inquiry served the interests of the Klingons much more efficiently than open conflict.

Alexander could not understand why Kirk did not return to earth to defend himself. It was as if he had surrendered without fighting, as if he did not care whether the inquiry condemned or vindicated him.

"Captain—"

"Yes, lieutenant."

"I'm receiving—" Suddenly, with a curse, the *Saratoga*'s Deltan science officer snatched the earphone from his ear. Sgeulaiches, the communications officer, yelped in pain and pulled the transmission membrane from its vibratory sensors.

"Mr. Ra-Dreii! What happened?"

"A transmission, captain, of such power that it overcame the volume filters. A rather stimulating experience," he said with irony. He listened to the earphone gingerly.

"Source?"

"The Neutral Zone, captain."

"The Romulans?"

"No. Nor the Klingons, unless they have completely altered their communications signature."

"Visual sensors."

"The energy density hinders localization," Sgeulaiches said.

Watchful excitement tingled along Alexander's spine.

"Volume filters back in service and intensified, captain," Chitirih-Ra-Dreii said.

"Let's hear it," Alexander said.

The transmission's cacophony filled the bridge.

"The universal translator—" Chitirih-Ra-Dreii said. He abruptly cursed again, using an epithet far up the hierarchy of Deltan curses. Deltans did not even bother with minor curses. "Overloaded, captain. Useless."

The gibberish bucked and broke over the speakers.

Alexander felt more excited than angry. This might make the months of patrol worthwhile. Every starship captain possessed the ambition to make a first contact: an encounter with something new, something unknown.

"I want to see our guest, Lieutenant Sgeulaiches," Alexander said. "And send out a universal greeting. Let them know we're here."

"Yes, captain."

Alexander detected no change in the wailing noise, no indication that the transmission's source detected her transmission, no acknowledgment of the *Saratoga*'s presence.

"Found it, captain! Maximum magnification."

An object caught starlight and flung it out again. All the information the sensors could glean about the object—damned little, Alexander noted—appeared in a stat window in the corner of the viewscreen. Alexander whistled softly. Whatever the object was, it was big.

"Evidence of Romulan ships?"

"None, captain."

Alexander frowned. "They should have seen that thing. They ought to be pursuing it. They ought to be accusing us of sending intruders into their territory. Where *are* they?"

The object approached.

"Helm—wait for it." This whole business reminded Alexander a little too strongly of the *Kobayashi Maru* test.

"Aye, captain," the helm officer said. The *Saratoga*'s impulse engines countered the ship's momentum.

"Overlay."

An information overlay dimmed the primary image on the viewscreen.

If the object remained on its current course, it would intersect the system of an average yellow star, Sol, the system of Alexander's home world, earth.

"Cancel," she said stiffly. The overlay dissolved. The intruder was much closer now.

The surface of the long, cylindrical construction erupted here and there with antennae. The construction's metallic skin bore a brushed finish. Or . . . a shiny finish had been dulled by eons of space travel, touched by micrometeoroids or stroked by stellar winds perhaps once a year, once a century, till a uniform pattern of microscopic scratches created its velvety skin.

"What do you make of it?"

"It appears to be a probe, captain," the science officer said. "From an intelligence unknown to us."

"Continue transmitting," Alexander said. "Universal peace and hello in all known languages. And get me Starfleet Command."

"Starfleet, captain."

"Starfleet Command," Alexander said, "this is the starship *Saratoga,* patrolling sector five, the Neutral Zone. We are tracking a probe of unknown origin on apparent trajectory to the Solar system. We have attempted first contact on all frequencies. We have received no intelligible response and no acknowledgment."

"Continue tracking, *Saratoga.* We will analyze transmissions and advise."

"Roger, Starfleet," Alexander said. "Relay transmissions."

The science officer relayed a copy of the probe's transmissions back to Starfleet. His sardonic smile as much as said, "Analyze away, and see what *you* make of it."

"*Saratoga* out," Alexander said.

"Range four hundred thousand kilometers and closing."

The ship reverberated with the probe's transmission. The bridge lights faded.

"Mr. Ra-Dreii, what's causing that?"

"Captain, their call is being carried on an amplification wave of enormous power."

"Can you isolate the wave?"

"Negative. It's affecting all our systems—"

The dim half-intensity illumination flickered as the probe's cry plunged through the *Saratoga* and overwhelmed it.

"Red alert," Alexander said calmly. "Shields up. Helm, reduce closing speed."

"Captain, our impulse engine controls have been neutralized!"

22

"Emergency thrusters." This was going the *Kobayashi Maru* test one better. Or one worse.

"No response, captain."

The probe plunged toward them. The volume of its transmission increased, as if the probe could grip the fabric of matter and space-time itself and force it to vibrate to its will. *Saratoga* quivered.

All power failed.

"Emergency lights!" Alexander shouted over the impossible scream of the probe.

In the feeble scarlet glow, the officers wrestled to win some reaction from deadened controls. The viewscreen wavered into a blurry half-intensity image.

"Damage report!" Alexander snapped.

"Captain, all systems are failing," Chitirih-Ra-Dreii said. "We are functioning on reserve power only."

The enormous bow of the probe plowed toward them. Its body stretched back endlessly.

"*Saratoga* is out of control," Alexander said. "Secure for collision."

The probe's immense length flashed past, just above the upper curve of *Saratoga*'s hull. It left them behind in a sudden silence and dimming scarlet light.

It headed toward earth.

"They've finished us," Chitirih-Ra-Dreii whispered, his voice hoarse. "And we don't even know why, we don't even know what they want."

"Give me whatever you've got on the emergency channel," Alexander said. "Mr. Ra-Dreii, prepare stasis."

The signal strength hovered at such a marginal level that Captain Alexander might drain the last of *Saratoga*'s reserves and never get through to Starfleet. But she had no choice.

"Starfleet Command, this is *Saratoga*," Alexander

said. "Can you hear me? Come in, please. Starfleet Command, come in." She paused, hoping for a response but receiving none. "Any Federation ship, Mayday, Mayday. Please relay this message to Starfleet. Earth is in danger. Repeat—"

The air grew heavy with exhaled carbon dioxide. Chitirih-Ra-Dreii and Engineering struggled to restore the life-support systems, but failed. Alexander ordered the rest of her crew into stasis and repeated the message of danger till the signal strength fell to zero.

The Federation did not reply.

Sarek of Vulcan stepped from the transporter center into the cool, damp brightness of earth. He could have beamed directly to Federation headquarters, but he preferred to make his way on foot. On any world where conditions permitted, he chose to walk in the open air and on the open ground. In this way he could make himself familiar with a new environment. This was something Amanda had taught him. He often wondered why Vulcans did not habitually do the same thing, for it was quite logical.

Sarek had expected never to return to diplomatic service after his retirement. He had never expected to visit earth again. But now, two journeys in three months disarranged his contemplative existence. He had made his first voyage to accuse James Kirk. He made this voyage to defend him.

The planetary government of Vulcan had come perilously close to forbidding the second voyage. Sarek had to delve deep into his reserves of logic and persuasion to win their agreement. Many members of the government claimed no interest in James Kirk's fate; they offered Sarek the hypothesis that since Kirk had neutralized a series of events that he himself had begun, a balance had been reached. Kirk must face the consequences of his actions alone. If Vulcans acted, the balance would be destroyed.

Perhaps, Sarek thought, the charge Representative T'Pring made is correct. Perhaps I have spent too much time on earth. I have certainly, in the eyes of other Vulcans, spent too much time in the company of human beings, or at any rate in the company of one human being. Yet I cannot imagine following any other path for my life, and, at the end of our debate, even the flawlessly logical sword-edged blade of T'-Pring's mind finally turned to my persuasion. She argued on my behalf.

As he walked, he reaccustomed himself to earth's low gravity and weather conditions. Fog, gathering beneath the catenaries of the Golden Gate Bridge, crept through the streets and flowed around the hills. Sarek drew his cloak around him, marring the fine pattern of condensation that collected on the heavy fabric.

Sarek arrived at Federation headquarters moments before he was scheduled to speak. In the foyer, Commander Christine Chapel hurried to meet him.

"Sarek, thank you for coming."

"I left Vulcan as soon as I was able after your message arrived. Do the findings of the inquiry still go against James Kirk and his shipmates?"

"It isn't going well for him. For any of them." She sounded worried. "He's made a lot of friends in his career. But a lot of enemies as well. There are people—outside the Federation, and in it too—who would like to see him brought down."

"But he saved Spock's life, and the life of Lieutenant Saavik," Sarek said. "Furthermore, he acted on my behalf and at my request. It is preposterous that he should be punished."

"Sir," Chapel said, "you've made enemies too."

"It is illogical," Sarek said. "But it is true."

"Mr. Ambassador, has Spock recovered?"

"He is recovering. However, the experience is not without effect. He has undergone changes, but he is Spock."

"I'm glad," she said.

Sarek followed Chapel into the surprising darkness of the council chamber.

A harsh glare flashed over the stepped ranks of seats and turned the councilors' varied complexions a uniform scarlet. The floor, the very air, shook with a subsonic rumble. On a holographic screen above the chamber, a violent explosion roiled and rumbled.

A thunderous voice filled the room. "All the members of the boarding party perished horribly in this Federation trap. All but one of Commander Kruge's heroic crew died by a devious hand, and Commander Kruge himself was abandoned, to perish on the surface of an exploding planet!"

The holographic image faded. The only light remaining radiated upward from the witness box, illuminating the flushed and angry heavy-featured face of Kamarag, the Klingon ambassador to the United Federation of Planets. Sarek had encountered Kamarag before. He knew him as an obdurate opponent.

A great starship appeared above Kamarag: the *Enterprise*, bright against a background of black space and multicolored stars. A second explosion filled the chamber with the actinic light of warp engines gone critical. Beside Sarek, Commander Chapel gasped. The nictitating membranes flicked across Sarek's eyes, protecting him from a glare that caused most of the sighted beings in the chamber to blink and murmur. When their vision cleared, they saw what Sarek observed: the destruction of the *Enterprise*. The battered ship struggled against its death, fighting to stay in the sky, but another explosion racked it, and another, and it fell from space into atmosphere. It glowed with the friction of its speed. It burned. It disappeared in ashes and in flames.

Distressed, Chapel turned away.

How very like a human, Sarek thought, to grieve over a starship.

"But one fatal error can destroy the most sinister plan," Kamarag said. "The mission recordings remained in the memory of our fighting ship! Officer Maltz transmitted them to me before he, too, died. Did he die, as the Federation claims, a suicide? Or was it convenient to eliminate the last objective witness?"

The image of a small band of humans appeared. The mission recorder focused on the face of James Kirk.

"There!" Kamarag shouted. "Hold the image! *Hold!*"

The image froze: James Kirk gazed at his dying ship.

"Observe!" Kamarag said in a low and dangerous voice. His brow ridges pulsed with anger; his heavy eyebrows lowered over his dark, deep eyes. "The quintessential devil in these matters! James T. Kirk, renegade and terrorist. He is responsible for the murder of the Klingon crew and the theft of their vessel. But his true aims were more sinister. Behold the real plot and intentions!"

One image of James Kirk dissolved into a second. The new image, uniformed, calm, well groomed, gazed out at the audience.

"To fully understand the events on which I report," Kirk said, "it is necessary to review the theoretical data on the Genesis device."

A complex diagram glowed into being.

"Genesis is a procedure by which the molecular structure of matter is broken down, not into subatomic parts as in nuclear fission, or even into elementary particles, but into subelementary particle-waves."

The diagram solidified into a torpedo, and the torpedo arced through space to land on a barren world. The effect of the device spread out from the impact like a tidal wave of fire, racing across and finally covering the rocky surface of the planetoid. When the glow faded, stone and dust had become water and air and fertile soil.

"The results are completely under our control," James Kirk said. "In this simulation, a barren rock becomes a world with water, atmosphere, and a functioning ecosystem capable of sustaining most known forms of carbon-based life."

Sarek knew about the Genesis device. He did not need to watch its simulation. Instead, he observed the councilors. Most had known little if anything about the secret project. They reacted with amazement or shock or silent contemplation, depending on their character and their culture.

"Even as the Federation negotiated a peace treaty with us, Kirk secretly developed the Genesis torpedo. This dreadful weapon, disguised as a civilian project, was conceived by Kirk's paramour and their son. It was test detonated by the admiral himself!"

Kamarag waited for silence among the agitated councilors. Sarek gathered his own energy. The holographic screen contracted upon itself, squeezing its image to nothingness. The chamber's lights rose.

"James Kirk called the result of this awesome

energy the 'Genesis Planet.' A gruesome euphemism! It was no more and no less than a secret base from which to launch the annihilation of the Klingon people!" He paused again, letting his outrage affect the council chamber. He drew himself up. "We demand the extradition of Kirk! We demand justice."

"The Empire has a unique point of view on justice, Mr. President," Sarek said. He strode into the chamber and descended the stairs. "It is not so many years past that the Empire recognized James Kirk as a hero, and honored him for preventing the annihilation of the Klingon people. One must wonder what political upheaval could have changed their opinion so precipitously."

"It is Kirk who changed!" Kamarag clamped his fingers around the edge of the lectern and leaned toward Sarek, fixing him with an expression of hatred and fury. "From concealing his treachery to exposing it, as Genesis proves!"

"Genesis was perfectly named," Sarek said. "Had it succeeded, it would have meant the creation of life, not death. It was the Klingons who drew first blood while trying to possess its secrets."

"Vulcans are well known," Ambassador Kamarag said coldly, "as the intellectual puppets of the Federation."

"Your vessel did destroy U.S.S. *Grissom*. Commander Kruge did order the death of David Marcus, James Kirk's son. Do you deny these events?"

"We deny nothing," Kamarag said. "We have the right to preserve our species."

"Do you have the right to commit murder?"

The councilors and the spectators reacted to Sarek's charges. Sarek stood in silence, unaffected by the noise rising around him. The president rapped the gavel.

"Order! There will be no further outbursts from the floor."

After quiet returned, Sarek mounted a dais and faced the council president. This put his back to Ambassador Kamarag. It was an action both insult and challenge.

"Mr. President," Sarek said, "I have come to speak on behalf of the accused."

"This is a gross example of personal bias! James Kirk retrieved Sarek's son." Kamarag's voice grew heavy with irony. "One can hardly blame Sarek for his bias—or for letting his emotions overwhelm a dispassionate analysis."

Sarek ignored the retaliatory insult. His attention remained on the council president. He refused to be distracted by Kamarag's outbursts or by the whispers and exclamations of the councilors. During his many years away from Vulcan, Sarek had learned that such reactions to an altercation did not necessarily indicate the intention to interfere. However high the technologies of their worlds, however polished their educations, most sentient beings could easily be diverted from important issues by the promise of entertainment. And a fight between Ambassador Kamarag and Sarek of Vulcan would be entertainment indeed.

Sarek greatly preferred the Vulcan way. Perhaps the council president had also studied Vulcan methods, for he remained calm until the uproar subsided.

"Mr. Ambassador," the president said to Kamarag, "with all respect, the council must deliberate. We will consider your views—"

"You intend to let Kirk go unpunished," Kamarag said, his tone low and dangerous.

"Admiral Kirk has been charged with nine violations of Starfleet regulations—"

"Starfleet regulations!" Kamarag snorted with disgust. "This is outrageous! There are higher laws than Starfleet regulations! Remember this well: there will be no peace as long as Kirk lives."

He swept down from the witness box and strode from the council chamber. In the shocked silence that followed his ultimatum, the heels of his boots thudded loudly on the polished floor. His security guards surrounded him; his staff snatched up their equipment and hurried after him.

Disturbed, finally, by Kamarag's reaction, the president turned his attention to Sarek. "Sarek of Vulcan, with all respect," he said. "We ask you to return Kirk and his officers to answer for their crimes."

The president's request told Sarek much. The inquiry would find that charges were justified. James Kirk and his friends would face court-martial.

Kirk and the others had risked their careers and their lives at Sarek's request. They had willingly gone through an ordeal that most of the beings in this chamber could not even imagine. This was their reward.

"With respect to you, Mr. President," Sarek said evenly. "There is only one crime: denying James Kirk and his officers the honor they deserve."

The president hesitated, as if hoping Sarek might relent. Cold and silent, Sarek met his gaze.

An aging sun gave the planet Vulcan its two simple constants: the appalling heat, and the dry red dust. The climate wrung Jim out. The atmosphere's scanty oxygen forced humans to take a maintenance level of tri-ox. Tri-ox made Jim almost as lightheaded as oxygen deprivation. He supposed that at least it caused less neuron loss.

For all their long civilization, Jim thought, Vulcans

31

never bothered to invent air conditioning. I wonder what logic explains that?

Near sunset, Jim crossed the plain at the foot of Mt. Seleya and paused by the Klingon fighting ship. In the long shadow of its swept-wing body the temperature fell a few degrees, but the inside of the ship would be an oven. He and the others worked on the ship at night. During the day they slept in the relative coolness of the mountain habitat, they did what work they could outside the Klingon fighter, and they worried. No one second-guessed either Jim's choice or their own decisions. But everyone worried.

Jim worried most about McCoy. Whatever the facilitation sessions were doing for Spock, they drained McCoy more completely as they progressed.

He heard a scraping noise above him. He went back outside and tried to see the dorsal surface of the ship from the top rung of the ladder.

"Who's there?" he called.

"Just me."

"Bones? Are you all right?" He chinned himself on the edge of the wing and climbed onto the ship. He was hypersensitive to any hint of odd behavior on McCoy's part, but he tried not to show it.

"T'Lar says Spock doesn't need any more facilitation sessions," McCoy said, without turning around. He sat back, regarded his handiwork critically, and made one last stroke with his paintbrush.

Jim looked over McCoy's shoulder. The doctor had struck out the Klingon identification script; above it he had spelled out "H.M.S. *Bounty*."

"We wouldn't want anybody to think this was a Klingon ship, would we?"

Jim chuckled. "You have a fine sense of historical irony, Bones."

"Jim, I think we've been here just about long enough. How about you?"

"Not just about long enough. Too long." He gripped McCoy's shoulder. "And everyone's had long enough to consider the question. We'll vote tonight."

They climbed down again. At the top of the ladder, Jim took a long breath, let it out, and entered the ship. The heat closed in around him. By dawn the temperature would be nearly tolerable. James Kirk was accustomed to living in the perfectly controlled environment of a starship. Back home he lived in San Francisco, a city with an even and moderate climate.

"I'm *never* going to get used to that smell," McCoy said.

The heat intensified the pungent, slightly bitter odor of the materials of an unfamiliar technology.

"It isn't that bad," Jim said. "You never used to be this sensitive to unusual smells."

"Don't tell me how I've changed, Jim," McCoy said. "I don't want to hear that anymore." His good mood vanished. "I've got work to do in sick bay." He disappeared down the corridor.

Jim walked down the long neck of the Klingon fighter to the command chamber. The differences far outnumbered its similarities to the *Enterprise*. He and his officers had all taken a crash course in the obscure dialect of Klingon in which the controls were labeled. Bits of tape with scribbled reminders littered all the consoles. Chekov's mnemonics were in Russian. Sulu's were in three different languages, only one of which used the Roman alphabet.

Jim sat at Uhura's station and glanced over her notes, which were in Standard. He turned on the system.

"Vulcan communications control."

"James Kirk, requesting subspace to Delta. Private channel, please."

"Subspace channels are blocked with heavy interference. Please try again at a later time."

Jim cursed softly. His every attempt to contact Carol Marcus had met with failure. Perhaps she was avoiding him, out of grief or out of fury. Or both. He remembered what she had told him the first time he and David had met: "You have your world, and I have mine. I wanted David in my world."

Her reluctance had been justified. James Kirk's world was wondrous and dangerous. In seeking out the wonder, David encountered the danger. It destroyed him.

Jim envied Carol's knowing the boy. What would his own life have been like, if he had been told about David and invited to participate in his childhood? But he had not. He had never known David as a child; no one would know David in his maturity.

Jim treasured his few memories of the arrogant and intelligent and sensitive young man who had been his son. He grieved for David's death and for lost chances.

At sunset, Jim cleared his throat, straightened his shoulders, and rose. It would be all too easy to withdraw into his grief. But he still had responsibilities, even if the end of his responsibility turned out to be leading friends to the ends of their careers, or worse.

He climbed down the ladder and waited for the officers of the destroyed starship *Enterprise* to gather.

Montgomery Scott was the first to straggle across the plain toward the *Bounty*. The chief engineer appeared exhausted. He had not been himself since the destruction of the *Enterprise*—nor had anyone in the group, but the starship's last mission had hit Scott particularly hard. He lost his beloved nephew, Peter Preston, during Khan Singh's suicidal attack. Then he lost his ship. Scott was chief engineer of the *Enterprise* before Jim took command and after flag rank took Jim away from starships and from space. Jim could hardly count the times Scott had pulled some mechanical or electronic rabbit out of an invisible hat to keep the *Enterprise* from certain destruction. This time Scott had done more than fail to save the starship. He had concurred in its annihilation.

"Good evenin', admiral," the engineer said.

"Hello, Scotty. Don't go in yet. We'll vote tonight."

"Aye, sir."

They waited. Pavel Chekov and Commander Uhura crossed the plain together. As they approached, Pavel, the youngest of the group, made another in a series of jokes about serving on ore carriers. The evening wind ruffled his dark hair. As collected and cool as always, Uhura managed to smile at Chekov's joke.

"We vote tonight," Jim said. Serving on an ore carrier was perhaps the best they could hope for. Even Chekov's usually irrepressible sense of humor crumbled.

As for Uhura, Jim could not tell what she felt or what she thought. During their entire three months on Vulcan, she had never revealed any discouragement. More than once, her strength and certainty had kept the group's morale from bottoming out.

Sulu ran toward the ship from the other side of the plain. Sweat plastered his straight black hair to his forehead.

In choosing to help Jim fulfill Sarek's request, the young captain had given up more than anyone else.

Had he remained on earth, he would now have his own command. The starship *Excelsior* had been taken from Sulu and given to another officer because of James Kirk. Sulu had never voiced a word of regret over the choice he had made.

During their exile, Sulu had begun studying a Vulcan martial art. Tonight, as he approached, Jim saw a new bruise forming on Sulu's wrist. The Vulcans described the art as meditative. Jim had watched one training session, and he considered the art brutal. Concerned about his officer, Jim had suggested two months ago that Sulu might consider getting more rest. Sulu replied in the most civil terms imaginable that Admiral Kirk should mind his own business.

And Sulu had been right. Now he looked as elemental as the blade of a saber, as if he had deliberately tested himself, seeking and finding a point beyond regret or fear. Vulcan's heat and gravity had purified him to essentials, and tempered him to steel.

McCoy climbed down the ladder. The group was complete.

"Have you all decided?" Jim said.

"Is nothing to decide, admiral," Chekov said. "We return to earth, with you."

"How do you know I'm planning to return?" Jim said.

At that, even Uhura looked shocked. "Admiral!"

"I bear the responsibility for what's happened," Jim said. "No, don't object. If I return alone, Starfleet may choose to overlook the rest of you. If I don't return, they may concentrate on finding me and leave you in peace. At the embassy back on earth, Sarek granted Uhura asylum. The Vulcans will never break that promise. If any of the rest of you request it, I'm certain Sarek will arrange your protection."

"And spend the rest of our lives learning logic on Vulcan?" McCoy said. "Not likely."

"Any of you who wish it could take the *Bounty* to one of the colony worlds, out by the boundary, where people don't ask too many questions."

Chekov laughed. "Even on boundary, sir, people would ask questions of human people flying Klingon fighter. Even disguised as it is." He gestured toward the ship's new name.

McCoy snorted. "Come on, Jim, enough of this. You're not about to become a colonist—or a pirate— and we all know it. Let's vote."

"Very well," Jim said. "All those in favor of returning to earth . . ."

Sulu raised his hand. His motion was like a challenge, not a gesture of defeat. McCoy and Uhura and Chekov followed his lead. Finally, listlessly, Scott joined the others.

"Scotty, are you sure?"

"Aye, sir, I just . . . I just keep thinkin' . . ."

"I know, Scotty. I know."

Jim, too, raised his hand. He gazed at each of the others in turn, then nodded.

"The record will show," he said, "that the commander and officers of the late starship *Enterprise* have voted unanimously to return to earth to face the consequences of their actions in the rescue of their comrade, Captain Spock." He hesitated. He tried to express his gratitude for their loyalty, but the words would not come. "Thank you all," he said, his voice tight. "Repair stations, please."

At first no one had believed the ship would fly again. At the beginning, Scott vehemently denied any possibility of making the ship spaceworthy. Sulu gracefully argued him into a challenge that interested him enough to put at least a hairline crack in his depression. Throughout the endeavor, Scott alternated between bleak despair at the monumental task and grim determination to conquer all the difficulties.

Every time they solved one problem, another came up. Now Jim understood how the captain of an eighteenth-century sailing ship must have felt, stranded in the New World, thousands of miles from home, attempting to repair a broken mast or a stove-in hull. But Jim could not go into the forest, cut down a tree, and fashion from it a new piece of equipment (Vulcan had no forests, in any event, and the citizens protected the few ancient trees that remained); he could not repair the hull, even temporarily, by stretching a canvas sail over the holes. His job had become one of convincing Vulcan quartermasters and bureaucrats that giving him and his people the equipment they needed made perfectly logical sense.

Jim would have preferred to go into a forest and cut down a tree.

Jim found Scott. The engineer stood beneath the body of the little ship, gazing critically at a patch on the hull.

"Mr. Scott, how soon can we get under way?"

"Gi' me one more day, sir," Scott said. "The damage control is easy. Reading Klingon is hard."

Jim nodded, straight-faced, and refrained from reminding Scott of all the times he had declared the project impossible. Scott climbed up the landing ladder and disappeared inside.

McCoy stopped next to Jim and folded his arms across his chest. "They could at least send a ship for us."

Jim had neglected to tell McCoy about his argument with Admiral Cartwright. The doctor did not need any more stress.

"What do you have in mind, Bones?" Jim said, trying to be jocular. "A nice little VIP yacht?"

"They should insist on it. Instead of a court-martial—!"

"I lost the *Enterprise,* Bones!"

"You lost the *Lydia Sutherland,* too. They didn't court-martial you that time."

"But I was a hero that time, Bones. This time . . ." He shrugged. "Starfleet could have waived court-martial. They didn't choose to. Besides, it isn't the trial that matters, it's the verdict."

"The verdict where we're all sentenced to spend the rest of our lives mining borite? It's adding insult to injury for us to have to come home in this Klingon flea trap."

"Don't let Captain Sulu hear you say that. Anyway, I'd just as soon go home under our own steam. And we could learn a thing or two from this flea trap. Its cloaking device cost us a lot."

McCoy glanced up the landing ladder and squared his shoulders. He took a deep breath of the dusty air, as if he could stock up before having to go inside. "I just wish we could use it to cloak the smell." He climbed up the ladder and disappeared into the *Bounty.*

Saavik sat cross-legged in her spare stone chamber. She let her hands rest lightly on her knees, closed her eyes, and settled her thoughts.

Saavik had dreamed of coming to Vulcan since she learned of its existence and of her own heritage. She felt more comfortable here than on any other world to which she had traveled, even earth, where she had spent some years, and Hellguard, where she had spent her childhood. Like most other Romulan-Vulcan half-breeds, she had been abandoned very young. Her usefulness to her Romulan parent ended with her birth. Hellguard's usefulness to the Romulans ended soon thereafter. Only the arrival of a Vulcan exploratory party saved Saavik from a short, hard life of struggle for subsistence. When they found her, she was a filthy and illiterate little thief. But Spock detected potential in her. When all the other members of the exploration team preferred to pretend the half-breeds never existed, Spock rescued her, arranged for her education, and sponsored her entrance into Starfleet.

Since his return from the Genesis world, Spock had not spoken to her. The revival had changed him. No one but Spock knew what he recalled from his past life, and what he had to relearn. Perhaps he had forgotten her. She was too proud to plead for his attention, and she was trying too hard to be a proper Vulcan to admit that she missed his friendship. Even if he did forget her, and never remembered her again, she would always be grateful to him for giving her the chance to become a civilized being.

In his earlier life, Spock had acknowledged her existence, but Saavik still did not know why. She believed herself to be the product of abduction and coercion, while Spock descended on his father's side from a Vulcan family reknowned and respected for centuries. He commanded respect with his very name, both because of his family and because of his own achievements. Saavik did not even possess a proper Vulcan name.

The single similarity between them was that neither was completely Vulcan. Even that similarity held great differences. Mr. Spock's mother was a human being. Amanda Grayson descended from a human family whose accomplishments could not be denied, even if its lineage could be traced only ten generations. Her own accomplishments rivaled any Vulcan's. Even if Amanda had possessed no background worth mentioning, Saavik would have respected and admired her. In their brief acquaintance, Amanda had shown her great kindness. She had made it possible for Saavik to stay on Vulcan.

Saavik, on the other hand, did not even know which of her parents had been Vulcan and which Romulan. She had gone to some trouble to avoid finding out, for tracing her Vulcan parent could gain her no acceptance.

She absently touched her shoulder, rubbing the complex scar of the family mark she bore. Someday the information it contained would reveal her Romulan parent, upon whom she had sworn revenge.

Saavik brought herself to a more recent past.

"Computer."

"Ready," replied the discipline's ubiquitous, invisible computer.

"Record deposition."

"Ready."

"I am Saavik, lieutenant of Starfleet. I last served on the starship *Grissom,* an unarmed exploratory vessel, Captain J. T. Esteban, commanding. Captain Esteban proceeded to the Mutara sector, conveying Dr. David Marcus to the Genesis world. Dr. Marcus was a member of the group that designed Genesis.

"*Grissom* warped into orbit around Genesis. David Marcus and I transported to the surface to investigate the effect of the Genesis torpedo. We found an earth-type planet with a fully evolved biosphere. Tracking the signals of a being more highly evolved than the Genesis data allowed, a being that should not have existed on the new world, we discovered a Vulcan child of the age of about ten earth-standard years. It was the opinion of Dr. Marcus that the

Genesis wave had regenerated the physical form of Captain Spock, who had been buried in space and whose casket and shroud we found empty on the surface of the world.

"Soon thereafter, we lost contact with *Grissom*. Some hours later, a Klingon expedition arrived on Genesis. They made prisoners of Dr. Marcus, the young Vulcan, and me. The Vulcan and the planet both aged rapidly. It became clear that the Vulcan would die if he were not removed from the influence of the degenerating Genesis wave."

Again, she did not reveal her knowledge of the reasons for the degeneration. A flaw in the Genesis program made the whole system dangerously unstable; it eventually caused the new world to decay into protomatter, to destroy itself. David had suspected this might happen, but in his enthusiasm for the project he persuaded himself he was wrong. Saavik saw no reason to tarnish his reputation as a scientist. Doing so could only cause more pain.

"The Klingon expeditionary force refused to believe the truth about Genesis, that the experiment had failed. They demanded the equations, believing Genesis to be a powerful weapon. Knowing that it could be used in such a way, David—Dr. Marcus—bravely refused to reveal the information, despite threats on all our lives.

"At this juncture, Admiral James T. Kirk returned to Genesis at the request of Sarek of Vulcan, to recover the body of Captain Spock. Commander Kruge, of the expeditionary party, demanded the Genesis equations of Admiral Kirk, and threatened him with the deaths of the hostages if he did not comply. To prove his determination, Kruge ordered a death. . . . He ordered my death. Dr. David Marcus, protesting, drew the attack to himself. He was unarmed. He was murdered. The killing was unprovoked."

Saavik's hesitation lasted only the blink of an eye, but during that moment, she reexperienced David's death. He should not have died. Saavik had the training and the responsibility to protect civilians. But he had interfered before she could stop him. She felt the warmth of his blood on her hands as she tried to save him by giving him some of her own strength. The Klingon war party forced her away from him and permitted him to die.

"Admiral Kirk and his companions escaped from the *Enterprise.* The majority of the Klingon warriors sought him on board the starship. It self-destructed, destroying them. On the Genesis world, Admiral Kirk fought Commander Kruge in hand-to-hand combat, defeated him, and tried to persuade him to surrender. Kruge preferred to perish with Genesis.

"I have no doubt," Saavik said, "that at the least Admiral Kirk's actions prevented two deaths: Captain Spock's, and mine. I believe it probable that he prevented Genesis from falling into the hands of an opposing power. Though the ideals of Genesis failed, Admiral Kirk prevented them from being perverted into a most terrible weapon.

"I am Saavik of Starfleet," she said again. "I have been assigned to Vulcan at the request of Dr. Amanda Grayson, but I will return to earth willingly to testify on behalf of Admiral Kirk and his companions. I swear on my oath as a Starfleet officer that the words I have spoken are true. End recording."

"Recording ended," the computer replied.

"Electronic copy."

The computer obediently created an electronically

readable copy of her testimony and delivered it to her chamber. Saavik slipped the memory chip into her pocket and hurried to the landing field.

James Kirk raised a hand in greeting.

"You have decided," Saavik said.

Kirk nodded. "We lift off tomorrow."

"To earth?" Saavik had always believed the admiral and his friends would choose to face their accusers.

"Yes."

"Admiral, I would like to continue my work on the ship until you leave."

"Thank you, Lieutenant Saavik."

She drew the memory chip from her pocket. "I have made a deposition."

"Thank you, lieutenant." He accepted the chip.

"If it is insufficient, I will return to earth to testify."

"Is Vulcan a disappointment, Saavik? Do you want to leave?"

"No, sir!" She collected herself once more. On Vulcan she felt strong and powerful; she felt completely in control of her life for the first time since she could remember. And this reaction struck her as very strange and wonderful, for she had no idea what the future would bring to her.

Saavik wanted to explain all this to Admiral Kirk, but the words were far too emotional.

"No, sir," she said again. "Amanda has made me welcome. She is teaching me many things."

"And Spock?"

"Mr. Spock . . . is in the hands of the students adept," Saavik said. "I have not spoken with him. I cannot help him here."

"You aren't alone," the admiral said. "No, Saavik. I appreciate your offer. But I think you should stay on Vulcan."

"Thank you, sir."

She climbed the *Bounty*'s landing ladder, taking the rungs two at a time. At the hatch, she glanced back at the admiral.

James Kirk stood alone in the dusk, gazing up at Mt. Seleya, his expression suddenly uncertain.

Chapter Two

THE TRAVELER CALLED, but it no longer expected any reply. The pain of the loss had begun to fade. The traveler brought other programs into play as it approached the insignificant blue planet. Because it had fallen silent, the traveler could act upon it. The world that had appeared so promising had proved inhospitable, and so must be changed. When the traveler had completed its work, the world would be ready for a rebirth of intelligent life.

The traveler ranged closer to the planet, plowing through the electromagnetic flux of the yellow star's spectrum. Other stray waves of radiation passed across the traveler, but it had been designed to withstand such energy, not to attend to it.

Soon its work would begin. The possibilities of the future began to wipe away the disappointment of loss.

From a balcony carved into the living rock of Mt. Seleya, Spock could see a great distance across the plains of his chosen home world. As the huge red sun set and twilight gathered, his attention focused on the landing field at the foot of the mountain. He watched as the small party of human beings who had brought him to Vulcan gathered beneath the battered wings of their Klingon warship. He deduced the purpose of their meeting; when they parted, he deduced their decision.

The Starfleet lieutenant who had also accompanied them to Vulcan joined Admiral Kirk and spoke to him briefly. Spock knew that she had been on the Genesis world, and he knew she had been instrumental in saving his life. But he knew very little else about her. This troubled him, for each time he saw her, he thought he knew everything about her. Then the knowledge faded, as unrecoverable as the memory of a dream. She became a stranger again.

Spock raised the hood of his heavy white robe and let the fabric settle around his face. During the past three months of intensive memory retraining, he should have recovered or relearned all the information he needed to conduct his life and his career. When he looked down the mountainside into the twilight and saw James Kirk, he could bring into his conscious memory an enormous amount of data about the man. He had first met James Kirk on the occasion of Kirk's taking over command of the starship *Enterprise* from Captain Christopher Pike. No Starfleet officer had ever attained the rank of captain at a younger age than James Kirk. His rate of promotion to flag rank had been similarly precocious. That much was in the records. But Spock also knew that at first he had doubted his ability to work with James Kirk, and the captain had a similar reaction to his new science officer. That was true memory, recovered from the *katra* left in McCoy's keeping when Spock died.

Only experience would reveal where Spock's true memory required more augmentation. It was time to complete his final testing.

On the landing field below, Admiral James Kirk looked upward, as if seeking Spock out. Without acknowledging him, Spock turned away and entered the domain of the students adept of the Vulcan discipline of ancient thought.

He paused in the entrance of the testing chamber. The computer had frozen all three screens: "MEMORY TESTING INTERRUPTED." Spock entered the chamber, sat before the screens, and composed himself.

"Resume."

Three problems appeared simultaneously. The computer demanded the chemical formula for yominium sulfide crystals; asked, "What significant legal precedent arose from the peace pact between Argus and Rigel IV?"; and presented him with a challenge in three-dimensional chess. He wrote the formula with one hand; replied, "It is not the province of justice to determine whether all sentient beings are created equal, but to ensure that all such beings are given equal opportunity and treatment under the law"; and moved his queen. White queen took the black knight. "Check," he said. The first screen demanded the electron structure of the normal state of gadolinium; the second requested an outline of the principal historical incidents on the planet earth in the year 1987; the third remained static. He typed "$1s^2 2s^2 2p^6 3s^2 3p^6 3d^{10} 4s^2 4p^6 4d^{10} 4f^7 5s^2 5p^6 5d^1 6s^2$" and recited the watershed events of earth, 1987, old dating system. He glanced at the chess screen. The computer had not yet answered his challenge. "You are in check," he said. The computer replied by presenting him with an image to identify. The second screen demanded, "Who made the first advances on toroidal space-time distortion, and where?" "The image is a two-dimensional projection of a three-dimensional theoretical representation of a four-dimensional time gate as proposed by the Andorian scientist, Shres; Ralph Seron did the original toroid work at Cambridge, Massachusetts, earth, in 2069, and you are still in check." The computer's rook took Spock's queen. Spock instantly moved his white pawn and captured the black rook.

"Checkmate."

All questions ceased. All three screens cleared. A legend appeared, in triplicate: "MEMORY TESTING SATISFACTORY."

The central screen dissolved and reformed: "READY FOR FINAL QUESTION?"

"I am ready," Spock said.

The question appeared before him and to either side, filling his vision, central and peripheral.

"HOW DO YOU FEEL?"

Confused, Spock gazed at the central screen. He drew his eyebrows together in thought. The screen flashed the question at him, urging him to reply.

"I do not understand," Spock said.

The screen continued to flash, demanding an answer.

Spock heard the faint rustle of soft fabric against stone. He glanced over his shoulder.

Amanda, student adept of the Vulcan discipline of ancient thought, Spock's human mother, stood in the doorway.

"I do not understand the final question," Spock said.

"You are half human," Amanda said. She crossed

the room, stopped beside him, and put her hand on his shoulder. "The computer knows that."

"The question is irrelevant."

"Spock . . . the retraining of your mind has been in the Vulcan way, so you may not understand feelings. But you are my son. You have them. They will surface."

Spock found this statement difficult to accept, for he could recall no evidence that what she said was true, no occasion when he had reacted as she said he must. Yet he trusted her judgment.

"As you wish," he said, "since you deem feelings of value. But . . . I cannot wait here to find them."

"Where must you go?" Amanda said.

"To earth. To offer testimony."

"You do this—for friendship?"

"I do this because I was there."

She touched his cheek. "Spock, does the good of the many outweigh the good of the one?"

"I would accept that as an axiom," Spock replied. Her touch revealed her concern, her disquiet, and her love.

"Then you stand here alive because of a mistake," Amanda said. "A mistake made by your flawed, feeling, human friends. They have sacrificed their futures because they believed that the good of the *one*—you—was more important to them."

Spock considered. "Humans make illogical decisions."

She looked at him, sadly, patiently; she shook her head slightly. "They do, indeed."

Spock raised one eyebrow, trying to understand the incomprehensible motives of human beings.

Dr. Leonard McCoy let the door of the *Bounty*'s sick bay close behind him. He sagged into a chair designed for someone of entirely different build. The ship, particularly his cabin, felt completely alien. He had managed to bring some familiarity to sick bay alone. He had begged, borrowed, and scrounged medical equipment and supplies on Vulcan. However short and safe the trip, he would not go into space without medical capabilities. Some of the *Bounty*'s instruments he had been able to adapt to humans and Vulcans; others he had found useless or incomprehensible.

He had had neither opportunity nor desire to make his sleeping quarters feel more homelike. He did not expect to spend much time on this alien ship. But where he would be spending his time in the future, he did not know.

He rubbed his temples, wishing away the persistent headache. Wishing had about as much effect on it as the medications he had tried and given up on.

McCoy was troubled. Despite T'Lar's assurances, McCoy still felt the presence of Spock in his mind. He hoped it was just a shadow, a memory of the memories he had carried during those few interminable days. Though he did not believe that he and Spock were entirely separate, he had said nothing. He did not want to go through any more facilitation sessions. They delved too deeply; they made him face parts of himself he preferred not to acknowledge. They opened him up to the Vulcans as surely as if he were being dissected. And the Vulcans could not understand. After each session they withdrew from him farther and farther, as if he were some experimental animal gone wrong, some freak of nature. Even Spock withdrew, never speaking to him before or after the sessions, though he should have understood McCoy better than any other being in the universe.

McCoy certainly understood Spock. That was one

of the things that troubled him. He could understand how appalled and repelled the Vulcans were when they stripped the civilized veneer from McCoy's emotions and left his psychic nerve endings bare. He could even understand their cold curiosity about him. The Vulcans had given him the ability to stand aside from his own being and act as an objective observer. It was not an ability he had ever encouraged in himself. He knew far too many doctors who prided themselves on their objectivity, who could separate themselves completely from a patient in pain. They might be technically competent, even brilliant; technically they might even be far better doctors than McCoy. But he could not work like that, and he had never wanted to. There was more to being a doctor than technical expertise. Now, though, McCoy felt as if he might be forced into such a mold. If he could no longer understand the feelings of his patients, he was worse than useless as a doctor.

McCoy could find only one defense, and that was to accentuate his reactions, both positive and negative, to let them loose instead of putting them under any restraints.

If Spock and the other Vulcans thought he was emotional before, just wait.

After a long night, Jim Kirk climbed down from H.M.S. *Bounty*. He breathed deeply of the cool thin air, trying to escape his persistent lightheadedness. The little ship hunched over him, ungainly on the ground, but spaceworthy again.

Vulcan's harsh and elegant dawn surrounded him. The cloudless sky turned scarlet and purple as the sun's edge curved over the horizon. Light reflected from the atmosphere's permanent faint haze of dust.

High above, a shape glided into sunlight from Mt.

Seleya's shadows. Jim watched in amazement as the wind-rider soared and circled. Few humans—indeed, few Vulcans—ever saw the rare creature. Too delicate to bear any touch less gentle than air, it lived always in the sky, hunting, mating, giving birth, and dying without ever touching the ground. Even after death it flew, until the winds dissociated its body into molecules, into elements.

It spiraled upward, directly over the *Bounty*. Vulcan's sun, low on the horizon, illuminated the wind-rider from below. Jim realized that at any other sun angle, the translucent creature would be nearly invisible. But with the light reflecting off the undersides of its wings, he could see the tracing of its glassy hollow bones beneath a tissue-thin skin covered with transparent fur. The creature soared spiraling to a peak. It arched over backward and dove straight toward him, its brilliant gold eyes glittering. Jim caught his breath, afraid the ground would smash it or the turbulence of the air rip it apart. Twenty meters overhead it swooped upward again. It sailed away.

Jim did not understand how a beast of such delicacy had survived the fall; but Jim Kirk was not the first person to be mystified by a wind-rider. No one, not even Vulcans, claimed to understand how they withstood the violent wind and sandstorms that sometimes racked the world.

Jim wondered if seeing a wind-rider meant good luck in Vulcan mythology; he wondered if any Vulcan would admit an omen of luck existed. For while Vulcans preserved their ancient myths, modern Vulcans were far too rational to believe in luck.

What Vulcans believed did not matter. Jim felt as if seeing a wind-rider meant good luck in his own mythology. He climbed back into the *Bounty*, heartened.

Sulu and Scott had directed the repair of the worst of the damage the *Enterprise* had done. Admiral James Kirk took his place in the control chamber of the Klingon fighter, doubting he would ever feel comfortable in the commander's seat. It had been designed for a member of a species that averaged rather larger than human beings.

"Systems report," he said. "Communications?"

"Communications systems ready," Uhura replied. "Communications officer—ready as she'll ever be."

"Mr. Sulu?"

"Guidance is functional. I've modified the protocols of the onboard computer for a better interface with Federation memory banks."

"Weapons systems?"

"Operational, admiral," Chekov said. "And cloaking device is now available in all modes of flight."

"I'm impressed, Mr. Chekov. A lot of effort for a short voyage."

Chekov grinned. "We are in enemy vessel, sir. I didn't wish to be shot down on way to our own funeral."

"Most prudent," Jim said. "Engine room. Report, Scotty."

"We're ready, sir. I've converted the dilithium sequencer into somethin' less primitive. And, admiral, I've replaced the Klingon food packs. They gi' me sour stomach."

"Appreciated by all, Mr. Scott."

In the silence that followed, Jim became aware that the attention of everyone on the bridge centered, expectantly, upon him.

"Prepare for departure," he said in a matter-of-fact tone.

Sulu began the prelaunch checklist, and in a moment Jim was surrounded by the low, intense chatter of preparation. This was always the moment when the captain of a starship sat at storm's eye, observing everything, responsible for everything, but with no physical tasks. He could only think of where he was taking his people, what he was taking them back to face.

He glanced around the bridge. In the shadows of the passageway that led into the neck of the *Bounty*, Saavik hesitated on the threshold, her uncertainty clear. She was not as unexpressive as a Vulcan.

Jim rose and joined her. "Well, Saavik, I guess this is good-bye."

"I should accompany you back to earth, admiral," she said hesitantly. "I have considered—I am prepared . . . I need nothing. I would request a moment to take my leave of Amanda."

"No, Saavik. Starfleet's put you on detached assignment to Vulcan, so you're staying on detached assignment to Vulcan." He spoke quickly to forestall her argument. She would undoubtedly present it with flawless logic, choosing responsibility over her own wishes. "There's no point in another of us being brought up on charges of insubordination, now, is there?"

"But—"

"Your recorded deposition will be sufficient for the inquiry, lieutenant. You'll follow your orders. Is that understood?"

She raised her head, her dark eyes narrowing in a flash of anger and rebellion, but the moment's lapse into emotion lasted only an instant before her Vulcan training overcame her Romulan upbringing.

"Yes, sir."

The *Bounty* vibrated at a low, throbbing frequency as it prepared for liftoff.

"Hurry, now," Jim said, trying to maintain a hearty

cheerfulness. "You have a great deal to learn on Vulcan. Almost as much as Spock. And you'll be a better Starfleet officer for your stay here. Besides, you're the only one who knows everything that happened on Genesis—" His own memories swept in close around him. His cheer failed and his voice caught. He recovered himself, not as quickly as a Vulcan. "You may be able to help Spock regain access to his true memories."

"My knowledge has not as yet been required in Captain Spock's refusion," Saavik said stiffly. "But I will follow my orders."

"Apparently we won't see Spock before we leave," Jim said, keeping his voice neutral. "If the subject should come up, tell him I wished him . . . good-bye and good luck."

"Should I converse with Captain Spock, admiral, I shall endeavor to give him your message."

Jim watched Saavik go. The hatch slid open at her approach. To Jim's astonishment, Spock appeared in the hatchway. He wore his long, pale robe. Saavik stopped.

"Good day, Captain Spock," Saavik said.

"Live long and prosper, lieutenant," Spock said, his voice and face expressionless.

He stepped past her, never glancing back. Saavik's control faltered with deep pain. She watched Spock, but when her gaze intersected Jim's, she brought herself up short, turned, and disappeared.

Apparently the Vulcans in charge of Spock's memory training had not thought it desirable to remind him of Saavik and his importance in her childhood. Perhaps time would bring him the recollection.

Spock stopped before him. "Permission to come aboard, sir."

"Permission granted," Jim said. "But we're preparing for liftoff, Spock. We've spent as much time on Vulcan as we can afford. I'm glad to have the chance to say good-bye—"

"I request permission to accompany you to earth, sir."

"To earth? What about your retraining? What about the elders?"

"My retraining is as complete as study permits. The elders . . . would prefer that I stay, but I have declined their invitation. Subject to your decision, of course."

"Of course I grant you permission, Spock. Welcome aboard."

"Thank you, admiral."

"Jim, Spock. *Jim.* Remember . . . ?" It startled Jim to have Spock revert to titles. "Your name is Jim," Spock had said to him, after the refusal. Jim wondered if the elders' program had re-formed Spock as a perfect Vulcan, without personality, character, or even the remnants of emotion to hold in check.

"It would be improper to refer to you as Jim while you are in command, admiral." Spock hesitated and glanced down at himself. "Also, I must apologize for my attire." He frowned slightly. "I . . . I seem to have misplaced my uniform."

"Well, I . . . find that understandable." Spock was not the only member of the group without a uniform. Jim started to smile.

Spock raised one eyebrow, questioning.

"I mean," Jim said, "you've been through a lot."

Spock did not respond.

Jim sighed. "Station, please," he said.

Spock crossed the bridge to the science station and took his position. Jim watched him, suddenly doubtful about the wisdom of taking Spock along. Spock did not yet seem to be quite his old self. But the trip to earth should be uneventful, and Spock was not under a council directive to appear and explain his actions.

Maybe this trip is just what Spock needs, Jim thought. Maybe.

Besides, Spock had made his decision to leave Vulcan many years ago. Jim did not want to involve himself in complicity with the Vulcan elders, supporting an "invitation" that might keep Spock here into the unforeseeable future.

"You sure this is such a bright idea?"

McCoy had appeared silently at Jim's shoulder. He gazed skeptically at Spock.

"What do you mean?" Jim said, irritated to have McCoy voice in such bald terms the same question he had been thinking.

"I mean *him,* back at his post, like nothing happened. I don't know if you've got the whole picture, but he isn't exactly working on all thrusters."

"It'll come back to him," Jim said, still trying to persuade himself.

"Are you sure?"

Dissembling was one thing; lying directly to his old friend was another. Jim glanced across the bridge to where Spock sat, communing with his computer.

"That's what I thought," McCoy said.

"Mr. Sulu," Jim said abruptly. "Take us home."

Saavik strode across the landing field. Behind her, the *Bounty* gathered itself for takeoff. Saavik did not alter her pace. Amanda waited at the edge of the landing pad, staring past her at the ship with an unreadable expression. The wind caught a stray lock of her hair and fluttered it against her throat.

Amanda held out her hand. Saavik hesitated, then grasped it and turned to stand with her as the ship lifted off. It rose on a cloud of dust and power, then plunged forward, climbing slowly as it vanished between the peaks and canyons of Mt. Seleya's range.

Saavik glanced at Amanda when *Bounty* had disappeared. Saavik suddenly felt glad that she had stayed, for tears tracked Amanda's cheeks, and her fingers felt very thin and frail in Saavik's strong hand.

Chief Medical Officer Christine Chapel stood in the midst of the chaos of Starfleet Command's major missions room. Huge curved windows presented a 180-degree view of San Francisco Bay, but no one inside could pay any attention to the calmness of the scene outside. Major missions vibrated with tense communication in many languages, many accents. All the news was bad.

An unknown object was approaching earth with appalling speed and appalling power. It passed Starfleet ships, and the ships ceased to communicate. Nothing even slowed it down.

Chapel had spent the morning coordinating efforts to reach the crippled ships. But she was running out of personnel, she was running out of rescue ships, and communications became progressively more difficult. The probe showed no sign of running out of ways to stop Starfleet vessels on its headlong plunge toward earth.

The president of the Federation Council entered. The chaos of the missions room hushed for a moment. The president joined Starfleet Commander Admiral Cartwright at the central command console. Chris hoped they knew something about the probe that she did not, but both men looked intent and grim.

Chapel joined Janice Rand at one of the consoles in the missions room.

"Janice?"

Rand looked up, her expression grim. "Every ship in ten days' radius is already on its way back."

She gestured toward her screen, a three-d representation of part of Federation space, centered on earth. A multitude of ships moved toward that center at high warp speeds. Some had already begun to gather in a protective phalanx. The unknown signal plowed steadily toward the phalanx. It left in its wake a scattering of motionless, dimming sensor points.

"As for the more distant ships . . . at the rate this thing is going, Chris, by the time they return, there may not be anything to return *to*."

"We don't *know* what the probe's intentions are," Chris said. "We can't be certain . . ."

Janice glanced up at her. Chris stopped grasping at spider-silk hopes that dissolved in her hands.

"If I call the ships back," Janice said, "I may be calling them to their destruction."

"We may need them," Chapel said. "For evacuation."

"They can't evacuate anybody if they're destroyed! We don't even know what happened to the *Saratoga* and the others! That . . . that *thing* has completely disrupted communications from the entire sector."

"It's my job to be prepared," Chapel said. "Evacuation may be our only choice."

"But where can they go?" Rand said softly. She returned her attention to her console. "That thing is getting stronger, Chris," Janice Rand said. Her shoulders slumped as she stared at the screen. "I wish Admiral Kirk were here now," she said. "I wish he were here with the *Enterprise*."

60

Chapter Three

THE TRAVELER REACHED the star system of the nondescript blue planet. The voices it sought remained silent. It passed the system's outer worlds, frozen rocky spheres and great gas giants, and it sang its grief to space and all worlds' skies. Its sensors traced the planet's surface, cutting through the electromagnetic radiation that often surrounded such worlds. It found several small spaceborne nodes of power and drained them.

This was a marginally acceptable world. The traveler could give it new voices. First its surface must be sterilized. The traveler would lower the temperature until glaciers covered the land and the seas froze solid. Whatever had destroyed the intelligence that once existed here would itself be destroyed. After a few eons, the traveler would permit the temperature to rise again, leaving a tropical world devoid of life. Then the traveler could reseed.

The traveler centered its attention on a wide expanse of ocean and began feeding power to the focus.

An enormous sea wave burst upward and exploded into steam. The traveler observed and approved the results. It intensified its power discharge, which plunged into the ocean and vaporized tremendous volumes of water. The vapor rose into the atmosphere and collected into a cloud cover that rapidly thickened and spread, obscuring the surface of the world.

On the surface of earth, it began to rain.

The invincible probe crossed the orbit of Jupiter. The Federation waited in hope and fear.

With terrifying rapidity, clouds gathered over the surface of the earth. Rain scattered, pelted, scoured the land.

The last hopes faded with the proof of the probe's malevolence.

Captain Styles pounded through the corridor and into the turbo-lift. His orders were specific and desperate: "Stop the intruder." Starfleet Commander Cartwright's intensity had penetrated the badly scrambled channel. "Captain, if you fail . . . it's the end of life on earth."

Styles did not consider failure. The prospect of action excited him. His ship, *Excelsior,* Starfleet's newest and most powerful, had been held in reserve as a last defense against the unknown. Now the waiting had ended.

It's a good thing, he thought, that Montgomery Scott's little trick with the engine control chips didn't damage *Excelsior* permanently. If we were crippled now. . . . Helping steal the *Enterprise,* even losing the obsolete old bucket, is a trivial charge compared to sabotage. People care what happens to this ship.

Anyway, Styles cared. He cared what other people

thought about it. He cared what people thought about him. He was determined to erase the memory of the humiliation Scott and Kirk had caused him. *Excelsior* would meet the unknown probe and vanquish it. Styles would save his home world, and everyone in the Federation would talk about *Excelsior* and its captain instead of bringing up the heyday of the *Enterprise* and James T. Kirk.

"Open channel to Spacedock control."

"Channel open, sir."

"Styles to Spacedock control."

"You're cleared to depart, captain."

The transmission broke into static as the controller ordered Spacedock doors to open.

"Would you like to clear up that channel a little, lieutenant?" Styles said to his communications officer.

"I'm trying, sir. This is a direct hookup; it shouldn't have any interference."

"I'm aware of that—" A shriek of gibberish squealed through the speakers. The communications officer flinched. Styles cursed. "Helm, prepare for departure."

The helm officer engaged the controls. "No response, sir!" she said. "*Excelsior* has no power!"

"Engineering!"

"Captain Styles, the impulse engines are drained, and warp potential is failing!"

"*Excelsior,* stand by," Spacedock control said. The voice buzzed and jumped through the interference. "Spacedock doors are inoperative! Repeat, malfunction on exit doors."

"This is *Excelsior,* control. Never mind the damned doors—we've got no power! What's going on?"

A second voice, almost indistinguishable, penetrated the weird interference. "Space doors not responding. All emergency systems nonfunctional."

Styles glanced up through the clear dome that covered *Excelsior*'s bridge. A Spacedock observation deck loomed overhead.

On it, all the lights were going out.

"Engage reserve power." Spacedock control was a whisper among screams of incomprehensible interference. "Starfleet command, this is Spacedock on emergency channel. We have lost all internal power. Repeat, we have lost all power . . ."

The signal faded to nothingness.

The probe sped past Mars with little opposition and settled into orbit around the earth.

Tokyo: cloud cover ninety-five percent. The spattering rain froze to sleet.

Juneau: cloud cover ninety-seven percent. Icy snow plummeted from the sky.

Leningrad: cloud cover one hundred percent. It was too cold to snow. The city hunkered in the freezing darkness, as if for an early winter of conventional brutality. Its citizens, accustomed to their winters, were well prepared to survive till spring.

But this time, spring might never come.

Sarek of Vulcan stood on the observation platform of Starfleet's major missions room. Through the hours he had watched as Federation personnel searched for some response to the probe, some way to stop or escape it. The hum of voices gradually receded before the increasingly frantic data stream from machines stretched to overload. The people were exhausted, for the information had been pouring in for hours and they had no response to give it.

Sarek stepped down from the platform and crossed the main floor, listening and watching, trying to form some synthesis of the data that might explain what had happened, and why. The probe's incomprehensible cry resonated through the information channels, erratically disrupting communications.

He paused beside Christine Chapel, who was trying to direct rescue and evacuation on a world which ships could not leave. She stood by Janice Rand, staring in despair at the information that told her she would fail. Sarek gazed at the same information without comment or expression.

All over the globe the temperature dropped rapidly, and the curve kept growing steeper, with no indication of any plateau.

Chapel raised her head. "In medicine, no matter how good you are, no matter how much you know and how powerful your equipment is, you always come to times when you're helpless. But . . . not like *this.*"

She put her hands on the back of Janice Rand's chair. Sarek observed the trembling of her hands before she clenched her fingers and regained her control.

A few centuries before, a group of earth scientists had calculated what would happen if a nuclear war blasted dirt and soot and water vapor into the atmosphere. The results would have been devastating: a years-long winter of total cloud cover, a nonexistent growing season, famine, plague, and death for human beings and most other species. That single paper offered understanding of the utter finality of nuclear war; it had helped human people learn to fight to understand each other as hard as they had previously fought to destroy each other. And so earth and its population survived to join and enrich a civilization that spanned a large portion of an arm of the galaxy.

The calculations that had warned earth's powers of their folly had been made under the assumption that most of the bombs would explode in the northern hemisphere. In that event, most of the atmospheric debris would circulate through the wind and weather currents north of the equator, leaving the southern hemisphere less affected.

The probe was not so kind. Its disruption affected the earth from poles to equator.

"The rescue ships are getting close, Chris," Janice Rand said. "We have to tell them something soon."

"I know," Chapel replied.

Rand's screen revealed a small fleet of ships, several already within the orbit of Pluto. Perhaps they were already within the grasp of the probe, for no one could show any evidence of limits to its power.

Sarek glanced at Chapel, one eyebrow raised.

"No ship has approached the probe without being neutralized," Chapel said to Sarek. "The approaching rescue ships may suffer the same fate. It seems unlikely that the probe will allow them to carry out any evacuation."

Above, on the observation level, the council president stood with Starfleet Commander Cartwright. He had the whole planet to worry about, not just a few ships whose arrival would make little if any difference to the fate of the earth and its people.

"Try to get through to them," Chapel said to Rand. "Tell them to stand off. Maybe if they wait, the probe will finish, and leave . . ."

Sarek nodded, approving of her logical conclusion. He turned without a word, climbed back to the observation level, and gazed out into the bay. Tall waves roughened the surface of the water, as if reaching to join the thick, dark clouds rolling in from the sea. Already the clouds had obscured the upper curves and peaks of the bridge. A bolt of lightning flashed across the water. Glass shivered and rattled in the rumble of thunder.

Nearby, the council president and Starfleet Commander Cartwright discussed the possibilities, which now were desperately limited. They had no more power than Chapel to overcome the probe. Perhaps it came from an intelligence so great that the Federation was nothing to it but an anthill or a beehive, or from an intelligence so cold that the destruction of sentient beings concerned it not at all. Perhaps it did not even perceive earth's transmissions as attempts at communication.

Sarek's acute hearing sorted the familiar voices of Cartwright and the president from the constant gibberish of computers offering more and more information that became less and less useful. The two men had to decide what, if anything, to do. Whatever they decided, without sunlight the earth could not long survive.

"Status report, please," the council president said.

His adjutant replied, his voice not quite steady. "The probe is over the South Pacific. No attempts at dissipating the clouds have had any effect. Estimate total cloud cover by next orbit."

"Notify all stations," Cartwright said suddenly. "Starfleet emergency, red alert. Switch power immediately to planetary reserves."

"Yes, sir."

The president joined Sarek by the observation window. "Sarek . . . Is there no answer we can give this probe?"

Sarek shook his head, for he had no resources to offer. "It is difficult to answer if you do not understand the question." He could conceive of only one logical response. The president could not save earth, but he might save other beings by offering a warning. If he transmitted all the information they possessed, some other world might discover a defense against the probe.

"Mr. President, perhaps you should engage the terminal distress signal, while we still have time."

The president gazed out the window. During his silence, the waves increased in amplitude and the rain increased its intensity. Huge drops hit with perceptible force and streaked down the glass as if to score its shining surface. When finally the president spoke again, his words surprised Sarek.

"You shouldn't be here, Sarek," he said. "You came to earth to aid a friend. Not to die. I wish I could change things. I am sorry."

"I see no reason to indulge in regrets for events I cannot alter," Sarek said. "I would ask only one thing."

"It's yours, if it's in my power to grant it."

"A moment on a communications channel, after the warnings have been transmitted. To call Vulcan."

"Of course."

The data stream echoing through major missions suddenly failed to silence. The threnody of the probe reverberated through the chamber.

Over the bay, snow began to fall.

The *Bounty* sped toward earth through warp space.

"Estimating planet earth, one point six hours, present speed," Sulu said.

"Continue on course," Admiral Kirk replied.

"Aye, sir." Sulu checked the systems. Some, especially the power plant, already showed signs of strain. The instrument readings hovered barely within normal ranges. The *Bounty* would convey the group to earth, but Sulu doubted the ship could give much more. He felt sorry for that. Sulu had many ambitions, and almost all of them centered on Starfleet, space travel, exploration. But he suspected that Starfleet would forbid him to fly another starship for a very long time. Even flying a battered captured enemy ship was better than being grounded.

But the enemy ship could also get him and his companions killed. If the power blew, the cloaking device would go first. The *Bounty* would appear as an intruder. It was essential for Starfleet to be aware of their approach, and so far the Federation had not replied to Uhura's subspace transmissions. Unusual interference permeated this region of space, and she had received in reply nothing but an eerie silence. So no one knew that the survivors of the *Enterprise* were flying to earth in a Klingon fighter.

Or they know, Sulu thought, and they've decided to let us sweat for a while.

"Mr. Chekov, any signs of Federation escort?" Kirk said.

And if we do get an escort, Sulu thought, will it escort us—or put us under arrest?

"No, sir," Chekov said. "And no Federation vessels on assigned patrols."

"That's odd," Kirk said.

"Admiral, may I speak with you?" Uhura said.

"Certainly, commander." Kirk rose and joined Uhura at her station.

"What have you got, Uhura?"

"I'm getting something awfully strange," Uhura said. "And very active. Overlapping multiphasic transmissions. . . . It's nothing I can translate. It's gibberish."

"Can you separate them?" Kirk said.

"I've been trying, sir. They're unfocused, and they're so strong they bleed out into adjacent frequencies and harmonics. And their positions . . . lead in the direction of earth."

"Earth!"

"Yes, sir. I'm trying to sort it out."

Like Sulu and everyone else in the command chamber, Spock overheard the conversation between Admiral Kirk and Commander Uhura. Curious, Spock picked up an earphone and listened in as Uhura attempted to extract a comprehensible message from the garble that filled the frequencies.

When Leonard McCoy appeared at the entrance to the control chamber, then strolled in, Spock took care to show no reaction. He had not spoken directly to McCoy since . . . before. He had not even been in his presence without T'Lar as a barrier between them. Speaking to McCoy should be no different from speaking to any other human being, and yet Spock felt a strange reluctance to do so.

"Hi," McCoy said. "Busy?"

"Commander Uhura is busy," Spock said. "I am monitoring."

McCoy looked at him with a strange expression. "Well. Just wanted to say—nice to have your *katra* back in your head, not in mine."

McCoy smiled. Spock could not imagine why.

"I mean," McCoy said, "I may have carried your soul, but I sure couldn't fill your shoes."

"My shoes?" Spock said. "What would you intend to fill my shoes with? And why?" Spock seldom wore shoes. On shipboard, in uniform, he wore boots. On Vulcan he ordinarily wore sandals. "I am wearing sandals," Spock said. This seemed wrong to him. "How would one go about filling a pair of sandals?"

"Forget it," McCoy said abruptly. "How about covering a little philosophical ground?"

Spock tried to reconcile McCoy's words and tone, which he interpreted as flippant, with the tension in his body, the intensity in his gaze.

"Life. Death. Life," McCoy said. "Things of that nature."

"I did not have time on Vulcan for deep study of the philosophical disciplines."

"Spock, it's me!" McCoy exclaimed. "I mean—our experience was unique."

"My experience was unique," Spock said. "Your experience was essentially the same as that of anyone accompanying a Vulcan to that Vulcan's death. It is true that you were untrained and unprepared; this caused T'Lar great difficulty in freeing my *katra*—"

"T'Lar!" McCoy exclaimed. "What about me? I thought I was going crazy! I was arrested, drugged, thrown in jail—"

"—and it caused you some distress," Spock said. "For this I apologize, but I could see no other choice."

"Never *mind* that," McCoy said. "Do you think I'm complaining about helping save your life? But, Spock —you really have gone where no man has ever gone before. And in some small part, I shared that experience. Can't you tell me what it felt like?"

The Vulcan elders had asked him the same question, and he had not replied. He continued to resist the demand that he delve into his memory of the subject. Yet he had no logical reason for his reluctance.

Even if he did force himself to recall the experience, he doubted he could express it to McCoy in words the doctor or any human—except perhaps Amanda Grayson, who had studied Vulcan philosophy—could understand. Spock was not altogether sure he could express it to any sentient being.

"It would be impossible to discuss the subject without a common frame of reference."

"You're joking!" McCoy exclaimed.

"A joke . . ." Spock said, sorting through his memory, "is a story with a humorous climax." He wondered why McCoy had accused him of making a joke. In the first place the comment seemed an utter non sequitur. Spock could not understand how it followed from their previous discussion. In the second place, McCoy must be under some serious misapprehension if he thought Spock would deliberately attempt to make a joke.

"Do you mean to tell me," McCoy said, "that I have to die before you'll deign to discuss your insights on death?"

The chaotic tangle of sound suddenly sorted itself out, distracting Spock from McCoy's unanswerable questions. "Most strange," Spock murmured.

"Spock!" McCoy said.

"Pardon me, doctor," Spock replied. "I am hearing many calls of distress."

"I heard a call of distress, too, and I answered it," McCoy said angrily. "You—" He cut off his furious protest. "What do you mean? What calls of distress?"

"Captain!" Uhura exclaimed.

Kirk strode to her side. "What did you find?"

"Overlapping distress calls. Maydays from starships, and—"

"Let's hear them!" Kirk said. "Have you got any visuals? Put them on screen."

Uhura complied. The Maydays flicked onto the holographic viewing area, each overriding the next, each different but very much the same: starships overtaken and drained by a huge spacegoing object that blasted their power supplies and sailed past at high warp, without answering their greetings or their supplications.

The blurry image of the president of the Federation Council formed before them. His message broke and dissolved, but Uhura had captured enough that its meaning could not be mistaken.

"This is . . . president of . . . grave warning: Do not approach planet earth . . . To all starships, repeat, do not approach!"

Shocked, Admiral Kirk cursed under his breath.

The president's image faded and the strange spacegoing construct replaced him.

"Orbiting probe . . . unknown energy waves . . . transmission is directed at our oceans. Ionized our atmosphere . . . all power sources failing. Starships are powerless." Suddenly the transmission came through with utter clarity. The president leaned forward, intent and intense.

"Total cloud cover has enveloped our world. The result is heavy rain and flooding. The temperature is dropping to a critical level. The planet cannot survive beneath the probe's force. Probe transmissions dominate all standard channels. Communication is becoming impossible. Earth evacuation plans are impossible. Save yourselves. Avoid the planet earth." He paused, closing his eyes wearily, opening them again to stare blankly from the screen. "Farewell."

Jim Kirk listened to the transmission with disbelief. What *is* that thing? he thought. "Uhura, can you let us hear the probe's transmissions?"

"Yes, sir. On speakers."

A blast of sound overwhelmed them with its eerie strangeness.

"Nothing we have can translate it," Uhura said. "Neither the *Bounty*'s original computer nor our universal translator."

"Spock, what do you make of it?" Jim said.

"Most unusual," Spock said. He gazed at the visual transmission, taking in all the available information, analyzing it, trying to synthesize an hypothesis. "An unknown form of energy, great intelligence, great power. I find it illogical that its intentions are hostile . . ."

"Really?" McCoy said sarcastically. "You think this is its way of saying 'Hi there' to the people of earth?"

"There are other intelligent life forms on earth, doctor. Only human arrogance would assume the message was meant for humanity."

McCoy scowled. He glanced sidelong at Jim. "I liked him better before he died."

"Bones!" Jim said in protest, knowing Spock could not help but have heard.

"Face it, Jim!" McCoy said. "Everything he used to have that made him more than a green-blooded computer, they've left out this time." He stalked away and stopped near the visual transmission, staring morosely at the images of destruction.

"Spock," Jim said, "are you suggesting that this transmission is meant for a life form other than human beings?"

"It is at least a possibility, admiral. The president did say that the transmission was directed at the earth's oceans."

Jim frowned, considering. "Uhura, can you modify the probe's signals by accounting for density, temperature, and salinity?"

"For underwater propagation? I'll try, sir."

He waited impatiently as Uhura played the communications console like a complex musical instrument, like a synthesizer creating an entire orchestra. The probe's signal mutated as she filtered it, altered its frequency, enhanced some parts of the sound envelope, and suppressed others. Slowly it changed, till it wailed and cried in a different voice, still alien, yet strangely and tantalizingly familiar. Jim searched his memory for the song, but the knowledge remained out of reach.

"This is what it would sound like underwater?"

"Yes, sir."

"Fascinating," Spock said. "If my suspicion is correct, there can be no response to this message." He strode toward the exit hatch of the control chamber.

"You recognize it, Spock?" Jim asked, but Spock offered no response. "Spock! Where are you going?"

"To the onboard computer room. To confirm my suspicions." He vanished through the hatchway without a word of explanation.

Jim headed after him. When he realized McCoy was following, he stopped and turned back. He was as concerned about McCoy's mental state as he was about Spock's. For all their vast knowledge and long history, Vulcans were neither omniscient nor omnipotent. They might not have freed McCoy as completely as they claimed.

And Bones might be right, Jim thought, trying to persuade himself that he was worrying to no purpose. Maybe they did use the opportunity of retraining Spock's mind to create the perfect Vulcan, a being of complete logic and no emotion at all . . .

"Stay here, Bones," he said.

"No way," McCoy said. "Somebody has to keep an eye on him."

"Yes. Me."

"Oh, no," McCoy said. *"You* think he's all right."

Spock gazed at the computer screen, waiting for the results. He felt as if he were taking still another memory test. He wondered if he would pass it. The result would be of intellectual interest.

Admiral Kirk and Dr. McCoy stood close behind,

their anxiety disquieting. He wondered why they were acting this way, for he had already told them that his hypothesis, even if true, could have no effect.

The computer replayed the probe's song, then played another, not identical but similar: a melody of rising cries and whistles, clicks and groans. He had heard it before, but only in a fragmented, half-remembered form.

The computer displayed the image of a huge creature, an inhabitant of earth's seas, and identified it: *Megaptera novaeangliae.*

Spock had passed his own memory test.

"Spock?" Admiral Kirk said, his voice tight.

"As I suspected," Spock said. "The probe's transmissions are the songs sung by whales."

"Whales?"

"In particular, the humpback whale, *Megaptera novaeangliae."*

"That's crazy!" McCoy exclaimed.

Spock found McCoy's highly emotional state to be most discomforting. He tried to ignore it.

"Who would send a probe hundreds of light-years to talk to a whale?" McCoy said.

"It's possible," Admiral Kirk said thoughtfully. "Whales evolved on earth far earlier than human beings."

"Ten millions of years earlier," Spock said. "Human beings regarded them, as they regarded everything else on the planet, as resources to be exploited. Humans hunted the whale, even after its intelligence had been noted, even after other resources took the place of what humans took from whales. The culture of whales—"

"No one ever proved whales *have* a culture!" McCoy exclaimed.

"No. Because you destroyed them before you had

the wisdom to obtain the knowledge that might form the proof." McCoy started to object again, but Spock spoke over him. "The languages of the smaller species of cetaceans contain tantalizing hints of a high intellectual civilization. Lost, all lost. In any event, the pressure upon the population was too great for the whales to withstand. The humpback species became extinct in the twenty-first century."

He glanced at the screen. The computer displayed the immense form of a humpback whale, bloated and graceless in death. Human beings flensed the carcass. Great thick chunks of the whale's body flopped onto the deck, and the whale's blood stained the sea dark red. Spock observed his colleagues. Kirk and McCoy watched, fascinated and horrified, unable to resist the scene of an intelligent creature's death and dismemberment.

"It is possible," Spock said, "that an alien intelligence sent the probe to determine why they lost contact. With the whales."

"My God . . ." McCoy whispered.

"Spock, couldn't we simulate the humpback's answer to this call?"

"We could replay the sounds, but not the language. We would be responding at best in rote phrases, at worst in gibberish."

"Does the species exist on any other planet?"

"It died out before humans had the ability to transplant it. It was indigenous to earth. The earth of the past."

"If the probe wants a humpback, we'll give it a humpback," McCoy said. "We've reintroduced other extinct species by cloning frozen tissue samples—"

"The same difficulty remains, Dr. McCoy," Spock said. "The reason great whales have not been reintroduced to earth's seas is that no great whales still exist to teach them survival, much less communication. You could clone a whale, of course—but you would create a lonely creature with no language and no memory of its own culture. Imagine a human child, raised in complete isolation. Imagine . . . my own existence, had you refused to undergo *fal-tor-pan*. No. A cloned whale, crying its despair, could bring only further destruction. Besides," he said, considering practicality, "I doubt earth could survive for the years it would take to grow a cetacean to maturity."

"That leaves us no choice," Kirk said. "We've got to destroy the probe before it destroys earth."

"The attempt would be futile, admiral," Spock said in a matter-of-fact tone. "The probe would neutralize us easily, as it has neutralized every other starship that has faced it, each one more powerful than the craft you command. Fleet Commander Cartwright's orders to all Starfleet vessels are to turn away."

"We can't! Orders be damned, I *won't* turn away from my home world! Isn't there any alternative?"

Spock considered Admiral Kirk's question as an interesting intellectual exercise.

"There is one, of course," he said. "The obvious one. I could not guarantee its success, but the attempt would be possible."

"The alternative isn't obvious to me," the admiral said.

"We could attempt to find some humpback whales."

"You just said there aren't any except on the earth of the past," McCoy said.

"Your memory is excellent, doctor," Spock replied. "That is precisely what I said."

"Then how . . . ?" McCoy glanced from Spock to Kirk and back again. "Now wait just a damned minute!"

Admiral Kirk made an instant decision. Spock recalled that this was James Kirk's characteristic behavior.

"Spock," Kirk said, "start computations for a time warp." He turned toward McCoy. "Come on, Bones. Let's pay Scotty a visit."

McCoy started to protest, but Kirk left the computer room, pulling McCoy along behind him. Spock watched them go, bemused. Kirk had asked him a question and he had answered it, never intending to base any action on his information. Still, it would be an interesting challenge to see if he could successfully solve the mathematical problem Admiral Kirk had posed him.

Turning back to the computer, Spock overrode the report on humpback whales and began to compose the complex equations.

Chapter Four

THE TRAVELER'S JOY overcame the distress of losing contact with the beings of this little world. The planet lay enshrouded in an impenetrable cloud. Great thunderstorms wracked it. Where they did not flood the land they seared it with lightning, setting fires that added soot and ash and gases to the roiling clouds. The globe's temperature continued to fall. Soon the rain would turn to snow from poles to equator. The insignificant life that remained would perish from the cold. After the world became sterile, and the clouds rained themselves out, and the particulate matter settled, the carbon dioxide left in the atmosphere would aid in the world's rapid warming. Then the traveler could begin its real work.

Until then, it need only wait.

Doggedly, McCoy followed Jim through the neck of the *Bounty*. The plan disturbed him deeply, but the reasons for his discomfort took time to puzzle out.

"Jim," he said, "are you sure this is the right thing to do?"

"I don't understand what you mean," Jim said.

"Time travel," McCoy said. "Trying to change the future, the past—"

"We aren't trying to change the future or the past, Bones. We're trying to change the present."

"But we're the past of other people's future."

"That's the most sophistic argument I ever heard," Jim said.

McCoy forged on, trying to ignore the edge in Kirk's voice. "What if we change something that makes a difference to history?"

"But that's the whole point, Bones. To make a difference."

"Don't evade my question—you know what I mean!"

Jim strode on in silence.

"In the old days, on the *Enterprise*," McCoy said, "we had the same kind of disaster to face. And sometimes we had to do the hardest thing in the universe. Sometimes we had to do nothing."

Jim's stride hesitated, but he kept going.

"Jim—what would the Guardian say?"

Jim swung around, grabbed McCoy by the front of his shirt, and shoved him against the bulkhead.

"Don't talk to me about the old days on the *Enterprise!*" Jim shouted. "Don't talk to me about the Guardian of Forever! I went back in time to save your life—and I had to stand by and watch someone else I loved die! I had to stand by while Edith died—*and do nothing!*"

"It was the right thing to do."

"You didn't think so at the time. I'm not sure I think so now. Ever since, I've wondered, what if I'd

81

saved her? What if I'd brought her back? Everything would have been . . . so different . . ."

"It wouldn't have worked. You couldn't have brought a twentieth-century person into a twenty-third-century world and expected her to adapt."

"You don't know that!"

"Jim," McCoy said, "she wouldn't have come."

"She loved me!"

"So what? She had a mission in her life, and she wouldn't have given it up to go with you. No matter how much she loved you. And if you'd brought her against her will, even to save her life, she would have seen it as a feeble excuse and she would have seen it as betrayal."

Jim stared at him, shocked by the blunt recital of the truth. "What's the matter with you, Bones?"

"Let go of me," McCoy said.

Jim loosed his rigid grip on McCoy's shirtfront. "You're telling me to stand back and watch what's left of my family die. You're telling me to write off my home world—and yours. I won't do it! And I can't believe you want me to! The future hasn't happened yet, Bones! If I start believing that nothing I do can—or should—change it, then what's the point of anything?"

"I don't know, Jim. I just know you shouldn't do this."

"And just how," Jim said, "do you propose to stop me?" He turned away and left McCoy standing in the corridor.

McCoy had no answer to James Kirk's rage, but as his old friend strode away, he still sought to counter the intuitive force of Jim's argument.

Upset and angry, Jim Kirk entered the engine room of the *Bounty*. Everything about McCoy's argument troubled him: the argument itself, the doctor's having proposed it, and the possibility that McCoy might be right. Could Spock's suggestion, if Jim carried it out, cause some traumatic change in the universe? The possibility, even the probability, existed whenever one began interfering with the vectors of space-time. Jim had faced enormous personal danger and worse emotional pain in order to keep from disrupting the past, and thus the future he lived in.

But I'm not going to disrupt the past, he thought. I'm going to enter it and remove something that's going to be destroyed anyway.

He intended to change his own present. He could not make himself believe that what he planned was wrong.

Besides, Jim thought, if the plan posed so much danger—beyond the obvious danger to my people and my ship, which I suppose Spock did not consider germane—Spock never would have suggested it in the first place.

If Jim did nothing, earth would die. He put McCoy's objections from his mind, for he feared that if he let them affect him he would fail. If he tried and failed, earth would die anyway.

"Scotty!"

"Aye, sir?" Scott said, appearing from behind a complex webwork of engine structure.

"Come with me to the cargo bay, would you?"

"Aye, sir."

The engineer accompanied him into the huge, empty chamber. McCoy followed in perturbed silence. Jim found it difficult to estimate the dimensions of the oddly proportioned and dimly lit space.

"Scotty, how long is this bay?"

"Abou' twenty meters, admiral."

"That ought to be enough. Can you enclose it to hold water?"

Scott pondered. "'Twould be easy wi' a forcefield, but there isna sufficient forcefield capability in the *Bounty*. 'Twould have to be done mechanically. I suppose I can, sir. Are ye plannin' to take a swim?"

"Off the deep end, Mr. Scott," McCoy said grimly.

Jim ignored him. "Scotty, we have to find some humpbacks."

"Humpbacked . . . people?"

"Humpback whales. They're fifteen or sixteen meters in length. They'll mass about forty tons."

"They willna have much room to swim."

"It doesn't matter. They won't have to stay in the hold for long. I hope."

"Long or short, sir, I canna be sure abou' the ship. 'Twill handle only so much mass."

"You'll work it out, Scotty. You've got to. Tell me what you'll need, and I'll do my best to get it for you. And remember: *two* of them."

"Two, admiral?"

"It takes two to tango, Mr. Scott."

As he headed for the bay hatch, he heard Scott mutter softly, "The great flood, and Noah's ark. What a way to finally go . . ."

Halfway across the cargo bay, McCoy caught up to him.

"You're really going to try this! Aside from everything else—time travel in this rust bucket?"

"We've done it before." The ship would make a full-power warp-speed dive toward the sun, letting the gravity field accelerate it. If it picked up enough velocity, it would slingshot around the sun and enter a time warp. And if not—

"If you *can't* pick up enough speed," McCoy said, as if reading his thoughts and completing them, "you fry."

"We could land on earth and freeze instead," Jim

said, his tone grim. "Bones, you don't really prefer me to do nothing—?"

"I prefer a dose of common sense and logic! Never mind the ethics of the situation. You are proposing to head backward in time, find humpback whales, bring them forward in time, drop them off—and hope they tell this probe what to go do with itself!"

"That's the general idea."

"That's crazy."

"If you've got a better idea, now's the time."

McCoy held his gaze a moment, then looked away. He did not have a better idea.

Jim entered the *Bounty*'s control chamber. Spock had returned to his station. Incomprehensible equations flickered across his computer screen. Jim took his place and turned on the intercom so his voice would reach Scott.

"Could I have everyone's attention, please." It seemed strange to him, but appropriate, to request their attention rather than expecting it. "Each of you has a difficult decision to make. The information that Mr. Spock and Mr. Scott have offered leads me to believe that it is possible, though risky, to go backward in time and obtain two humpback whales, the species with which the probe is trying to communicate. If the attempt is successful, it could mean the survival of earth. But we have no guarantee of success. The *Bounty* could be destroyed. We might all die."

He paused, waiting for a reaction. No one spoke. Finally Sulu gave him a curious glance.

"You mentioned a difficult decision, admiral."

"I intend to make the attempt, Captain Sulu. But anyone who wishes to remain in our own time is free to take one of the rescue pods and leave the ship before we enter the probe's apparent sphere of influence. An entire flotilla of rescue craft is hovering outside the solar system, unable to risk a close approach to earth. It's likely they could rendezvous with a rescue pod within a few minutes—a few hours at most. Remaining behind is probably . . . the sensible thing to do."

"You need somebody to fly this beast," Sulu said, and turned back to his console.

"Would anyone care to cast an opposing vote?"

Spock glanced up only long enough to cock one eyebrow.

"I think what you have here is consensus, admiral," Chekov said, and also returned to his console.

Uhura acted as if Jim had never asked if anyone cared to abandon the group. "Conditions on earth appear to be getting worse, sir," she said.

"Scott here, admiral. Wi' the proper materials—the proper twentieth-century materials—I'll be able to build ye a tank."

"Thank you, Mr. Scott." Jim glanced at McCoy.

"You know how I feel about this, Jim," McCoy said.

"Then you'd better take a pod and get out fast."

"Who said anything about getting out? I'm not getting into any rescue pod."

"Very well," Jim said. "We will proceed without delay. . . . Thank you all." He turned to the science officer. "Mr. Spock, your computations?"

"In progress, admiral."

"Uhura, get me through to Starfleet Command."

"I'll try, sir."

In all his years on Vulcan, on earth, and on many worlds in between, Sarek had never observed such weather. Waves of rain and sleet pounded against the windows. A repair crew had tried to shore up the glass, but the seals had sprung again. Water sprayed through the cracks and pooled on the floor. Lightning burst continuously, turning the night's darkness brighter than earth's yellow day.

Sarek always felt cold on earth. In the past, he had always found it possible simply to acknowledge the fact and then ignore it. He had been well trained to ignore the trivial matter of physical comfort. But now, as Starfleet Command diverted all its remaining power in an attempt to maintain communications, the temperature within the building fell to match the ambient temperature outside, which itself continued to fall. Sarek felt colder than he had ever felt in his life. He tried to increase the metabolism of his body to compensate, but he could not outdistance the chill.

Shivering, Sarek gazed through the observation window. Torrential rain whipped across the waves of the bay and pounded against the glass. The clouds darkened overhead. Lightning bursts illuminated each individual raindrop to form an instant's still picture of a billion tiny glowing spheres. Simultaneous thunder shook the platform, the building, the world.

Apparently serene amid the chaos, Sarek listened to Cartwright and the council president and Chief Medical Officer Chapel attempting to maintain some coherence among the rescue attempts. Sarek did not offer his aid, because he knew he could do nothing. No one could be evacuated from earth because of the probe, but the probe ignored the movement of people from coastal regions to higher elevations.

Perhaps it ignores them, Sarek thought, because it knows any such attempts to be futile. People will be saved from drowning only to freeze; people may be saved from freezing only to starve.

He had been offered a place on a transport to the interior of the continent; he had refused.

He found a certain irony in what had happened. In returning to earth to plead on behalf of the man who had saved Sarek's son's *katra,* and his life, Sarek would lose his own life and soul. For he had accepted that he would die here on earth. His *katra* would never be transmitted to the hall of ancient thought, because no one would be left alive to accept it.

Snow had already begun falling just a few kilometers inland. The hills to the east, like mountains, bore caps of snow. As Sarek gazed through the window, the rain driven in off the bay ceased to streak the glass and began instead to burst upon it and stick and flow in wet, slushy droplets of sleet.

Communications within Starfleet Command continued to deteriorate. Sarek could barely make out the reflections of the screens' blurry images. Humans scurried back and forth in futile activity. Chief Medical Officer Chapel had been on duty for nearly forty-eight hours. She slumped in a chair with her face in her hands. Fleet Commander Cartwright clenched his hands around the railing of the observation platform, tense with strain.

Sarek had spent the past few hours preparing himself, permitting himself a moment to consider his successes and releasing his regrets. Only one remained: no reserve power could be spared, no communications channel remained clear enough, for him to transmit a message to Vulcan, to Amanda. He had written to her, but he doubted she would ever receive his message. All he wished to tell her must remain forever unsaid.

"Sir!" Janice Rand turned toward Cartwright. Her rain-streaked image wavered in the glass. "I'm picking up a faint transmission—it's Admiral Kirk!"

"On screen!" Cartwright said.

Sarek turned from the shadow world of the reflections to the real world behind him. The blurry image on the screen was hardly sharper than its reflection, and Kirk's words came through utterly garbled. The picture faded to nothingness, to a resonance of the probe.

"Satellite reserve power," Cartwright said. "Now."

The screen flickered, cleared, blurred. Sarek made out Kirk's form, and the control boards of the Klingon fighter ship . . . and the vague silhouette behind him, unmistakably of a Vulcan, unmistakably Spock. Kirk said something, but static muffled his words.

He is coming to earth, Sarek thought. All ships have been ordered away. But instead of obeying, he will come. He has been ordered to earth. But instead of disobeying, he will come.

James Kirk was incapable of standing by while his home world died. But Sarek also knew that there was no logical way to save it. The Klingon ship would face the probe and be destroyed. So, too, Kirk and all his companions would die.

"Analysis," Kirk said. His voice rose and faded in the static and the resonance. A strange cry whistled and moaned in the background. For a moment Sarek thought it was the probe, and then he realized it was not. "Probe call . . . Captain Spock's opinion . . . extinct species . . . humpback whale . . . proper response . . ."

His voice and image both failed, but Sarek had already gleaned Spock's explanation of the probe's intent and desire. A bright stroke of pride touched the elder Vulcan's equanimity.

"Stabilize!" Cartwright exclaimed. "Emergency reserve!"

"Do you read me?" Kirk said clearly. His image

snapped into focus, then immediately deteriorated. "Starfleet, if you read, we are going to attempt time travel. We are computing our trajectory . . ."

"What in heaven's name—?" the fleet commander said.

The power failed utterly.

"Emergency reserve!" Cartwright said again, his voice hoarse.

"There *is* no emergency reserve," the comm officer said.

The groan of tortured glass and metal cut through the scream of the wind and the pounding of rain and waves. Sarek understood what Kirk proposed to do. Somehow, in the madness of its desperation, the plan possessed an element of rationality.

"Good luck, Kirk," Sarek said. "To you, and to all who go with you."

The shoring struts on the window failed. The glass imploded, spraying cold sharp shards. Cries of fear and freezing needles of sleet and wind formed Sarek's last perception.

Chapter Five

THE SUN BLAZED across the viewscreen. The *Bounty* plunged toward it. The light grew so intense that the screen blacked it out, creating an artificial eclipse. Tongues of glowing gas, the corona, stretched in a halo around the sun's edge.

"No response from earth," Uhura said. "The solar wind is too intense. We've lost contact."

"Maybe it's just as well."

The artificial gravity of the *Bounty* wavered. The acceleration of impulse engines on full punished the ship. The solar storms stretched and grasped for the *Bounty* as it sped toward a fiery perihelion just above the surface of the star.

"Ready to engage computer, admiral," Spock said.

"What's our target in time?" Jim asked.

"The late twentieth century."

"Surely you can be more specific."

"Not with this equipment. I have had to program some of the variables from memory."

"Just how many variables are you talking about?"

"Availability of fuel components, change in mass of the vessel as it moves through a time continuum at relativistic speeds, and the probable location of humpback whales. In this case, the Pacific basin."

"You've programmed that from memory?"

"I have," Spock said.

Beside him, McCoy looked at the ceiling in supplication. "'Angels and ministers of grace, defend us.'"

"Hamlet," Spock said. "Act one, scene four."

"Mr. Spock," Jim said with some asperity, "none of us has doubts about your memory. Engage computer. Prepare for warp-speed."

Sulu collected the *Bounty* for transition. "Ready, sir."

"Shields, Mr. Chekov."

"Shields up, admiral."

"May fortune favor the foolish," Jim said softly.

"Virgil," Spock said. "The *Aeneid*. But the quote—"

"Never mind, Spock!" Jim exclaimed. "Engage computers! Mr. Sulu, warp-speed!"

The warp engines impelled the ship forward. The light of the sun's corona shimmered. The *Bounty* plunged through successive bands of spectral color as the frequency of the light increased through yellow, to intense blue-white, to a penetrating actinic violet.

"Warp two," Sulu said.

The *Bounty* shuddered within the drag and twist of warp drive, within the magnetic field and the gravity of the sun.

"Warp three . . ."

"Steady as she goes," Jim said.

"Warp five . . . warp seven . . ."

A tentacle of the corona reached out and entwined the *Bounty,* squeezing it mercilessly.

"I don't think she'll hold together, sir!" Scott's voice on the speaker sounded faint and tinny. The ship struggled for its life.

"No choice now, Scotty," Jim said.

"Sir, heat shields at maximum!"

"Warp nine," Sulu said. "Nine point two . . . nine point three . . ."

"Mr. Sulu, we need breakaway speed!"

"Hang on, sir . . . nine point seven . . . point eight . . . breakaway threshold . . ."

"Steady," Jim said. "Steady . . ."

A mass of data swept over the viewing area. It would be close, all too close, too close to the sun and too close to the speed, with no margin left.

"Now, Mr. Sulu!"

The heat of the sun overrode the shields. A tendril of acceleration insinuated itself through the gravity.

The *Bounty* blasted out of its own dimensions of space and plunged into time.

Jim remembered . . .

Glimpses of his past returned to him at random. He saw the *Enterprise* exploding out of space and burning in the atmosphere of Genesis. He saw David Marcus lying dead among the ruins of his dreams. He saw Spock as a youth—on Genesis, Spock had aged. But Jim's memory crept backward and the aging reversed. The Vulcan's living body grew younger. As the images flowed faster and faster, Jim watched all his friends become younger and younger. Spock had changed least, in the time that Jim had known him, for the life of a Vulcan spanned more time than any human's. McCoy lost the lines that years in space had drawn in his face, till he looked as he had when James T. Kirk, lieutenant's stripes fresh on his sleeves, first met him. Jim remembered Mr. Scott, who had been doubtful at first of a brash young captain's ability to command the finest ship in Starfleet. He remembered Carol Marcus, as she had been when he returned her to earth, as she had been when they parted so many years before, as she was when they first met.

Jim's mother smiled and shook her head, bemused by some exploit, and as he watched she too grew younger, though she seemed hardly to change whether the years passed forward or backward.

Jim recalled Uhura the evening he met her, singing an Irish folk song and playing a small harp; he recalled Sulu, a youth just out of the Academy, beating him soundly in a fencing match; he recalled meeting Chekov, an ensign on duty during low watch, when late at night Jim haunted the bridge of his new ship. He saw his nephew, Peter Kirk, change from a young man at peace with himself and his past to a young boy, grief-stricken after the loss of both his parents.

And among those clear images drifted memories fainter and more ghostly. Jim saw his sister-in-law, Aurelan, dying in shock as the parasitic creatures of Deneva took over her mind. He saw his older brother, Sam, already dead of the same awful infestation. And yet he also saw them on their way to Deneva, in happier times, and he saw Sam as a youth, laughing, challenging him to a race across the fields of the Iowa farm; as a boy, climbing to their tree house; and as a child, looking down at him, one of the first memories Jim Kirk could recall. He saw his friend Gary Mitchell, mad with power, dying in a rock slide on an alien planet, and at the same time he saw him as an ambitious lieutenant, and as a wild midshipman their first year at the Academy. Jim heard echoes of their discussions: what they would do, where they would go, and all that they would achieve.

And Jim caught a quick, vague glimpse of his

father, George Samuel Kirk, a remote and solitary man, who seemed alone even when he was with his family.

Finally he saw nothing but a long and featureless gray time.

A tremendous noise roused him from his fugue. The ship had survived its plunge through solar winds. Heat penetrated from the *Bounty*'s seared skin and pooled in the control chamber. Sweat trickled down Jim's back. The instruments showed all systems within the limits of normalcy. Everyone else on the bridge—even Spock—gazed dreamily into nothingness. The temperature began to fall as the ship radiated energy back into space.

"Mr. Sulu," Jim said. He received no reply. "Mr. Sulu!"

Sulu glanced around, startled from his own reverie. "Aye, sir?"

Jim watched as they all drew themselves back from their reveries to now . . . but when was *now?*

"What is our condition?"

Sulu glanced at his control panel. "Braking thrusters have fired, sir."

"Picture, please."

A blue and white globe rotated lazily, its clouds parting here and there to reveal familiar continents.

"Earth," Jim said softly. "But when?" At least they had outdistanced the probe, for the probe's impenetrable, roiling cloud cover no longer enclosed the planet. "Spock?"

"Judging by the pollution content of the atmosphere, I believe we have arrived at the late twentieth century."

"Well done, Mr. Spock."

"Admiral!" Uhura exclaimed. "I'm picking up

whale songs on long-range sensors!" She patched the signal into the speakers. The eerie cries and moans and whistles filled the control chamber.

"Home in on the strongest signal," Jim said. "Mr. Sulu, descend from orbit."

"Admiral, if I may," Spock said. "We are undoubtedly already visible to the tracking devices of this time."

"Quite right, Spock. Mr. Chekov, engage cloaking device."

Chekov complied. The *Bounty* remained visible inside itself, yet it lost a certain substantiality. Jim had a brief impression of riding toward a phantom planet in a phantom ship. Perhaps McCoy should have named the Klingon fighter *Flying Dutchman*.

The *Bounty* swept down out of space, drawing its wings into their sleek and streamlined atmospheric configuration. The ship bit into the air, slowing as it used friction and drag to help its braking.

The leading edges of its wings glowed with heat. Ionized molecules of gas rippled from the heat shields over the bow. The *Bounty* passed into night. The ship rode a fiery wave toward earth, a brilliant shooting star in the dawn sky.

"We've crossed the terminator into night," Sulu said.

"Homing in on the west coast of North America," Spock said.

"The individual whale song is getting stronger. This is strange, admiral. The song is coming from San Francisco—"

"From the city?" Jim said. "That doesn't make sense."

"Unless they're stranded in the bay," Sulu said. "Or—held captive?"

"It's the only one I can pick up," Uhura said. "And it's being broadcast. But there's no way to tell if it's live or from a recording."

"Is it possible . . ." Jim said. "Is it possible that they're already extinct in this time?"

"They are not yet extinct," Spock said.

"Then why can't Uhura find more than one?" Jim snapped.

"Because," Spock said evenly, "this is the wrong time of year for humpbacks to sing."

"Then why—"

"I do not know, admiral. Information on great whales is severely limited in our time. Much has been lost, and much was never learned. May I suggest that we begin by discovering the origin of these signals?"

"Admiral!" Scott's voice overrode the song of the whale on the speakers. "Ye and Mr. Spock—I need ye in the engine room."

Jim rose immediately. "Continue approach," he said, and headed out of the control chamber. Spock followed at a more dignified pace.

When Spock entered the engine subroom beside the power chamber, he understood the trouble before Scott spoke. The glow of dilithium crystals should have provided a brilliant illumination. Instead, the transparent power chamber radiated only the dimmest of multicolored light from the planes and angles of the crystalline mass. The dilithium now consisted of a crystal lattice changing into a quasicrystalline form. The crystals were diseased. As Spock watched, the plague spread. It was as if diamonds were decomposing into graphite or coal. For the *Bounty*'s purposes, the dilithium crystal was essential, the dilithium quasi-crystal utterly useless.

"They're givin' out," Scott said. "Decrystallizin'.

97

Ye can practically see 'em changin' before ye. After a point, the crystal is so compromised that ye canna pull any energy from it at all."

"How soon before that happens, Mr. Scott?" Kirk said. "Give me a round figure."

Scott considered. "Twenty-four hours, give or take, stayin' cloaked. After that, admiral, we'll be visible, or dead in the water. More likely both. We willna have enou' power to break back out of earth's gravity. I willna even mention gettin' back home."

Kirk glared at the crystals. Spock wondered if he thought that the force of his anger could make them shift their energy states in an impossible spontaneous transformation.

"I can't believe we've come this far, only to be stopped," Kirk said. "I won't believe we'll be stopped." He chewed thoughtfully on his thumbnail. "Scotty, can't you recrystallize the dilithium?"

"Nay," Scott said. "I mean, aye, admiral, 'tis theoretically possible, but even in our time we wouldna do it. 'Tis far easier, never mind cheaper, to go and mine new dilithium. The recrystallization equipment, 'twould be too dangerous to leave lyin' abou'."

"There *is* a twentieth-century possibility," Spock said. During his brief study of his mother's species' history and culture, he had been particularly intrigued by the human drive, one might almost say instinct, to leave extremely dangerous equipment "lyin' abou'."

"Explain," Kirk said.

"If memory serves," Spock said, "human beings carried on a dubious flirtation with nuclear fission reactors, both for energy production and for the creation of weapons of war. This in spite of toxic side effects, the release of noxious elements such as plutonium, and the creation of dangerous wastes that still exist on earth. The fusion era allowed these reactors to be replaced. But at this time, some should remain in operation."

"Assuming that's true, how do we get around the toxic side effects?"

"We could build a device to collect the high-energy photons safely; we could then inject the photons into the dilithium chamber, causing crystalline restructure. Theoretically."

"Where would we find these reactors? Theoretically?"

Spock considered. "The twentieth-century humans placed their land-based reactors variously in remote areas of low population, or on fault lines. Naval vessels also used nuclear power. Given our destination, I believe this latter possibility offers the most promise."

Thinking over what Spock had said, Jim headed back to the control chamber.

At the helm, Sulu looked out across twentieth-century Earth. He kept the Bounty hovering above San Francisco. The city avalanched in light down the hillsides that ringed its shore. The lights ended abruptly at the bay, as if the wall of skyscrapers caught them and flung them upward.

"Is still beautiful city," Chekov said. "Or was, and will be."

"Yes," Sulu said. "I've always wished I had more time to get to know it. I was born there."

"I thought you were born on Ganjitsu," Chekov said.

"I was raised on Ganjitsu. And a lot of other places. I never lived here more than a couple of months at a time, but I was born in San Francisco."

"It doesn't look all that different," McCoy said.

Jim returned to the control chamber, and overheard McCoy's comment.

"Let's hope it isn't, Bones," he said.

But it did look different to Jim. He traced out the city, trying to figure out why the scene made him uneasy. Unfamiliar tentacles of light reached across the water: bridges. In his time, the Golden Gate Bridge remained as a historical landmark. But the other bridges no longer existed. The lights must be the headlamps of ground cars, each moving a single person. Jim located the dark rectangle of undeveloped land that cut across the eastern half of the city.

"Mr. Sulu," he said, "set us down in Golden Gate Park."

"Aye, sir. Descending."

As the *Bounty* slipped through the darkness, Jim discussed the problems they had to solve with his shipmates.

"We'll have to divide into teams," he said. "Commanders Chekov and Uhura, you draw the uranium problem."

"Yes, sir," Chekov said. Uhura glanced up from the comm board long enough to nod.

"Dr. McCoy, you, Mr. Scott, and Captain Sulu will build us a whale tank."

McCoy scowled. "Oh, joy," he said, almost under his breath.

"Captain Spock and I," Jim said, "will attempt to trace the whale song to its source."

"I'll have bearing and distance for you, sir," Uhura said.

"Right. Thanks." Jim gathered them together with his gaze. "Now, look. I want you all to be very careful. This is terra incognita. Many customs will doubtless take us by surprise. And it's a historical fact that these people have not yet met an extraterrestrial."

For a second no one understood what he meant. They lived in a culture that included thousands of different species of sentient beings. To think that they would meet people for whom a nonhuman person would be an oddity startled and shocked them all.

They looked at Mr. Spock.

Spock, who often felt himself an alien even among his own people, did not find Admiral Kirk's comment surprising. He considered the problem for a moment.

When he had in the past been compelled to pass for human among primitive humans, his complexion had aroused little comment and no suspicion. His eyebrows had engendered comment, but only of a rather pernicious kind that could easily be ignored. Of the several structural differences between Vulcans and humans, only one had caused him any difficulty: his ears.

He opened his robe, untied the sash of the underrobe, and retied the sash as a headband. The band served to disguise his eyebrows, but, more important, it covered the pointed tips of his ears.

"I believe," he said, "that I may now pass among twentieth-century North Americans as a member of a foreign, but not extraterrestrial, country."

James Kirk gave a sharp nod of approval. "This is an extremely primitive and paranoid culture. Mr. Chekov, please issue a phaser and communicator to each team. We'll maintain radio silence except in extreme emergencies." Jim glanced around to see that everyone understood the dangers they faced. Given the fears of the people of the late twentieth century, perhaps it would be better if his people did not look official. "Scotty, Uhura, better get rid of your uniform insignia."

They nodded their understanding and complied.

"Any questions?" Kirk said.

No one spoke.

"All right. Let's do our job and get out of here. Our own world is waiting."

Monday mornings were always worst as far as garbage was concerned. His heavy gloves scraping on the asphalt, Javy scooped up the loose trash and pitched it into the park garbage can. He and Ben were only supposed to empty the cans, but Javy hated seeing Golden Gate Park trashed after every weekend, so sometimes he broke the rules.

Belching diesel fumes into the foggy, salt-tinged air, the truck backed toward him. Javy hoisted the can onto his shoulder and pitched the contents into the garbage crusher. His first few weeks on the job, he had thought of a different metaphor for the machine every day, but there existed only a limited number of variations on grinding teeth or gnashing jaws. His favorite literary image contained a comparison of the garbage-crushing mechanism to a junkyard machine smashing abandoned cars into scrap. Minor garbage and major garbage. He had not quite got it worked out yet. So what else was new? He tried comparing the unfinished metaphor to the persistently intractable novel he was trying to write in the same way he compared the garbage crusher and the car crusher. Minor unfinished business and major unfinished business. Maybe he should try putting the manuscript into the garbage crusher.

You're really straining your symbolism here, Javy, he told himself.

He hoisted the second can and dumped the contents into the crusher.

Sometimes he wondered if he should go back to

teaching. But he knew that if he did, he would get less work done on the novel than he did now. He needed a job of physical labor. Now the book went better than before. But he still could not finish it.

Javy jumped on the back of the truck and hung on till the next pickup spot, where a whole row of cans waited. Ben climbed down and joined him.

"And then what happens?" Ben said.

Javy was telling him a scene from the novel. Every book on writing and every creative writing teacher he knew of said that writers who talked about their stories never wrote them. For years Javy believed it and never told anyone anything till after he had written it down. But recently he had met a writer, an actual published writer.

"Everybody's different, Javy," the writer had said. "Don't ever let anybody tell you you've got to work the same way they do. Don't let them make your rules for you. They'll screw you up every time. You're supposed to be in the rule-breaking business." He was drunk, so maybe it was all bull, but just as an experiment, Javy broke that first law of writing and talked about a story. To Ben, as it happened. And then he went home and wrote it. He had not sold it yet, but at least he had finished the damned thing. So far it had three reject slips. Javy was getting attached to his reject slip collection. Sometimes that worried him.

He grabbed a crumpled newspaper off the ground and flung it after the other garbage.

"Come on, Javy, what happens?" Ben said. He dumped a can of trash into the crusher. Javy tried not to pay too much attention to what all went past. His first couple of weeks on the job, he noticed with fascination what people threw away, but now the stuff grossed him out. He supposed he would eventually become oblivious to it, but then maybe it would be time to start looking for another job.

"'So I told her,'" Javy said, in the voice of the character in the scene, "'if you think I'm laying out sixty bucks for a goddamn toaster oven, you got another think coming.'"

The onshore breeze came up. It blew away the diesel fumes and brought a marshy, low-tide smell from the sea. Soon it would disperse the mist. Javy liked working the early shift; even on foggy days he liked dawn. A few minutes ago, before sunrise, he and Ben had seen a shooting star, surprisingly distinct in the fog.

"So what'd she say?" Ben asked, as if Javy were telling him about a real argument with a real person. Ben was a great audience. The only trouble was, he never bought books. He watched TV. Once in a while he went to a movie. Javy wondered if he ought to try writing the novel as a movie script instead—it would never make it as a TV movie; it was too rough and raw for TV—and take it down to L.A.

The onshore breeze freshened, then stiffened.

Suddenly the loose trash scuttled past Javy's feet like fleeing crabs and the wind blew trash out of the cans, knocking the cans over, swirling up whirlwinds of dust and leaves, whipping past so hard that even Ben had to grab the side of the truck to keep from being pushed over too. Javy stumbled and Ben grabbed him.

The wind stopped as abruptly as it had started. It did not die down or fade away; it simply ceased.

"What the hell was that?" Javy said.

He winced at a sharp pain in his ears. The pain became a high-pitched shriek, a zoned-out whine. Light fell out of the gray dawn. He looked toward it—

—and saw, amid the fog, on a terraced bank above him, a ramp descending, from nothingness, a light shining, from nothingness, and people appearing, from nothingness. He stared, speechless.

Ben grabbed him by the arm and pulled him toward the front of the truck.

"Let's get outta here!"

Too stunned to resist, Javy stumbled up into the driver's seat. Ben shoved him over, flung himself inside, grabbed the wheel, and snatched at the gearshift. He jammed his foot on the gas pedal and released the emergency brake with a jolt as the truck lurched forward.

"Wait!" Javy shouted. He lunged for the door on his side. Ben grabbed him by the shirt collar and dragged him back. Javy struggled with him, but Ben was about twice his size. "Did you see that?"

"No!" Ben shouted. "And neither did you, so shut up!"

For a minute Javy considered jumping out of the truck, but Ben had it going nearly fifty. Javy tried to see behind them in the side mirror, but the light and the ramp had vanished, and he could make out only shadows.

Jim led the way out of the *Bounty* and signaled for the ramp to withdraw. It disappeared into the cloaking field. The hatch closed, cutting off the interior light.

"Do you hear something?" Sulu said.

A low rumble changed pitch, fading.

"It's just traffic," Jim said. "Ground cars, with internal combustion engines. Shouldn't be too many around this early, but later the streets fill up with them."

The oily smoke of the ground cars' exhaust hung

105

close. Trash littered the path and the meadow. Someone had turned over a row of garbage cans and spread their contents around the park. Jim worried about how he and his people would be able to get along within a culture that took so little care of its world, the world that would be theirs. In Jim's time, earth still bore scars from wounds inflicted during the twentieth century.

Under his breath, McCoy grumbled about the smell. Spock gazed about with detached interest, his only visible reaction to the fumes a slight distension of the nostrils.

"We'll stick together till we get oriented," Jim said. "Uhura, what's the bearing to the whales?"

Uhura consulted her tricorder and gave him the distance and bearing. Before they departed, Jim fixed the surroundings in his mind. He could find the *Bounty* by tricorder, but he could also imagine needing to get back inside the ship without pausing for an instrument reading.

They set off across the meadow in the direction Uhura indicated.

"Everybody remember where we parked," Jim said.

Chapter Six

JIM AND HIS shipmates left the park and entered the city at dawn. The sun burnished adobe houses with gold and burned away the fog. Long, fuzzy shadows shortened and sharpened.

Jim had not walked through his adopted home town in a long while. Climbing the steep hills, he began to wish he had come on the voyage in a good pair of walking shoes instead of dress boots.

Ground cars and pedestrians crowded the streets and sidewalks. Jim's tension eased when no one gave him and his group more than a second glance. Even Spock received little notice. Jim could not help but wonder why no one bothered about them, especially when they reached an area in which everyone wore similar clothes—dark jackets, matching trousers or skirts, lighter shirts, a strip of material tied around the neck—and carried similar dark leather cases. But here Jim's group did not even get first glances—

A man suddenly stopped and glared.

"What's *your* problem?"

"Nothing," Jim said, suppressing an irrational urge to tell him. "I don't have a problem."

"You will if you don't watch who you stare at." He shoved past Jim, then looked back. "And how you stare at them!" He turned, nearly ran into Spock, snarled as he circled him, and strode angrily away.

Jim *had* been staring at the people he passed, but he did not understand why one individual had reacted so strongly. He kept going, and he still watched people, but he watched more surreptitiously. He wondered why everyone dressed more or less alike, though not alike enough to be described as "in uniform," at least as he understood the term.

He stopped at an intersection with the other pedestrians. They waited, gazing at lines of ground cars that moved at a crawl in one direction and stood dead still on the cross-street.

A group of glass-screened boxes clustered together, each chained to a steel post.

Good, he thought. News machines. They might tell me what I need to know. If I can key on whales . . .

He glanced quickly over the headlines: "I was abducted by aliens from space!"

Jim frowned. Had he stumbled into a first encounter of human beings with another sentient species? If so, he would have to keep his people and his ship well out of the way. But he distinctly remembered—he thought he remembered—that the first contact happened in the twenty-first century. It happened when humans left their solar system, not when another species visited earth. And he certainly did not recall anything about abductions of humans by extraterrestrials. He would have to ask Spock if he knew for certain, but not here on a crowded street corner where their conversation could be overheard.

Other headlines: "Talk Service Exposé." "Congloms Glom VidBiz." "Dow Jones Bull Turns Bear." The first two he found completely incomprehensible. He assumed the third to be a report on genetic engineering, though he did not quite understand why Jones would want to change a bull into a bear.

"Nuclear Arms Talks Stalled." That one he understood.

"It's a miracle these people ever got out of the twentieth century," McCoy said.

Jim waited for the headline to dissolve into a news story, but nothing happened. He wondered if the news machine were broken. Probably street machines were not as reliable now as they were in his own time. He looked for a way to key it to the subject he needed, but saw no controls. Perhaps it was more sophisticated than it looked and could be operated by voice.

"Excuse me." A man in quasiuniform stepped around Jim, bent over the news machine, inserted metallic disks into it, and opened it. Jim thought he was probably going to repair the machine so its screen would display more than headlines. Instead, the man took a folded bunch of paper from a stack of similar bunches of folded paper inside the machine. It was not an electronic news machine at all, but a dispenser of printed stories. Newspapers? That was it. The antique novels he had read sometimes mentioned newspapers, but never newspaper machines. They described young newspaper carriers running down the street crying "Extra!" Jim wondered how anyone kept up with the news here. These headlines must be hours old.

The man folded his paper under his arm and let the machine's spring door slam. The disks he had fed into it rattled in their container.

"Damn," Jim said softly. "They're still using money. We're going to need some."

"Money?" Chekov said. "We should have landed in Russia. There, we would not want money."

A couple of the twentieth-century people standing around them reacted to Chekov's comment with irritation. Jim heard somebody mutter, "Pinko commie exchange student." He recalled that the stalled nuclear arms talks referred to in the newspaper were arms talks between North Americans and Russians.

"In Russia," Chekov said, "to each according to their need, from each according to their ability." He smiled at a glowering citizen of twentieth-century North America.

The traffic pattern changed. The crowd at the corner flooded into the intersection, dashing around and between ground cars and sweeping away the belligerent citizen. The cars on the cross-street lurched forward, honking and screeching and outmaneuvering each other.

"Mr. Chekov," Jim said, *sotto voce,* "I think that keeping quiet about the glories of Russia would be the better part of valor. At least while we're walking around on the streets of North America."

"Very well, admiral," Chekov said, plainly mystified.

On the other hand, Jim thought, it would be awfully convenient if we could receive according to our need just long enough to do what we need to do. Maybe we could have vanished before anybody asked us what our abilities might allow us to contribute.

At any rate, they needed some money, physical money, and they needed it soon. Jim's conspicuous group would not get far with a zeroed-out credit balance.

He tried to remember more history. He thought

that the age of electronic credit either had not yet begun or had not yet taken hold. Staring glumly at a sign across the street, "Antiques: We Buy and Sell," he recalled that the economy of twentieth-century earth was still based on buying and selling.

He had some pieces in his collection back home that even here, a couple of hundred years in the past, might be worth something. But if he sold anything he had brought with him from his own time, he would introduce anachronisms into history. This he must not do. Besides, he could hardly hope to pass off a tricorder or one of McCoy's medical instruments as an antique.

Then he remembered something.

"You people wait here," he said. "And spread out. We look like a cadet review. Spock—"

The others moved apart, looking almost as self-conscious as when they clustered together. Jim started across the street without thinking. Spock followed.

A high shriek, an oily burned smell—a ground car's wheels spread black streaks on the gray street and the nose of the car stopped a handsbreadth from Jim's leg.

"Watch where you're going, you dumb ass!" the driver shouted.

"And—and a *double* dumb ass on you!" Jim yelled, startled into a reaction and still trying to fit in. Flustered, he hurried across the street. The driver blew a deafening blast of the ground car's horn. The car accelerated, leaving a second set of black streaks on the pavement.

On the far curb, Spock gave him an odd look, but said nothing. Jim's pulse raced. It would be ridiculous to travel years and light-years through space-time in order to meet his end under a primitive vehicle in the street of the city where he lived.

He would have to be more careful. All his people would, especially Spock. If the Vulcan had an encounter with contemporary medical authorities, no matter how rudimentary their techniques, his headband would not conceal his extraterrestrial characteristics.

Back on the curb, the shipmates breathed a collective sigh of relief that Kirk and Spock had made it past the traffic.

How disorienting it is, Sulu thought, to be in a place that looks so familiar yet feels so alien.

"Ah! Hikaru oji san desu ka?"

Sulu started. He turned to see who had called him by his given name, and called him "uncle" as well. A young boy ran up to him, and addressed him in Japanese.

"Konna tokoro ni nani o shiteru'n desu ka?" The voice spoke informally, as if to a close relative, asking what he was doing here.

"Warui ga, bōya wa hitochigai nasaremashita," Sulu said. To tell the little boy that he had mistaken him for someone else, Sulu had to reach into his memory for his disused Japanese, learned in the classroom and from reading novels not three hundred but a thousand years old.

"Honto desu ne!" the little boy said. *"Anata no nihongo ga okashii'n desu."*

Sulu smiled. I'm sure he's right, and my Japanese *is* strange, he thought. I probably sound like a character from *The Tale of Genji.*

Embarrassed, the little boy started to back away.

"Bōya, machina," Sulu said gently. At his request, the boy stopped. *"Onamae wa nan da?"*

"Sulu Akira desu." The little boy told Sulu his name.

Sulu sat on his heels, and looked at him. The child,

112

Akira Sulu, already possessed the intense gaze and the humor one could see in pictures of him as an adult and as an elderly man.

"Ah sō ka," Sulu said. *"Tashika ni bōya wa shogaianraku ni kurasu."*

The boy blinked, startled to be told by a stranger who looked like his uncle but clearly was not, that he would have a long and happy life.

"Ogisama arigato gozaimasu," he said, thanking Sulu politely.

Sulu stood up again. The little boy ran away down the street.

"What was that all about?" McCoy said. "Who was that?"

"That, doctor," Sulu said, still watching the little boy, "was my great-great-great grandfather."

McCoy, too, gazed after the child.

On the other side of the street, Jim opened the door of the antique shop and entered, leaving the noisy traffic behind. His vision accustomed itself to the dimmer light of the interior. He stared around, astounded by the items in the shop. Antiques of this quality were nearly impossible to find, at any price, in his time. The years had been too hard on them.

"Can I help you, gentlemen?"

The proprietor, a man of about forty, wore his graying hair long and tied at the back of his neck. Jim believed the period of his costume to be somewhat earlier than the present: antique, perhaps, to fit in with his shop. The antique dealer wore gold spectacles with small round lenses, wide-bottomed blue trousers, patchy and pale with age, leather sandals, and a vest that looked to Jim like museum-quality patchwork.

"What can you tell me about these?" Jim said. He drew his own spectacles from his pocket. They resembled those of the proprietor, but his had rectangular lenses. Light flowed and flared along the cracks in the glass.

The dealer took them and turned them over reverently. He whistled softly. "These are beautiful."

"Antique?"

"Yes—they're eighteenth-century American. They're quite valuable."

"How much will you give me for them?"

"Are you sure you want to part with them?"

"I'm sure." In fact he did not want to part with them at all, but he had no choice, no room for sentiment.

The antique dealer looked at them more carefully, unfolding them and checking the frame. He crossed the shop to get his magnifying glass from the counter, then squinted at the fine engraving on the inner surface of the earpiece.

Spock bent toward Kirk. "Were those not a birthday present from Dr. McCoy?"

"And they will be again, Spock," Kirk said. "That's the beauty of it." He joined the owner on the other side of the shop. "How much?"

"They'd be worth more if the lenses were intact," the antique dealer said. "But I might be able to restore them. It would take some research . . ." He glanced at the glasses again. Jim could tell he wanted them. "I'll give you two hundred bucks, take it or leave it."

"Is that a lot?" Jim asked.

He looked at Jim askance. "I think it's a fair price," he said defensively. "But if you don't like it—" He offered Jim the glasses back.

"My companion did not mean to impugn your fairness," Spock said. "He has been . . . out of the area . . . for some time, and I am only visiting. I am not familiar with prices, or with your current word usage. What is a buck?"

"A buck is a dollar. You know what a dollar is?"

Neither Spock nor Kirk replied.

"The main unit of currency of the good old U.S. of A.? You can buy most of a gallon of gas with it, this week anyway, or most of a loaf of decent bread, or a beer if you choose your bar right. Either you guys have been gone forever, or . . . did we ever meet in the sixties?"

"I think not," Spock said.

They were getting out of their depth. "Two hundred bucks would be fine," Kirk said quickly.

"You aren't interested in selling your belt buckle, are you? Does it have any age on it, or is it contemporary? I've never seen anything quite like it, but it looks a little bit deco."

Jim felt tempted, but he had already pushed his luck by selling his spectacles. McCoy had had the lenses ground to Jim's prescription in their own time. Jim had no idea what an analysis of the glass would show, but he doubted that the results would resemble something from the eighteenth century any more than his belt buckle would look like an alloy from old date nineteen-twenty.

"No," he said. "It . . . doesn't have any age on it. I don't think it would be worth much."

"Okay. Let me draw you a check for these."

Jim followed him to the back of the shop. The antique dealer sat at a beautiful mahogany roll-top, opened a black lacquer lap desk, took out a spiral-bound book, and unscrewed the top of a fountain pen.

"Who should I make this out to?"

"I beg your pardon?"

"What's your name, man?" The owner frowned. "I have to know your name so I can write you a check so you can get your money."

"Can't I just have the money?" Jim said.

The owner turned in his chair and hooked one arm over the back rest. He gestured toward the spectacles, glittering gold on his desk. "Look, man, do you have any paperwork on these?" His voice held a hint of suspicion.

"Paperwork?" Jim said, confused.

"You know, like a sales receipt? Any proof of ownership? I've never had any trouble with stolen stuff, and I'm damned if I want to start now."

"They aren't stolen!" Jim said. Spock's story was wearing rather thin. "I've . . . had them for a long time. But I don't have any paperwork."

"Do you have some I.D.?"

At least he knew what I.D. was, unless the usage had changed between now and then. He shook his head. "I . . . er . . . lost it."

"What about your friend?"

With perfect serenity, Spock said, "I have lost mine as well. Our transportation lost our luggage, thus we find ourselves in our present difficulty."

The dealer's attitude changed abruptly. "Jeez, why didn't you say so in the first place? What a bummer. Did you come all the way from Japan? I always wanted to go there, but I never made it. I spent a lot of time in Asia. Nepal, Tibet, and, well, Nam, but I hardly ever tell anybody that anymore, they think you're going to wig out in front of them, you know?" He cut off his words. "Sorry," he said shortly. He closed his fountain pen and put the checkbook back into the lap desk. He gazed at Jim closely. "You know what?"

"What?" Jim said, not sure he really wanted to know.

"Those glasses better not be stolen, man, because I don't want any trouble with the cops. Or the narcs. Or the feds. The feds are the worst, man, I don't want anything more to do with the feds, ever again. So if you're screwing me around, and you're really a couple high-class coke-heads ripping off your rich friends for your next score, it'll go on your karma, you got that?"

"I got that," Jim said. He got the message, even if the details eluded him. "The spectacles are not stolen." He hoped he was telling the truth. It occurred to him that it was perfectly possible that sometime in their long history his spectacles had been stolen.

"Okay." The antique dealer rose and strode to his cash register. It flung itself open with ringing bells and the crash of its drawer. "Here's your money, no questions asked." He handed Jim a wad of green and gray printed rectangles of paper. "Small bills." He suddenly grinned. "I guess I've got a little anarchy left in me yet."

"I guess so," Jim said. He took the money. "Thank you."

As he stepped out into the sunshine, Jim drew a long breath and let it out slowly.

"Thank you, Mr. Spock," he said. "I'm not sure we got away clean, but at least we got away."

"I merely spoke the truth, admiral," Spock said. "Our transportation did destroy my belongings. The *Enterprise* held virtually everything I possessed."

"Yes . . ." Jim did not want to think about the *Enterprise*. "Spock, I'm not in command of anything right now. You've got to get used to calling me Jim, at least while we're here. Calling me admiral might draw attention."

"Very well," Spock said. "I will try to form a new habit."

They rejoined the rest of their group, being more careful about crossing the street.

"We were about to send out the cavalry," McCoy said.

"The cavalry, even in its mechanized form, ended some decades ago, Dr. McCoy," Spock said.

"No!" McCoy exclaimed. "Really? I'm devastated!"

Jim fended off another quarrel by showing everyone the money. He explained what he knew of its value. He divided it as evenly as the denomination of the bills allowed among the three teams. He gave seventy bucks—dollars?—to Uhura, seventy to Sulu, and kept sixty for himself and Spock. Perhaps he should have kept strictly to rank order and given the tank team money to McCoy or to Scott, but in all the years Jim had known Scott, the engineer had never had an iota of sense about money. As for McCoy . . . Jim did not know what was going on with McCoy. He almost wished he had kept him on the whale team, where he could keep an eye on him. But then he would have to act as buffer between McCoy and Spock, and he did not know how long his temper would hold if he had to do that.

"That's all there is," he said, "so nobody splurge. Are we set?"

Like him, they put a good face on it. He worried more about sending his people into the past of their own world than he ever had about sending them to the surface of a completely alien planet.

He and Spock headed north. The crush in traffic eased. Ground cars still filled the streets, but the masses of people in quasiuniform gave way to a more casual crowd.

"Well, Spock," Jim said, "thanks to your restored memory and a little bit of luck, we are now in the streets of San Francisco looking for a pair of humpback whales."

Spock did not reply. He certainly did not laugh.

"How do you propose to solve this minor problem?" Jim said.

"Simple logic will suffice," Spock said. "We need a map. That one should do."

Showing not the least surprise at discovering one immediately, he led Jim to an enclosure. It sheltered a bench on which a number of people sat. Near a list of street names, some of them still familiar, and numbers, none of which meant anything to Jim, a diagrammatic map had been painted.

"I will simply superimpose the coordinates on this map and find our destination."

Spock glanced at the map, as if an instant of casual attention would solve the problem. Then he looked more closely. The streets and boundaries had been drawn in a formalized way that had little connection with the true geography of the region. The thick colored lines painted over it helped not at all.

As Spock puzzled over the map, a larger than average ground car pulled up. It belched oily smoke, further polluting air already saturated with suspended fumes and particulates. The doors of the vehicle folded open and the people on the bench lined up to enter it. Jim realized this must be contemporary public transportation.

Then he read the sign on the vehicle's side: "See George and Gracie, the only two humpback whales in captivity. At the Cetacean Institute, Sausalito."

"Mr. Spock," he said.

"One moment, admiral. I believe that in time I can discover a solution—"

119

"Mr. Spock. I think we'll find what we're looking for at the Cetacean Institute. In Sausalito. Two humpbacks called George and Gracie."

Spock turned to him, more puzzled than before. "How do you know this?"

"Simple logic," Jim said.

The driver leaned toward them. "You guys getting on the bus or not?"

"Come on, Spock."

Jim led the way through the front doors of the bus.

A moment later, fuming, he descended from the rear exit.

"What does it mean," Spock said, perplexed, " 'exact change'?"

Sulu followed Scott and Dr. McCoy down the street. Scott forged ahead as if he knew where he was going, but if he did he had not let Sulu or McCoy in on the secret.

"Would you mind telling me," McCoy said, "how we plan to convert the cargo hold into a tank?"

"Ordinarily," Scott said, "'twould be done wi' transparent aluminium."

"You're a few years early for that," Sulu said.

"Aye, lad, I know it. 'Tis up to us to find a twentieth-century equivalent."

Sulu wished that Scott would stop calling him lad. They walked along in silence for another fifty meters. Halfway down the next block, a billboard loomed over the street: "Can't find it? Try the yellow pages!"

Sulu pointed to it. "What about that?"

Scott squinted to read it.

"Does look promising. But can ye tell me," he said, "what's a yellow pages?"

"Beats me," Sulu said. "We'll have to ask somebody." Preferring a straightforward approach, he headed toward the nearest pedestrian.

McCoy grabbed his arm. "Wait a minute," the doctor said. "That billboard—you're obviously supposed to know already what yellow pages are. Or is. For all we know, maybe we're supposed to know what 'it' is, too. If we go around asking questions blind, somebody's bound to get suspicious."

"'Tis true," Scott said.

"So maybe they'll think we're a little strange," Sulu said. "Maybe they'll think we're from out of town. But I don't think we have to worry about anybody's suspecting that we're space travelers from the future!"

"Out of town . . ." McCoy said. "Sulu, that's a good idea." He regarded Sulu, then Scott, speculatively. "Which one of us is most likely to be able to pass for somebody from out of town?"

All their clothes were just different enough to stand out, but not different enough to attract inordinate amounts of attention; none was physically remarkable in comparison to the general population of San Francisco.

"Mr. Scott," McCoy said. "I think you're elected. Your accent—"

"Accent!" Scott exclaimed. "Ye canna be sayin' that I speak wi' an accent!"

"But . . ." McCoy let his protest trail off. "Everybody here does, so in relation you'll sound like you're from out of town. It's that, or I'll have to do my Centaurian imitation—"

"Never mind!" Scott said. "If I'm elected, I'm elected." He straightened his uniform jacket, glanced around, and left their group to speak to the next pedestrian.

"Begging your pardon, sir," he said. "But I'm from out of town, and I was wondering—"

The pedestrian walked past without acknowledging Scott's presence. Scott watched him go, frowning. He rejoined Sulu and McCoy.

"What d'ye make of that?"

McCoy shrugged. "I can't imagine."

"Try again," Sulu said.

Again Scott straightened his coat; again he approached a pedestrian.

"If I might have a moment of your time, sir—"

"Get out of my face!"

Scott backed off, startled. The pedestrian stormed away without a backward glance, muttering something about panhandlers, tracts, and street crazies.

"This isna working," Scott said to Sulu and McCoy. "Doctor, maybe ye'd better attempt the Centaurian imitation after all."

"Come on, Scotty, once more," McCoy said. "Third try's the charm."

Scott approached a third pedestrian. As he neared her, she dropped something. Scott picked it up.

"Excuse me, ma'am, ye dropped this."

She turned back. "Are you speaking to me?"

"Aye, ma'am, that I am, ye dropped this." He offered her the folded leather parcel.

"That's very kind of you," she said, "but I've never seen that wallet before. Maybe we'd better see if there's any identification inside." She took the wallet, opened it, and looked through it.

"Aye, ma'am, I'm sure ye'd know what's best to do wi' it, but I'm from out of town, and I was wondering—"

"Oh, my goodness," she said. "There isn't any identification, but look at this." She displayed a wad of bills. "There must be a thousand dollars in here!"

Scott had not yet got used to twentieth-century money. It all looked the same to him, so all he could tell was that there was a good bit more of it in the wallet than Admiral Kirk had given Sulu. He shrugged.

"I'm sure ye'd know better than me," Scott said. "In the meantime, could ye tell me what the term 'yellow pages' means?"

"Look, if we turn this in to the police, they'll just disappear it even if somebody claims it. Why don't we split it? We'll both put up some of our own money to show our goodwill, and—" She stopped. "What did you say?"

"I asked ye if ye knew what 'yellow pages' means."

"You're not from around here, are you?"

"I told ye that, too," Scott said, wishing he could figure out why it was so difficult to get a simple answer to what he hoped was a simple question.

"Where are you from?"

"Why, Scotland."

"Don't they have phone books in Scotland?"

"What's a phone book?"

"A directory of phone numbers. The yellow pages are the commercial part. You don't have those in Scotland?"

"Nay," he said. Her expression indicated the necessity of some further explanation. "'Tis all computerized, ye see."

"Oh." She shook her head, bemused. "I suppose your money is computerized, too, and you don't have any cash on you. I bet you don't have any cash money in this country at all."

"Aye," he said, then suddenly wondered if he had said too much. "Why d'ye ask?"

She sighed. "Never mind, it isn't important. If you need some yellow pages, all you have to do is find a phone—you do have phones in Scotland, don't you?"

"Aye," he said, "I mean, well, in a manner o' speaking."

"Phone." She turned him around and led him to a tall, narrow, glass-sided box. He stood before it, waiting for the door to open. She reached out and pulled the handle, folding the door.

'Tis mechanical, Scott thought, startled by its primitiveness.

"Door," she said. She hoisted a heavy, black-covered book that hung by hinges. She put it on a shelf, opened it, backed out of the booth, and pointed again. "Yellow pages."

"Thank ye kindly, ma'am," Scott said. "Ye've been of great help."

"Just call me a good Samaritan," she said. "You have a nice day, now." She started away.

"Ma'am?"

"What is it?"

"That wallet—ye seemed to think 'twould cause ye difficulty. Would ye want me to turn it in for ye? I could try to find the time."

She cocked her head. "No," she said. "No, don't worry about it. I know what to do with it."

"Thank ye again."

She raised her hand in acknowledgment and farewell, already striding down the street.

Scott went into the phone booth and paged through the phone book. After a moment, McCoy and Sulu joined him.

"What was all that about?" McCoy said.

"All what, doctor?"

"What took you so long?" the doctor snapped. "I thought you were going to take her out on a date."

"I wouldna jeopardize our mission wi' such a digression," Scott said, affronted. "Nay, she found a wallet—I mean, I found a wallet—" As he began to get his bearings in the yellow pages—he found it easier if he thought of it as a printed technical manual—he repeated the conversation to McCoy and Sulu. When he finished, all three agreed that the encounter was incomprehensible.

"Hah!" Scott exclaimed, pointing to a section of a yellow page. "Acrylic sheeting! 'Tis bound to be just what we need. Burlingame Industrial Park. Off wi' us, then."

A few blocks and a few phone booths away, Chekov found what he was looking for. He clapped the reinforced cover of the phone book shut and rejoined Uhura on the sidewalk.

"Find it?" she asked.

"Yes. Under U.S. Government. Now we need directions." He stopped the first passerby he saw. "Excuse me, sir. Can you direct me to Navy base in Alameda?"

The man looked at Chekov, looked at Uhura, and frowned. "The Navy base?"

"Yes," Chekov said. "Where they keep nuclear vessels?"

"Sure," the man said slowly. "Alameda. That's up north. Take BART—there's the station over there—toward Berkeley and all the way to the end of the line. Then catch a bus to Sacramento. You can't miss it."

"*Spasiba*," Chekov said. "Thank you."

Harry watched the Russian biker in the leather suit and the black woman in the paramilitary uniform head toward the BART station. He scowled after them. Then he smiled with one corner of his mouth. He entered the same phone booth they had left, picked up the receiver, wiped the mouthpiece with his pocket handkerchief, and dialed a number from memory.

It took quick thinking to divert a couple of trained spies like that. He had never expected anything like this to happen to him, right out on the street. He never expected to have this kind of chance.

"FBI."

"This is Gamma," Harry said. He recognized the agent's voice. He had talked to him before. He did not know his name, so he called him Bond. Bond never sounded very sympathetic when Harry called, but he always listened and he always claimed to have taken down the information. Harry suspected Bond never did anything with it, though, because the TV and the newspapers never announced the apprehension of any of the spies Harry detected. Someday Gamma would show Bond what he was worth to the government. Maybe this was the time.

Harry assumed the brief pause on the FBI's end of the line was for Bond to turn on a tape recorder.

"What do you want now?"

"I just talked to two spies."

"Spies. Right."

Harry explained what had happened. "What else could they be but commie spies? They asked for directions to Alameda but I sent them to Sacramento instead. You ought to be able to catch them up at the bus station at the end of the BART line."

"Okay. Thanks much."

"You aren't going to do anything, are you?" Harry said angrily.

"I can't release information about investigations over the phone," Bond said. "You know that."

"But—he was a Russian, I tell you. And that woman with him, I bet she was from—from South Africa. Aren't you guys always saying the Russkies are trying to take over Africa?"

Bond did not reply for so long that Harry wondered if he had to change the tape in the recorder.

"A black South African spy," Bond said.

About time I got through to him, Harry thought. "Yeah. Had to've been."

"Right. Uh, thanks very much." The line went dead.

Harry replaced the receiver. Finally he had Bond listening to him. The FBI man must have hung up fast so he could get a squad of agents out after the saboteurs.

The spies had spent a lot of time in and around this phone booth. Maybe another spy had left something for them to pick up. Or maybe *they* had left something to be collected! That would be something to show to Bond, all right. He searched on top of the phone, around the shelves, above the door, even inside the coin return. City grime covered everything with a thin, dusty film. It made him want to wash his hands. He found a quarter, but nothing in the way of secret documents. Maybe he was looking for a microdot. The trouble was that he had no idea what a microdot looked like. He inspected the quarter carefully but found nothing out of the ordinary.

Then he recalled another sneaky thing the government had found out the Russians did. They covered doorknobs and telephones and money and whatever they could get their hands on with poison dust that glowed, or emitted radiation, or something.

He dropped the quarter, kicked it into the corner of the phone booth, and bolted outside.

Suddenly fearful of being spied on himself, Harry glanced suspiciously around. They left the quarter as bait, and marked it, so the spies must have fingered him as an enemy. He rubbed his contaminated hands down the sides of his trousers. He would have to find a place to wash. But he was too smart to let them trick him into leading them right to his home. He would follow the first pair of spies instead. That would fool the ones following him, all right, if he led them to their cohorts and let them run into each other. Maybe Bond and his group could scoop them all up at once.

He headed for the BART station.

Sliding smoothly underground in the Bay Area Rapid Transit train, Uhura read the advertisements on the walls of the car. She hoped they would tell her something about the culture she was trying to hide inside, but they were all written in a sort of advertising shorthand, almost a code, in which a few words meant a great deal to a member of the community, but very little to a stranger. She turned her attention to the schematic map of the transit routes.

"Pavel," she said. "That fellow sent us off in the wrong direction."

"What? How is this possible?" He jumped up and looked at the map.

Uhura traced the route the man on the street had indicated. "I don't know where Sacramento is," she said, "but if we go through Berkeley and then turn east, in the first place we'll be headed away from the sea, not toward it. At least I don't remember that there's been a sea in that direction for a lot longer in the past than we've come. In the second place, Berkeley is north of us, and we want to go to Alameda, which is south." She touched the city on the map.

"You're right," Pavel said.

"We'll have to get off on the other side of the bay and transfer," she said. "I wonder how much it will cost? This is getting expensive."

"I wonder why he told us wrong thing," Pavel said.

Uhura shook her head. "I don't know. Maybe he's from out of town, too, and just didn't want to seem ignorant."

"That must be explanation."

At the first station on the other side of the bay, they got off, waited, and boarded a train going south. Uhura sat down gratefully, glad to be headed in the right direction without an unnecessary digression. She looked out the window. Another train, heading north, stopped beside them.

"Pavel—look!"

The man who had sent them in the wrong direction sat in the northbound car. Someone sat down next to him. He shifted closer to the window and looked away. His gaze locked with Uhura's. As her train pulled out going south, and his train pulled out going north, he jumped up and stared after her with an expression of shock and anger.

Chapter Seven

CHANGING PAPER MONEY into a metallic form suitable for use on the bus took more time and more powers of persuasion than obtaining the paper money in the first place. Admiral Kirk walked angrily out of the first two establishments in which they sought help. The first proprietor pointed to a hand-lettered sign stuck to his counter with adhesive strips of transparent plastic: "No change." The second proprietor snarled, "What am I, a bank?" He did not react sympathetically when Spock tried to explain about their lost luggage. He muttered something about foreigners and invited Spock and Kirk to depart.

"My disguise appears to be successful," Spock said when they were once more out on the street.

"Too damned successful," Kirk said.

"Admiral," Spock said, "my understanding is that the amounts of money we possess are not too small to permit us onto the bus, but too large."

"Very astute, Mr. Spock."

"In that case, we must purchase something that costs less than the difference between one piece of paper money and the amount of metallic money we must give to the bus."

"Astute again."

"It is simple logic."

"So simple I even figured that one out for myself. I've been trying to avoid buying something nonessential. But I don't see any alternative." Scowling, he strode into a third shop. Spock followed. Kirk plucked a small foil-wrapped disk from a bowl on the counter. "I'll have one of these," he said, and handed the clerk a bill.

She pressed keys on a machine that emitted buzzes and a small slip of paper. She handed Kirk a handful of change and a handful of bills. She put the disk into a plastic bag, folded the slip of paper over the bag's top, and fastened it all securely with a small device that inserted a small piece of wire. This was a ceremonial ritual with which Spock was not familiar. The clerk handed Kirk the bag. "Anything else for you today?"

"Yes, thank you," Kirk said. "I'd like some more of these." He showed her the metallic money and offered her another bill.

"Look, mister, I'm sorry. The boss really gets on my case if I give people bus change—that is what you need, isn't it?—and run out of quarters halfway through the afternoon. If it was up to me—"

"Never mind," Kirk said through clenched teeth. "I'll have *two* of these." He picked up another disk, went through the process all over again, and stalked out of the store. "Here, Spock," he said when they were once more on the street. "Have a mint."

Spock disassembled the package, unwrapped the foil, and sniffed the wafer inside. Kirk ripped open the bag he carried and ate his wafer quickly; Spock put his wafer in his mouth and allowed it to melt as he analyzed the outer and inner tastes.

A bus stopped; they entered; they paid. Once they had prepared themselves, the task became simple.

As is true of so many other endeavors, Spock thought.

They sat in the only remaining seat. A young person sat in the seat in front of them, feet stretched across the second seat, attention centered on a large, rectangular, noise-producing machine.

"Admiral," Spock said, "I believe this confection you have given me contains sucrose."

"What?" Kirk said.

Spock wondered why he spoke so loudly. "Sucrose," he said again, showing Kirk the foil wrapper.

"I can't hear you!" Kirk shouted, and Spock realized the admiral was having trouble sorting voices from the sounds produced by the noise-making machine. The admiral leaned toward the next seat. "Excuse me," he said. He received no response. "Excuse me! Can you please stop that sound?"

The young person glanced up, blinked, raised one fisted hand with the middle finger extended, then pushed the machine aside and stood.

"Want to try to make me?" The young person leaned over the back of his seat toward Admiral Kirk.

"That could be arranged," the admiral said.

The young human punched him. But the admiral blocked the blow. The young man's fist smacked against Kirk's palm.

Before the altercation could escalate, Spock placed his fingers at the junction of the neck and shoulder of the young person. He applied slight pressure. The young person sagged, unconscious. Spock settled him securely in the corner of the seat, inspected the controls of the noise-box, and pressed the control marked "on/off." The noise ceased.

Suddenly the other riders on the bus began to applaud. Spock realized, to his surprise, that they were applauding him.

"Domo arigato gozaimashita!" someone shouted at him. Spock had no idea what that meant. Feeling conspicuous, he sat down again. Admiral Kirk settled beside him. To Spock's relief, the applause subsided and the attention of the other riders returned to their own concerns. He could only assume that the audience had enjoyed the minor spectacle.

"As you observed," Spock said, "a primitive culture."

"Yes," Kirk said rather too loudly in the absence of the noise. He lowered his voice abruptly. "Yes."

"Admiral, may I ask you a question?"

"Spock, dammit, don't call me admiral!" Kirk whispered. "Can't you remember? You used to call me Jim."

Having been told the same thing by several people whose word he trusted, Spock believed this to be true; but another truth was that he did not actually remember it. He said nothing. He felt rather strange. He tried to shake off the effects of the sucrose and the other active chemicals in the mint.

"What's your question?" Kirk said.

"Your use of language has altered since our arrival. It is currently laced with—shall I say—more colorful images: 'double dumb ass on you,' and so forth."

"You mean profanity. That's simply the way they talk here." He shrugged. "Nobody pays any attention to you if you don't swear every other word. You'll find it in all the literature of the period."

"For example?"

"Oh . . ." Kirk considered. "The complete works of Jacqueline Susann, the novels of Harold Robbins . . ."

"Ah," Spock said. He recognized the names from a list he had scanned: the most successful authors of this time. "The giants."

The bus roared onto the Golden Gate Bridge. Kirk and Spock let their discussion of literature drop, for the Pacific stretched away to one side and the bay and the golden California hills stretched in the other, and the cables of the bridge soared above it all.

Following other visitors to the Cetacean Institute, Jim stepped down from the bus, Spock close behind. The wide, white, multileveled building stretched along the shore before them. The sun warmed the pavement and the salt air sparkled. Jim laid out a few more of the precious dollars for admission. He passed through the doors, entering a huge, cool, high-ceilinged display hall. Life-sized replicas of whales hung overhead, swimming and gliding through the air above a group of visitors.

"Good morning." A young woman faced the group. "I'm your guide today," she said. "I'm Dr. Gillian Taylor. You can call me Gillian. I'm assistant director of the Cetacean Institute. Please follow me, and just give a yell if you can't hear. Okay?"

She was twenty-five or thirty, and she had a lot of presence for someone so young. She had a good smile, too. But Jim got the impression that escorting tourists did not completely occupy her attention. He moved closer. Spock lagged at the back, but Jim supposed the Vulcan could not get himself in too much trouble. He had agreed, for the moment, to let Jim ask the questions. They both assumed Jim had a better chance of fitting in with this culture. Jim hoped they both were right.

"The Cetacean Institute is devoted exclusively to whales," Gillian Taylor said. "We're trying to collect all the research that exists on cetaceans. Even if we succeed, our information will be minuscule compared to what we still have to learn—and what we think we know that's wrong. The first common misconception is that whales are fish."

She passed a striking series of underwater photographs of whales. Jim wanted to inspect them more closely, but he also wanted to listen to Gillian Taylor. Gillian Taylor won out.

"Whales aren't fish," she said. "They're mammals, like us. They're warm-blooded. They breathe air. They produce milk to nurse their young. And they're very old mammals: eleven million years, give or take."

A little boy waved his hand to attract her attention. "Do whales really eat people, like in *Moby Dick?*"

"Many whales, baleen whales, like George and Gracie, don't even have teeth," Gillian Taylor said. "They strain plankton and shrimp out of vast amounts of sea water, and that's the limit of their hostility. Moby Dick was a sperm whale. He did have teeth, to hunt giant squid thousands of feet beneath the surface of the sea. But there are very few documented cases of attacks on people by whales. Unfortunately, their principal enemy is far more aggressive."

"You mean human beings," Jim said.

She glanced at him and nodded. "To put it bluntly. Since the dawn of time, people have 'harvested' whales." She accentuated the word *harvested* with considerable sarcasm. "We used the bodies of these creatures for a variety of purposes—most recently for dog food and cosmetics."

Jim noticed that she used few cosmetics herself; the blue of her eyes was natural, unaccented, and intense.

"Every single product whales are used for can be duplicated, naturally or synthetically, and usually more economically than by hunting whales. A hundred years ago, using hand-thrown harpoons, people did plenty of damage. But that was nothing compared to what we've achieved in this century."

She led the group to a large video screen and touched a button. Images appeared, grainy and ill defined by Jim's standards, but affecting nonetheless. The films in the *Bounty*'s computer had been grotesque. These, of a modern whale-processing operation, were gruesome. A helicopter spotted a pod of whales. Following directions from the air, a powered boat singled out the largest whale and pursued it. A cannon blasted a harpoon into the whale's side. The harpoon itself exploded. In a moment, an immense and powerful entity changed to a bleeding, dying hulk. The hunt had been replaced by assembly-line killing and butchery.

The harpoon boat left the whale floating and set out after another victim. The dying whale moved its flukes convulsively, erratically, as if somehow the creature could free itself, escape, and live. But it was not to be. The factory ship engulfed the whale and dismembered it into oil and bones, flesh and entrails.

"This is humanity's legacy," Gillian Taylor said. "Whales have been hunted to the edge of extinction. The largest creature ever to inhabit the earth, the blue whale, is virtually gone. Even if hunting stopped right now, today, we've got no assurance that the population would be able to recover."

Gillian's bitterness cut Jim deeply. Her intensity drew him into bearing some of the responsibility for what had happened in their past, for what was happening in her present, and for what would occur in Jim's present, in the future.

"Despite all attempts to ban whaling, countries and pirates continue to engage in the slaughter of these inoffensive creatures. In the case of the humpback, the species once numbered in the hundreds of thousands. Today, less than seven thousand individuals still live, and the whalers take smaller and smaller victims because the whales no longer have time to reach their full growth. And since it's hard to tell whether a whale is male or female, whalers even take females carrying unborn calves."

"To drive another species to extinction is not logical."

Gillian glared at the back of the crowd, at Spock.

"Whoever said the human race was logical?" Anger tinged her voice, but she repressed it. "If you'll all follow me, I'll introduce you to the Institute's pride and joy."

Gillian led the group out into the sunlight. A wide deck surrounded an enormous tank.

"This is the largest sea water tank in the world," Gillian said. "It contains the only two humpback whales in captivity."

Jim scanned the surface of the water, squinting against the dazzle on the wavelets.

"Our pair wandered into San Francisco Bay as calves. Whales, especially humpbacks, seem to have a well-developed sense of humor. So we call our whales George and Gracie."

On the other side of the tank, the arched black back of a whale broke the surface. The whale's small dorsal fin cut through the water. The whale gathered itself, hesitated, flipped its flukes into the air, and smoothly disappeared.

"They're mature now," Gillian said. "They weigh about forty-five thousand pounds each. Gracie is forty-two feet long and George is thirty-nine. They're mature, but they aren't full-grown. Humpbacks used to average about sixty feet—when full-grown humpbacks still existed. It's a measure of our ignorance of the species that we don't even know how long it will take these individuals to reach their full size."

Jim heard a loud splash. Some members of the audience gasped, but Jim's attention had been on Gillian Taylor, and he had not seen the whale leap. A wave splashed at the edge of the deck.

"That was Gracie leaping out of the water," Gillian said. "What she did is called breaching. They do it a lot, and we don't know why. Maybe it's a signal. Maybe it's courtship. Or maybe it's because they're playing. Their scientific name is *Megaptera novae-angelica;* we call them humpbacks because of their dorsal fin. But the Russians have the perfect name. They call them *'vessyl kit,'* merry whale."

Jim faded to the back of the group to rejoin Spock.

"It's perfect, Spock!" he whispered. "A male, a female, together in a contained space! We can beam them up together and consider ourselves damned lucky!"

Spock raised an eyebrow.

The whales swam to the edge of the tank nearest Gillian, rose, and spouted the mist of their breath. Gillian knelt on the deck, reached into the water, and stroked one of the whales.

"Aren't they beautiful?" Gillian said. "And they're

extremely intelligent. Why shouldn't they be? They're swimming around with the largest brains on earth."

Jim moved to the front of the group again. All he could make out of the whales was two huge dark shapes beneath the bright water.

"How do you know one's male and one's female?" Jim asked. They looked the same to him. Gillian Taylor glanced at him. She blushed.

"Observational evidence," she said, and quickly continued her lecture. "Despite all the things they're teaching us, we have to return George and Gracie to the open sea."

"Why's that?" Jim asked, startled.

"For one thing, we don't have the money to feed them a couple of tons of shrimp a day, and it takes the whole morning to open all those little cans."

Everybody laughed except Jim, who had no idea what was so funny.

"How soon?" he asked. A month, he thought. Even a week. By then we'll be gone, and you won't have to worry about feeding them anymore. I'll take them to a good home, Dr. Gillian Taylor, I promise you that.

"Soon," Gillian said. "As you can see, they're very friendly. Wild humpbacks would never come this close to a person. Whales are meant to be free. But I've . . . grown quite attached to George and Gracie." She strode across the deck. "This way." Her voice sounded muffled.

She led the group down a set of spiral stairs, through an arched doorway, and into a blue-lit chamber with one curving wall of glass. At first Jim could see only the water beyond. The glass wall, a section of a sphere, arched overhead. Some meters above, the surface rippled smoothly.

Suddenly a great *slap!* thundered through the chamber. An enormous shape, obscured by bubbles, plunged through the surface toward them.

Gillian laughed. The bubbles rose in a swirling curtain, revealing the colossal shape of a humpback whale.

"This is a much better way to see George and Gracie," Gillian said. "Underwater."

None of the pictures, none of the films, even hinted at the sheer size and grace of the creature. It used its long white pectoral fins like wings, soaring, gliding, banking, turning. It rose surfaceward and with a powerful stroke of its tail it sailed through the surface and out of sight. Its entire majestic body left the water. A moment later, ten meters farther on, it plunged into the water upside-down, flipped around, and undulated toward the viewing bubble. At the limits of vision through the tank's water, a second whale breached, then swam, trailing bubbles, to join its partner at the glass. They glided back and forth across the curve of the window. For a moment Jim felt as if he were enclosed and the whales were free.

Jim had expected the tremendous creatures to be clumsy and lumpish, but underwater their supple bodies moved easily, balancing on their flippers, muscles rippling. They looked as if they were flying, as if they were weightless. Speakers on the walls emitted an occasional whistle, or a groan, and the smooth, silky sound of the whales' motion.

George and Gracie undulated past and away, now parting, now coming together to stroke each other with their long flippers.

Spock kept himself at the back of the crowd, but he too watched the humpback whales cavort and play. Their grace and elegance and power transfixed him. Vulcan possessed no creatures the size of whales. Though Spock knew he had observed enormous creatures in his earlier life, he could remember only pictures, recordings, descriptions.

Spock wondered if it was proper Vulcan behavior to be amazed by two creatures playing. He decided he did not care, for the moment, about proper Vulcan behavior. He merely wanted to watch the whales. Nevertheless, the object of the *Bounty*'s mission remained in his mind. Only now did he fully realize the magnitude of the task. If the two whales found themselves beamed into the storage tank without any knowledge or understanding of why they were being transported or where they were being taken, they might panic. Perhaps twenty-third-century materials could withstand the force of the powerful body of a terrified whale. But Spock had no doubt that the structural integrity of a tank jury-rigged from contemporary materials would be severely compromised by such stress.

Spock felt quite strange. He wondered if he were being affected by human emotions. T'Lar and the other Vulcan adepts had warned him against them. Yet his mother, also an adept, had urged him to experience them rather than shutting them out. Spock wondered if now might be the time to take her advice.

"Humpback whales are unique in a number of ways," Dr. Taylor said. "One is their song." She touched a control on a wall panel.

A rising cry soared from the speakers, surrounding the audience.

"This is whale song that you're hearing," Dr. Taylor said. "It isn't the right season to hear it live; this is a tape. We know far too little about the song. We can't translate it. We believe it's only sung by male humpbacks. George will sing anywhere from six to thirty minutes, then start the song over again. Over time, the song evolves. In the ocean, before the era of engine-powered seagoing vessels, the song could be heard for thousands of miles. It's possible—though it's impossible to know for sure, because human beings make so much noise—that a single song could travel all the way around the world. But the song can still travel long distances, and other whales will pick it up and pass it on."

Gracie glided past the viewing window again. As her eye passed Spock, he had the sensation of being watched. He wondered if she sensed the presence of him and Admiral Kirk; he wondered if the whales had some intimation of the intentions of the visitors from the future.

Will they believe they are being stolen? Spock wondered. No, not stolen. Stolen implies that someone owns them, and this is not the case. I doubt that Dr. Taylor believes she owns them. Perhaps some governmental body claims possession, but that could have no effect on what the whales perceive. The whales may believe they are being kidnapped or abducted. Suppose they do not wish to leave this time and place? In that case, do we have the right to take them against their will? If, in fact, we do take them against their will, would our actions not defeat our own purpose? If two beings who have been wronged answer the probe, it may respond with more and wider aggression.

Spock could imagine only one solution to the dilemma: communication. And since Dr. Taylor admitted that human beings could neither communicate with the whales nor translate their songs, Spock saw only a single way of achieving the solution.

He moved to the exit, turned, and swiftly climbed the spiral staircase to the surface level of the whale tank. One of the creatures slid past at his feet, curving its back so its dorsal fin cut the water. It dove again, and he could see only its shadowy form, its white pectoral fins, beneath the ripples. At the far end of the tank, the second whale surfaced and spouted with a blast of vapor and spume. Despite the impressive size of the tank, it was little more than a pond to a creature who could dive one hundred fathoms, and whose species regularly migrated a quarter of the circumference of earth.

The hot sunlight poured down on Spock. He gazed across the surface of the pool, dropped his robe, and dove.

The cold salt water closed in around him and whale sounds—not a song, but curious creaks and squeaks and moans—engulfed him. The vibrations traveled through the water and through his body; he could both feel and hear them. The whales turned toward him, curious about the intruder, and the inquiring sounds became more intense, more penetrating. One whale swam beneath him and breathed out bubbles that rose around him and tickled his skin. She turned and ascended and hovered at Spock's level. Her great eye peered directly into his face. The warmth of her body radiated through the frigid water.

He reached toward her, slowly enough that she could glide out of his reach if she chose. She hung motionless.

Spock touched the great creature, steeling his psyche for mind-melding's assault.

Instead, a gentle touch soothed and questioned him. The peace of the whale's thoughts surrounded him, incredibly powerful, yet as delicate as a windrider.

The touch questioned, and Spock answered.

Inside the observation chamber, Jim Kirk listened

to Gillian Taylor talk about the whales. He was both fascinated by the information and impatient for the lecture to end so he could speak to her alone.

One of the whales glided past the observation window, drawing Spock along with it. Jim smothered a gasp of astonishment.

Damn! he thought. Of all the harebrained things to do, in front of fifty people! Maybe Bones is right—

A murmur of surprise rippled over the crowd as one person brought the odd sight to the notice of the next.

And if Spock's headband slips off, Jim thought, we're going to have a lot more to explain than why my crazy companion wants to take a dive in a whale tank.

At least Gillian Taylor had not noticed. Perhaps no one would say anything directly . . .

"The song of the humpback whale changes every year. But we still don't know what purpose it serves. Is it navigational? Part of the mating ritual? Or pure communication, beyond our comprehension?"

"Maybe the whale is singing to the man," said one of the spectators. Jim flinched.

Gillian turned. "What the hell—!" She stared at Spock, disbelieving, then spun and sprinted for the stairs. "Excuse me! Wait right here!"

Ignoring her order, Jim rushed after her. At the top of the spiral he burst out into the bright sunlight, blinking.

Spock raised himself from the tank with one smooth push. Water splashed and dripped around his feet. He straightened his headband and shrugged into his robe.

"Who the hell are you?" Gillian shouted. "What were you doing in there?"

Spock glanced toward Jim.

144

I can't take the chance of us both getting arrested, Jim thought.

"You heard the lady!" Jim said.

"Answer me!" Gillian said. "What the hell do you think you were doing in there?"

"I was attempting the hell to communicate," Spock replied.

"Communicate? Communicate what?" She looked him up and down. "What do you think you are, some kind of Zen ethologist? Why does every bozo who comes down the damned pike think they have a direct line to whale-speak?"

"I have no interest in damned pikes," Spock said. "Only in whales."

"I've been studying whales for ten years and *I* can't communicate with them! What makes you think you can come along and—never mind! You have no right to be here!"

In silence, Spock glanced at Jim. Jim tried once more to hint that they should pretend not to be acquainted.

"Come on, fella!" he snapped. "Speak up!" He realized too late that Spock would take him literally.

"Admiral, if we were to assume these whales are ours to do with as we please, we would be as guilty as those who caused their extinction."

"Extinction . . . ?" Gillian said. She glanced from Jim to Spock and back. "O-*kay*," she said. "I don't know what this is about, but I want you guys out of here, right now. Or I call the cops."

"That isn't necessary," Jim said quickly. "I assure you. I think we can help—"

"The hell you can, buster! Your friend was messing up my tank and messing up my whales—"

"They like you very much," Spock said. "But they are not the hell your whales."

"I suppose they told you that!"

"The hell they did," Spock said.

"Oh, *right*," she said, completely out of patience.

In short order Jim and Spock found themselves escorted with politeness, firmness, and finality from the Cetacean Institute by an elderly unarmed security guard. They could have resisted him easily, but Jim did not even try to talk his way into staying. He thought he could do it, but he also thought that if he did he would attract more attention and cause himself more trouble than if he left quietly.

He trudged down the road, a few paces ahead of Spock. They had found out most of what they needed to know.

But *damn!* Jim thought. I'll just *bet* I could have found out when they're planning to release the whales if I'd had a few more minutes . . .

Spock lengthened his stride and caught up to him.

"I didn't know you could swim, Spock," Jim said with some asperity.

"I find it quite refreshing, though I wonder if it is proper Vulcan behavior," Spock said, oblivious to Jim's irritation. "It is not an ability that is common, or even useful, on my home world. Admiral, I do not understand why Dr. Taylor believed I wanted the hell to swim with damned pikes."

"What possessed you to swim with damned whales?" Jim exclaimed.

Spock considered. "It seemed like the logical thing to do at the time."

"In front of fifty people? Where's your judgment, Spock?"

Spock hesitated. "It is perhaps not at its peak at the moment, admiral. Sucrose has been known the hell to have this effect on Vulcans. I do not usually indulge."

"Indulge? Spock, do you mean to tell me you're *drunk?*"

"In a manner of speaking, admiral." He sounded embarrassed.

"Where did you get it? Why did you eat it?"

"You gave it to me. I did not realize that the wafer's main constituent was sucrose until I had damned already ingested it."

Jim abandoned that line of conversation. "Listen, Spock," he said.

"Yes?"

"About those colorful idioms we discussed. I don't think you should try to use them."

"Why not?" Spock said.

"For one thing, you haven't quite got the hang of it."

"I see," Spock said stiffly.

"Another thing," Jim said. "It isn't always necessary to tell the truth."

"I cannot tell a lie."

"You don't have to lie. You could keep your mouth shut."

"You yourself instructed me to speak up."

"Never mind that! You could understate. Or you could exaggerate."

"Exaggerate," Spock said in a thoughtful tone.

"You've done it before," Jim said. "Can't you remember?"

"The hell I can't," Spock said.

Jim sighed. "All right, never mind that, either. You mind-melded with the whale, obviously. What else did you learn?"

"They are very unhappy about the way their species has been treated by humanity."

147

"They have a right to be," Jim said. "Is there any chance they'll help us?"

"I believe I was successful," Spock said, "in communicating our intentions."

With that, Spock fell silent.

"I see," Jim said.

Chapter Eight

GILLIAN TRIED NOT to be too obvious about hurrying the audience along, but as soon as the last of them finally disappeared through the museum doors, she ran through the lobby, up the spiral staircase, and out onto the deck around the whale tank. George and Gracie sounded and swam toward her, their pectoral fins ghostly white brush strokes beneath the surface. Gillian kicked off her shoes and sat down with her feet in the water. Gracie made a leisurely turn, rolled sideways, and stroked the bottom of Gillian's foot with her long fin. Her movement set up a wave that sloshed against the side of the tank and splashed over the other side.

Both whales rose and blew, showering Gillian with the fine mist of their breath. Gracie lifted her great head, breaking the surface with her knobby rostrum, her forehead and upper jaw. Unlike wild humpbacks, Gracie and George would come close enough to be touched. Gillian stroked Gracie's warm black skin.

Underwater, the whale's eye blinked. She blew again, rolled, raised her flukes, and lobbed them into the water. Gillian was used to being splashed.

Both whales seemed upset to Gillian, not agitated but anxious. She had never seen them act like this before. Of course, this was the first time a stranger had ever actually dived in with them, which was probably lucky. Heaven knows enough nuts picked whales to fixate on.

Maybe, Gillian thought, I ought to be surprised nobody ever got in the tank before now. But I should have realized something odd was going on with those two guys, the way they were dressed, and the one so quiet, the other so intense and with so many questions.

"It's all right," she said. "Yes, I know." George nuzzled her leg with one of the sensory bristles on his chin. "It's okay. They didn't mean any harm."

At the sound of footsteps she turned quickly, wondering if the two strangers had returned.

Instead, the director of the Cetacean Institute looked down at her and grinned sympathetically.

"Heard there was some excitement." Bob Briggs kicked off his shoes and rolled up his slacks too. He sat beside her and eased his feet into the cold water.

"Just a couple of kooks," Gillian said. But if they were only harmless kooks, she thought, why were they so interested in when we're letting the whales free?

Gillian wished Bob would leave her alone with George and Gracie. With some effort, she could get along all right with her boss. He was not deliberately malicious, but his offhand condescension annoyed the hell out of her.

"How're you doing?"

"Fine," she said. "Just fine."

"Don't tell me fish stories, kiddo. I've known you too long."

"It's tearing me apart!" she snapped.

Damn! she thought. Suckered in again.

"Want to talk about it? It'll help to get your problems out in the open."

"You've been in California too long," she said.

She stared at the water and at the two whales drifting just under the surface at her feet. Every few minutes one would rise above the glimmer of water, exhale noisily, inhale softly, and sink again.

"I know how you feel," Bob said. "I feel the same. But we're between a rock and a hard place, Gill. We can't keep them without risking their lives and we can't let them go without taking the same chance."

"Yeah," she said. "Why are you lecturing me about this? It was my idea to free them in the first place! I had to fight—"

"I'm lecturing you," he said, "to help you get over your second thoughts."

"I'm not having any second thoughts!" she snapped. She immediately regretted her outburst. "I want them to be free. I want them to be safe, too, but there isn't any place in the world where that can happen. And . . . I'll miss them."

"Gill, they aren't human beings! You keep looking for evidence that they're as smart as we are. I'd be *delighted* if they were as smart as we are. But there isn't any proof—"

"I don't know about you, but my compassion for someone isn't limited to my estimate of their intelligence!" She glared at him angrily. "Maybe they didn't paint the *Mona Lisa* or invent the dirt bike. But they didn't ravish the world, either. And they've never driven another species to extinction!" Water splashed as she rose. Gracie and George moved away from the noise and swam to the center of the tank. "Sorry if I spoke out of turn," Gillian said bitterly.

"Not at all," Bob said. He never lost his temper. That was one of the reasons he was director, and one of the ways he made Gillian so mad. "You always give me things to think about. Gillian, why don't you go home early? You sound pretty wrecked."

"Thanks for the compliment," she said.

"Come on. You know what I mean. Really. Why don't you go home? Stare at the ceiling for a while."

"Yeah," Gillian said. "Why don't I?" She picked up her shoes and walked away.

Gillian flung her shoes into the back of her Land Rover, cranked the ignition, shoved a Waylon Jennings tape into the tape deck, and drove out of the parking lot faster than she should have. The speed helped, though she could not run from the dilemma of the whales. She did not want to run from it. She only wanted to let it blow away with the wind for a little while.

The incident with the two strangers refused to blow away with the wind. Why had the one in the tank referred to George and Gracie as extinct? Endangered, sure. Maybe he was just sloppy with his word choice.

But he sounded like he knew what he was talking about, Gillian thought. Just what the hell does he know that I don't?

Waylon was singing "Lonesome, On'ry and Mean." Gillian turned the volume up too loud and put her attention to driving, to the speed and the road and the blast of hot autumn air.

Back at the Institute, Bob Briggs watched the two whales surface and blow at the far end of the tank. With everyone but Gillian, George and Gracie acted like wild whales, coming close enough to watch but not to touch.

The track of Gillian's small wet footprints had begun to dry. He was worried about her. When she left the whales, she always looked as if she feared she would never see them again. And this time . . .

He shrugged off his doubts. He knew he had made the right decision. Gillian would be grateful to him later.

His assistant came out of the museum, blinking in the sunshine, and joined him on the deck.

"All squared away?"

"Looks like it," Bob said.

"She's gonna go berserk."

"It's for her own good," Bob said. "It's the only way. She'll call me names for a while, but then she'll calm down. She'll understand."

"Alameda Naval Base!" Pavel Chekov exclaimed. "Finally!"

"No thanks to our helpful friend," Uhura said. She glanced around.

"What is wrong?"

"Nothing. I just keep expecting to see him again. Lurking. Hiding behind a bush or a shrub."

"I am sure he just made mistake," Pavel said.

"Maybe."

"It was coincidence to see him on train. He realized he gave us incorrect directions. He was embarrassed. He has no earthly reason to feel suspicion."

"No earthly reason?" Uhura said. Pavel grinned.

The trees parted before them. Sunlight glittered off the water of the harbor.

Uhura saw the ship. *Enterprise,* CVN 65.

She stopped. She shivered suddenly; the last time

she had seen the huge craft, it was in a photo displayed on board the starship *Enterprise*.

Through generations of ships, from space shuttle to system explorer to early star voyager, the name descended to the starship on which Uhura had spent most of her adult life. In this time and this place, the name belonged to an aircraft carrier. She moved toward it, awed by its size, fascinated by the destructive power it represented. In Uhura's time, structures much larger than this were commonplace, but they were built in space, without the restrictions of gravity and air and water pressure. This century's *Enterprise* existed in spite of those factors. The hull swept upward, then flared out to accommodate the landing deck. Uhura and Pavel entered the shadow of its curving side.

Pavel gestured toward the name. Uhura nodded. Pavel opened his communicator; Uhura set to work with her tricorder.

Pavel transmitted the communicator code. "Team leader, this is team two. Come in please . . ."

Uhura studied the readings. "I have the coordinates of the reactor. Or, anyway, coordinates that will have to do."

Pavel gazed at the carrier. "This gives me great sense of history."

"It gives me a great sense of danger." The emissions from the reactor added distortion to Uhura's information, making it impossible to get a precise idea of the layout of the ship. "We have to beam in *next* to the reactor room, not *in* it."

"Team leader," Pavel repeated, "this is team two. Come in please . . ."

On the other side of the bay, Jim trudged down the road leading from the Cetacean Institute. Several buses had passed them by, despite Jim's waving whenever he saw one coming. Public transportation must stop only at spots marked by shelters like the one in the city, but he had not yet found one on this road. He still wished he had brought a pair of walking shoes. Spock, of course, made no complaint; he simply strode along nearby as if they were on a field trip. Every so often he stopped to inspect some dusty plant by the side of the road. More often than not he would nod and murmur, "Fascinating. An extinct species."

"Spock, dammit!" Jim said. "If you keep referring to plants and animals in this world as extinct, somebody is going to start wondering about you."

"I think it unlikely that anyone will reach the proper conclusion about my origin," Spock said.

"You're probably right. But they might reach an improper conclusion about your sanity, and that could cause us trouble."

"Very well," Spock said. "I shall endeavor to contain my enthusiasm. But are you aware, admiral, that during this period of humanity's history, your species managed to eradicate at least one other species of plant or animal life each day? That frequency increased considerably before it decreased."

"Fascinating," Jim said grimly. "It's your species, too. In case you've forgotten."

"I have not forgotten," Spock said. "But it is a fact on which I prefer not to dwell."

"You ignore everything about earth and about humans that you possibly can, yet it was you who recognized the humpback's song! Why *you*, Spock?"

"I believe . . ." Spock hesitated. "I remember . . . I have told you that I taught myself to swim, many years ago on earth. Once, I swam too far. The current caught me. Its force overcame me. When I had nearly lost myself, I felt a creature nearby. I expected a shark

155

to tear my flesh, to kill me. But when the creature touched me, I felt the warmth of a mammal, and I discerned a young and bright intelligence. A dolphin swam beneath me. She supported me and helped me toward shore. One reads of such behavior in mythology, but I had never given the tales credence. We . . . communicated." Spock reached down and touched a dusty, nondescript plant by the side of the road. "This species, too, is extinct in our time. Like the great whales. But the smaller cetaceans, the dolphins, survive. They preserve the memories of their vanished cousins. They remember—they tell stories, in pictures created of sound—the songs of the humpback. They hold themselves aloof from humans, and who can blame them? But I am not a human being. Not entirely. The dolphin sang to me."

In his imagination, Jim could see the endless ocean and feel the depths of its cold; he could feel the supple warmth of the dolphin and hear its echo of the humpback's call.

"I see, Spock," he said softly. "I understand."

Jim's communicator beeped the signal code. He started, pulled it out, and opened it.

"This is team two. Come in please."

"Team two, Kirk here."

"Admiral," Chekov said, "we have found nuclear vessel."

"Well done, team two."

"And, admiral, this ship is aircraft carrier . . . *Enterprise.*"

Jim felt a pang of regret for his own ship. He kept his voice carefully controlled. "Understood. What is your plan?"

"We will beam in tonight, collect photons, and beam out. No one will ever know we were there."

"Understood and approved," Jim said. "Keep me informed. Kirk out."

He started to call in to Scott, but heard a vehicle speeding down the road behind him. He quickly put away his communicator.

The ground car screeched to a halt behind them, passed them slowly, and stopped again.

Jim kept walking at a steady pace.

"It's her," he said sidelong to Spock. "Taylor, from the Institute. Spock, if we play our cards right, we may learn when those whales are really leaving."

Spock glanced at him. Jim knew he had one eyebrow quirked, even though the headband obscured it.

"How," the Vulcan said, "will playing cards help?"

Using the rearview mirror, Gillian watched the two men approach. She put the Rover in first gear and started to let out the clutch, then changed her mind and jammed the gearshift to reverse. She backed up the Rover and stopped.

"Well," she said. "If it isn't Robin Hood and Friar Tuck."

"I'm afraid you have us confused with someone else," the one in the maroon jacket said. "My name is Kirk, and his is Spock."

She let the Rover ease forward to keep up with him. "Where're you fellas heading?"

"Back to San Francisco," Kirk said.

"That's a long way to come, just to jump in and swim with the kiddies."

"There's no point in my trying to explain what I was doing. You wouldn't believe me anyway."

"I'll buy that," Gillian said. She nodded toward Spock. "And what about what he was trying to do?"

"He's harmless!" Kirk said. "He had a good reason—" He cut himself off. "Look, back in the sixties he was in Berkeley. The free speech movement, and all that. I think . . . well, he did too much LDS."

"LDS? Are you dyslexic, on top of everything else?" She sighed. A burnt-out druggie and his keeper. She felt sorry for them, now that she was sure they posed no danger to the humpbacks. "Let me give you a lift," she said. She smiled ruefully. "I have a notorious weakness for hard-luck cases. That's why I work with whales."

"We don't want to be any trouble," Kirk said.

"You've already been that. Get in."

Spock got in first, then Kirk slid in and slammed the door. Spock sat stiff and straight and silent. When Gillian reached for the gearshift, her hand brushed past his wrist. His body radiated heat, as if he had a high fever. But he did not look flushed. He drew away and slid his hands into the sleeves of his long white robe.

"Thanks for the ride," Kirk said.

"Don't mention it," Gillian said. "And don't try anything, either. I've got a tire iron right where I can get at it."

"I appreciate it, but I don't need help with a—tire iron?"

"You will, if—oh, never mind."

"What's that noise?"

"What noise?" She listened for a problem with the engine.

"That—" Kirk hummed a few notes off-key with the gravelly voice on the tape.

"That's not noise, that's Waylon Jennings!" She turned it down a little. "Don't you like country-western?" She was used to that reaction from her colleagues. "There's some rock in the box on the floor. Not much sixties, I'm afraid. Some Doors, though."

Kirk moved the tape box and looked around. "I don't see a door down here—oh." He opened the glove compartment. Road maps folded inside out and emergency supplies spilled into his lap. Gillian lunged over and grabbed a handful of stuff and pushed it into the glove compartment.

"What is all this?"

"Just junk, shove it all back. I didn't say 'door,' I said 'Doors.' How could you get through the sixties in Berkeley without knowing about the Doors?"

"I didn't say I was at Berkeley, I said Spock was at Berkeley."

"Yeah, but, still—"

"The Doors were a musical group, admiral," Spock said. "Mid-nineteen-sixties to—"

"Yes, Spock, I get the idea, thank you."

"Want to hear something really different?" Gillian asked. "I've got some Kvern. And 'Always Coming Home' is in there someplace."

"I'm not much on music," Kirk said. "That's more Mr. Spock's department. Can you turn it off? Then we could talk."

"Oh. Well. All right." She turned off the tape and waited for Kirk to start talking. She drove along for a time during which neither man spoke.

"So," she said to Spock, determined to get some kind of straight information out of at least one of them, "you were at Berkeley."

"I was not," Spock said.

"Memory problems, too," Kirk said.

"Uh-huh," she said skeptically. "What about you? Where are you from?"

"I'm from Iowa."

"A landlubber," Gillian said.

"Not exactly."

"Come on," Gillian said. "What the hell were you

159

boys really doing back there? Men's club initiation? Swimming with whales on a dare? If that's all, I'm going to be real disappointed. I hate the macho type."

"Can I ask *you* something?" Kirk said suddenly.

She shrugged. "Go ahead."

"What's going to happen when you release the whales?"

Gillian clenched her hands on the wheel. "They're going to have to take their chances."

"What does that mean, exactly?" Kirk said. " 'Take their chances'?"

"It means that they'll be at risk from whale hunters. Same as the rest of the humpbacks."

"We are aware of whale hunters," Spock said. "What I do not understand is the meaning of 'endangered species,' or the meaning of 'protected,' if hunting is still permitted."

"The words mean just what they say," Gillian said. "To people who agree with them. The trouble is, there isn't any way to stop the people who *don't* agree with them. A bunch of countries still allow whale hunting, and our government always seems to find it expedient not to object." She frowned at Spock. "What did you mean when you said all that stuff back at the Institute about extinction?"

"I meant—"

Kirk interrupted. "He meant what you were saying on the tour. That if things keep on the way they're going, humpbacks will disappear forever."

"That's not what he said, farm boy. He said, 'Admiral, if we were to assume these whales are ours to do with as we please, we would be as guilty as those who *caused*'—past tense—'their extinction.' " She waited. Kirk did not reply. "That *is* what he said."

Spock turned to Kirk. "Are you sure," he said, "that it is not time for a colorful idiom?"

Gillian ignored Spock. "You're not one of those guys from the military, are you?" she said to Kirk. "Trying to teach whales to retrieve torpedoes or some dipshit stuff like that?"

"No, ma'am," Kirk said sincerely. "No dipshit."

"That's something, anyway," she said. "Or I'd've let you off right here."

"Gracie is pregnant," Spock said.

Gillian slammed on the brake and the clutch. Spock moved quickly, bracing one hand on the dashboard even before the tires squealed on the pavement. But the sudden stop flung Kirk forward.

"All right," Gillian shouted. "Who are you? Don't jerk me around anymore! I want to know how you know that!"

Kirk pushed himself back. He looked shaken. "We can't tell you," he said.

"You'd better—"

"Please. Just let me finish. I can tell you that we're not in the military and that we intend no harm to the whales." He leaned forward, one hand reaching out, open.

"Then—"

"In fact," Kirk said, "we may be able to help—in ways that you can't possibly imagine."

"Or believe, I'll bet," Gillian said.

"Very likely. You're not exactly catching us at our best."

"That much is certain," Spock said.

"That I *will* believe." Gillian drove on in silence for a mile or so.

"You know," Kirk said, his cheer sounding a little forced, "I've got a hunch we'd all be a lot happier talking over dinner. What do you say?"

Gillian wondered what she had let herself in for. If they were a danger to the whales, she ought to dump them out on the highway right now—except then she would not be able to keep an eye on them.

"You guys like Italian food?" she said.

They looked at each other as if they had no idea what she was talking about.

"No," said Spock.

"Yes," said Kirk.

Gillian sighed.

In the factory reception room, Montgomery Scott paced back and forth with unfeigned agitation. He pretended to be angry, but in truth he had a serious case of nerves.

He glanced at the door leading to the inner office. McCoy had been in there for a very long time.

In the manager's office, Dr. Nichols peered at the screen of his small computer. He was middle-aged and balding, wearing glasses and a rumpled cardigan sweater. He used a fist-sized mechanical box with a button on top to flip through the plant schedule. Each click of the button put a new page on the screen. When he moved the box across the desktop, a pointer on the computer screen moved on an identical path. Nichols frowned with perplexity.

"I don't understand why there's nothing down here about your visit," he said. "Usually the PR people are all too efficient."

"But Professor Scott's come all the way from Edinburgh to study your manufacturing methods. Obviously there's been a mix-up, but the university said the invitation was all arranged. I should have checked—you know academics."

"I do know academics," Nichols said. "Used to be one myself, as a matter of fact."

"Er . . ." Gliding over his *faux pas*, McCoy tried

creative hysteria. "Professor Scott is a man of very strong temperament," he said. "I don't know if the university got its signals crossed, or he got the date wrong. All I know is that I'm responsible for bringing him here. If he came all this way and goes all the way back for nothing, I get to be responsible for that, too. Dr. Nichols, he'll make my life a living hell."

"We can't have that," Nichols said with a smile. "I think the office will survive without me for an hour or so. Wouldn't do to have a visiting dignitary go back to Edinburgh with unpleasant memories of American hospitality, would it?" He rose and headed for the outer office. McCoy followed.

"Professor Scott," Nichols said, extending his hand. "I'm Dr. Nichols, the plant manager."

Scott stopped pacing and drew himself up, hands on his hips.

"I'm terribly sorry about the mix-up," Nichols said, overlooking Scott's snub. "Would you believe no one told me about your visit?"

Scott glared balefully at McCoy.

"I've tried to clear things up, Professor Scott," McCoy said quickly. "They didn't have any idea you were coming—"

"Dinna ha' any idea!" Scott exclaimed. He used an impenetrable Scots burr. "D'ye mean t' say I ha' come millions o' miles—"

Dr. Nichols smiled patiently. "Millions?"

"Now, professor, it's only thousands," McCoy said in a soothing tone. "It's understandable that you're upset, but let's not exaggerate."

"—thousands o' miles, to go on a tour o' inspection to which I was *invited*—and then ye mean to tell me ye never invited me i' the first place? I demand—"

"Professor Scott, if you'll just—"

"I demand to see the owners! I demand—"

"Professor, take it easy!" McCoy said. "Dr. Nichols is going to show us around himself."

Scott stopped in the middle of a demand. "He is?"

"With pleasure," Dr. Nichols said.

"That's verra different," Scott said.

"If you'll follow me, professor," Nichols said.

"Aye," Scott said. "That I will. And—'twould be all right if my assistant tags along as well?"

"Of course."

Dr. Nichols led them from the receptionist's office. Following him, Scott passed McCoy.

"Don't bury yourself in the part," McCoy muttered.

Sulu approached the plastics company's big huey, entranced. He had seen still photos and battered old film of this helicopter, but none had survived, even in museums, to his time. The huey was as extinct as the humpback whale. He stroked one hand along its flank.

He climbed up and looked into the cockpit—incredible. Hardly any electronics at all, all the gauges and controls mechanical or hydraulic. Flying it would be like going back to horse-and-buggy days. And he had never driven a horse and buggy.

The craft's engine cowling closed with a loud clang. Sulu heard footsteps.

"Can I help you?"

Sulu turned. "Hi." He gestured toward the helicopter. "Huey 205, isn't it?"

"Right on." The young pilot wiped his hands on a greasy rag. "You fly?"

"Here and there," Sulu said. He patted the helicopter's side. "I flew something similar to this in my Academy days."

"Then this is old stuff to you."

"Old, maybe. But interesting." He jumped to the ground and offered his hand. "I'm Sulu—with the international engineering conference tour?"

The pilot shook his hand. "I didn't know about a tour. They just tell me fly here, fly there, don't drop the merchandise. International, huh? Where you from? Japan?"

"Philippines," Sulu said, just to be safe. He had Japanese in his ancestry, but more of his family came from the Philippines, and he knew far more of its history.

"Hey. You folks really did it. Repossessed your country. What about all the loot, though? Think that will ever make it home again?"

"Oh, I think so, eventually," Sulu said, trying not to sound too certain. He drew the conversation back to the huey. "I was hoping I'd find a pilot when I saw this helicopter. Mind if I ask a few questions?"

"Fire away."

They chatted about the copter for a while. The pilot glanced at his watch. "I've got to make a delivery," he said. "Want to come along?"

"I'd like nothing better."

The chopper lifted off in an incredible clatter of noise. Sulu watched the pilot work, itching to take over. The young man glanced at him. "If anybody asks," he said, "you never flew this thing."

"If anybody asks," Sulu said, "I've never even been *in* this thing."

The young pilot grinned and turned over the controls.

All day Javy tried to talk about what he and Ben had seen in Golden Gate Park, and all day Ben tried to act as if they had seen nothing. He froze up every time Javy mentioned the shooting star or the wind or the lights or the ramp.

When they got off that afternoon, Javy still felt hyper. He had been awake since three and working since four. He usually went home, dove into the shower, slept for a couple of hours, got up, and stared at half-finished pages in his typewriter for a while. Today, all that changed.

He got into his battered gold Mustang and turned on the radio, but it only worked on alternate Fridays and leap days that fell on Wednesday. He tried to pick out news reports through the static and jumps of a traveling short circuit, but heard nothing about the lights.

He needed a shower. This would look different after he got some sleep. Ben was probably right all along.

But instead of going home, he drove down Van Ness, then turned onto Fell, back to the park. He pulled his car up beside the garbage cans, which he had not finished emptying. He tried to smile at the thought of trying to explain why to their supervisor.

The truck had left a patch of rubber on the street where Ben floored it. It was not easy to lay rubber with a garbage truck.

Javy stayed in his car and looked toward the place where he thought he had seen . . . what? In the mist and the dark, perhaps he had not seen anything. Some people out for a stroll, their flashlights glinting off the fog? In daylight, he could not even be sure where he thought he saw what he thought he saw. Whatever it was, nothing remained of it. He decided to watch for a while anyway, just for interest's sake. He settled back in the driver's seat.

Within a few minutes, he had fallen fast asleep.

* * *

Scott followed Dr. Nichols through the plant, wondering how on earth the people in this time had ever managed to achieve anything, much less the beginnings of space exploration. With their incredibly primitive methods, he could just see his way to doing what he needed to do with their materials. He wanted to get away to someplace quiet and think for a bit. Twentieth-century factories were unbelievably noisy.

As the tour progressed, Dr. McCoy drew Dr. Nichols out. The engineer's sharp and ambitious intelligence chafed within the bureaucracy of management.

"I've put in for a transfer back to research," Nichols said. "Upper management never understands when you want to go back to what you're best at doing."

"Aye," Scott said, recalling all the times Starfleet had tried to promote him out of engineering. "'Tis true."

"Especially if you're working for a plastics company and your first love is metallurgy. I've got some ideas about metallic crystalline structure—" He stopped. "But of course you're interested in acrylic production, Professor Scott."

"Professor Scott—'tis too formal. Call me Montgomery, if ye would."

"Certainly," Nichols said. "If you'll return the courtesy. My name's Mark."

"Verra well, Mark. Not Marcus? Ye are Marcus Nichols?" He grabbed Nichols's hand and pumped it. "I'm verra glad to meet ye! The work ye've done, the inventions—"

Behind Nichols, McCoy waved his hands in warning. Scott realized what he had said. He stopped abruptly.

"My inventions?" Nichols said, startled. "Professor

Scott, I only hold two patents, and if you've heard of either in Edinburgh, I'm surprised, to say the least."

"But—er—well—"

"You must have him confused with another Marcus Nichols," McCoy said quickly. "That's the only logical—" He stopped as abruptly as Scott.

"But—I mean, aye, that must be it." Scott subsided, face flaming with embarrassment.

"I see," Nichols said.

Nichols led Scott and McCoy into a glass-walled observation cubicle. Its door swung shut, cutting the sound to nearly nothing.

"So much for the tour of our humble plant." Nichols leaned one hip on the back of a leather-covered couch and gave Scott a long, searching appraisal. "I must say, professor, your memory for names may not be terrific, but your knowledge of engineering is most impressive."

"Why, back home," McCoy said, "we call him the miracle worker."

"Indeed . . ." Nichols gestured toward the bar at the back of the cubicle. "May I offer you gentlemen anything?"

McCoy and Scott exchanged a glance.

"Dr. Nichols," Scott said tentatively, "I might have something to offer *you.*"

Nichols raised an eyebrow at this turn of the conversation. "Yes?"

"I notice ye are still working with polymers," Scott said.

"Still?" Nichols frowned, mystified. "This is a plastics company. What else would I be working with?"

"Ah, what else indeed? Let me put it another way. How thick would ye need to make a sheet of your acrylic"—Scott hesitated a moment, converting meters to feet, wishing the twentieth century had finished getting around to the change—"sixty feet by ten feet, if ye wished it to withstand the pressure o' 18,000 cubic feet o' water?"

"That's easy," Nichols said. "Six inches. We carry stuff that big in stock."

"Aye," Scott said. "I noticed. Now suppose—just suppose—I could show ye a way to manufacture a wall that would do the same job but was only an inch thick. Would that be worth something to ye?"

"Are you joking?" Nichols folded his arms. His body language revealed skepticism, suspicion—and interest.

"He never jokes," McCoy said. "Perhaps the professor could use your computer?"

"Please," Nichols said, gesturing toward it.

Scott sat before the machine. "Computer."

The computer did not reply. McCoy grabbed the control box he had seen Nichols using earlier and shoved it into Scott's hand. Scott thanked him with a nod and spoke into it.

"Computer."

No reply.

"Just use the keyboard," Nichols said, "if you prefer it to the mouse."

"The keyboard," Scott said. "'Tis quaint."

He laced his fingers together and cracked his knuckles. Fast and two-fingered, he started to type.

Information filled the screen. Scott condensed each formula into a few words as he worked. After half an hour, he pressed a final key.

"And if ye treat it by this method, ye change the crystalline structure so 'twill transmit light in the visible range."

A three-dimensional crystalline structure formed on the computer screen. Scott sat back, satisfied.

"Transparent aluminum?" Nichols said with disbelief.

"That's the ticket, laddie."

"But it would take years just to figure out the dynamics of this matrix!"

"And when you do," McCoy said, "you'll be rich beyond the dreams of avarice."

Nichols's attention remained centered on the screen, which fascinated him far more than dreams of avarice.

"So," Scott said, "is it worth something? Or shall I just punch 'clear'?" He extended one finger toward the keyboard.

"No!" Nichols exclaimed. "No." He stared at the screen, frowning, uncomfortable. "What did you have in mind?"

"A moment alone, please," McCoy said.

Scott started to object.

"Please," McCoy said again.

Unwillingly, Nichols left them alone.

"Scotty," McCoy said, "if we give him the formula, we'll be altering the future!"

"How d'ye know he didn't invent the process?" Scott said.

"But—"

"Dr. McCoy, do ye no' understand? He *did* invent it! Have ye ne'er heard his name?"

"I'm a doctor, not a historian," McCoy growled. He had gone into this masquerade willingly, but now he found himself possessed with the need to make as few changes in the past as he could. The intensity of Jim Kirk's argument for their actions warred with another, alien impulse.

"'Tisna necessary to be a historian to know o' Marcus Nichols! Why, 'twould be as if I never heard o' . . . er . . ."

"Pasteur?"

"Who?"

"Yalow? Arneghe?"

"Nay, well, ne'er mind, the point is, Nichols *did* invent transparent aluminum! And that was only the beginnin' o' his achievements. 'Tis all right that we gi' the formula to him—perhaps 'tis essential!"

McCoy looked at him with his head cocked in a familiar and yet very un-McCoyish way.

"Then, Scotty, does that mean we succeed? We get the whales and get back to our own time and—"

"Nay, doctor. It means we gi' him the formula—or he recalls enough o' what I've already shown him to reproduce the effect. What happens back in our time . . . 'tis up to us."

McCoy nodded. He squared his shoulders and opened the door, beckoning Nichols into the transparent cubicle again. The scientist had been standing with his back to the windows, nervously giving his uninvited guests their privacy.

"Now, Dr. Nichols—Mark—" Scott said.

"Just a moment." He paused and took a deep breath. "You know what it is you're offering me."

"Aye," Scott said. "That I do."

"Why?"

"Why? Why what?"

"Why are you offering it to me?"

"Because we need something ye have."

"Such as what? My first-born child? My soul?"

Scott chuckled. "Nay. Acrylic sheets, large ones. Acrylic epoxy. The loan o' transportation."

"What you're asking for is worth a couple of thousand dollars at most. What you're offering in return is worth—if it's true—a whole lot more. As well as recognition, respect . . ."

"But, you see, Mark," McCoy said, "we don't have

171

a couple of thousand dollars. And we need the acrylic sheets. Desperately."

"Does the phrase 'too good to be true' mean anything to you?"

McCoy clapped his hand over his eyes. "What a time to run into an honest man!"

Nichols glanced at the tantalizing computer screen. "What you've shown me looks real," he said. "It's just a beginning, but it feels right. It feels like an answer—and I've been trying just to ask the question for the last two years. On the other hand, scientists smarter than me have been taken in by perpetual motion machines and heaven knows what-all kinds of absurd devices. How do I know—"

"Ye think we're tryin' to trick ye!" Scott exclaimed, astonished.

"The possibility did occur to me," Nichols said mildly. "You could be snowing me with fake formulae. You could be trying to plant some other company's research on me in order to embarrass my company with a charge of industrial espionage."

"I hadna thought o' that," Scott said, downcast.

Nichols glanced at McCoy with a wry grin. "Academics," he said.

"What can we do to persuade you we're legitimate?" McCoy said.

"Are you?"

"Er . . . in a way. In that we're not trying to cheat you or defraud you. Or embarrass your company."

"But if this is real, you could sell it—"

"Do ye no' understand?" Scott cried. "We have no time!"

Nichols hitched one hip on his desk, deliberately turning his back to the information on the computer screen.

"Ordinarily, if you wanted to sell something like

this—no, let me finish—you'd take it to a company and license it in return for a royalty."

"But 'tisna royalties we need. 'Tis—"

"Mark," McCoy said, "we don't have time for this. We're going to make this trade with someone. It ought to be you. Don't ask me to explain why. If it is you, I think we can be sure it will be well used. If it'll make you feel better to assign the royalties to your favorite charity, or your Aunt Matilda, go ahead. But we're pretty desperate. If we have to go elsewhere, to find someone with fewer scruples, we will."

Nichols drew one knee up, folded his hands around it, and gazed at them both. Then he turned to the computer, carefully saved Scott's work, and moused a purchase order up on the screen. Beneath "Bill to" he typed "Marcus Nichols."

"Tell me what you need," he said.

Chapter Nine

GILLIAN'S LAND ROVER wound through Golden Gate Park along Kennedy Drive.

"Are you sure you won't come with us, Mr. Spock?" Gillian said. "We don't have to have Italian food. I'll take us to a place where you can get a hamburger if you want."

"What is a hamburger?" Spock said.

"A hamburger? It's, you know, ground-up beef. On a bun. With a little lettuce, maybe some tomatoes."

"Beef," Spock said. "This is meat?"

"Yes."

"Sounds pretty good, Spock," Kirk said.

Spock looked green. Uh-oh, Gillian thought, a vegetarian. She had never seen anyone actually turn green before. Maybe it was a trick of the light on his sallow complexion. But he sure looked green.

"I shall prefer not to accompany you," Spock said.

"Okay."

Spock looked at Kirk. "I thought that among my acquaintances only Saavik eats raw meat," he said. "But, of course, she was raised a Romulan."

"It isn't raw!" Gillian exclaimed. "They cook it! Raw hamburger, bleah."

"I don't think we should discuss Saavik, Mr. Spock," Kirk said. "And I hate to disillusion you, but I enjoy a bit of steak tartare on occasion myself."

Mr. Spock looked at Kirk askance. Gillian wondered why he reacted like that to the idea of raw meat, considering what sushi is made out of. She considered offering to change their plans and go to a Japanese restaurant instead. Then she wondered what country or city people called Romulans lived in. Maybe Mr. Spock's friend Saavik came from a country where the people called themselves something that had nothing to do with the country's name, like Belgium and Walloons. Or maybe Mr. Spock did not speak English as well as he seemed to, and he really meant his friend who liked raw meat was Roman. But who ever heard of steak tartare Romano, and what kind of a Japanese name was Spock anyhow?

But if he *is* Japanese, or from anyplace in Asia, Gillian thought, suddenly suspicious—

"How do I know you two aren't procurers for the Asian black market in whale meat?" she said angrily.

"What black market?" Kirk said.

"Human beings *consume* whale meat? The flesh of another sentient creature?" Mr. Spock sounded appalled. His reaction surprised Gillian. Up until now he had seemed rather cold and unemotional.

"You two pretend to know so much about whales— then you pretend not to know anything—"

"I did not pretend to know that human beings *ate* whales," Spock said.

"Gillian," Kirk said, "if we were black market

procurers, wouldn't it be awfully inefficient to come to California to steal two whales, when we could go out in the ocean and hunt them?"

"How should I know? Maybe your boat sank." She jerked her head toward Spock. "Maybe he wants to take Gracie and George away and pen them up like cattle and start a whale-breeding program back in Japan or someplace—"

"I do not intend to take George and Gracie to Japan," Spock said. "I am not from Japan. I have never been to Japan."

"Oh, yeah? Why are you walking around in that Samurai outfit, then? If you're not from Japan, where are you from?"

"I am from—"

"Tibet," Kirk said. "He's from Tibet."

"*What?*"

"He's from Tibet," Kirk said again. "It's land-locked. It's thousands of meters above sea level. What could he do with a pair of whales back in Tibet?"

"Christ on a crutch," Gillian said.

The Land Rover approached a meadow.

"This will be fine," Kirk said.

Gillian pulled into a parking lot. She did not spend much time in San Francisco proper; she did not like cities. She wondered if it was safe to be in this park at night. Probably not. Though dusk had barely begun to fall, only one other vehicle remained in the lot: a beat-up old muscle car with a young man sleeping in the driver's seat. Gillian felt sorry for him. He probably had nowhere else to stay.

Kirk opened the door and let his strange friend get out.

"Are you sure you won't change your mind?" Gillian said.

176

Spock cocked his head, puzzled. "Is something wrong with the one I have?"

His tone was so serious that Gillian could not decide whether to laugh or answer in the affirmative.

"Just a little joke," Kirk said quickly. He waved to Mr. Spock. "See you later, old friend."

Gillian left the Land Rover in neutral. "Mr. Spock, how did you know Gracie's pregnant? Who told you? It's supposed to be a secret."

"It is no secret to Gracie," Mr. Spock said. "I will be right here," he said to Kirk, and strolled across the meadow toward a terraced bank planted with bright rhododendrons.

"He's just going to hang around in the bushes while we eat?" Gillian said to Kirk.

"It's his way." Kirk shrugged and smiled.

Gillian put the Land Rover into gear and drove away.

Javy woke with a start.

"Hey, bud, you can't sleep here. Come on, wake up!" The cop rapped sharply on the Mustang's roof.

"Uh, good evening, officer."

"I know things get tough sometimes," the cop said. "But you're not allowed to sleep here. I can give you the address of a couple of shelters. It's getting late to get into either one of them, but maybe—"

"I don't need a shelter!" Javy said. "You don't understand, officer. I'm . . ." He got out of his car, pulled out his wallet, flipped it open to flash his city I.D., and flipped it shut again. "We've had trouble with vandalism. I'm supposed to be keeping an eye out." He grinned sheepishly. "I'm kind of new. I thought it'd be easy to keep awake on stakeout, you know, like on TV? But it's boring."

"No kidding," the cop said.

A sparkle of light against the darkness caught Javy's attention.

"Jeez, did you see that?"

He bolted past the cop and sprinted a few steps into the meadow. He stopped. The light and the man-shaped figure both had vanished.

"See what? There's nobody out there, bud. Let me see that I.D. again."

Still staring toward the vanished light, Javy pulled out his wallet. Once the cop had more than a glance at it, he realized what department Javy was really in.

"What do you think you are, detective trash class? Look, I don't know what you're trying to pull, trying to sleep on taxpayers' money, or what—"

"I start work at four a.m.!" Javy said angrily, defensively. He gestured toward his Mustang. "That look like a garbage truck to you?"

"Looks like it belongs *in* a garbage truck," the cop said. "But I'm tired and the shift's almost over and I can't think of any reason to take you in, acting stupid not being against the law. But if you make me—"

"Never mind!" Javy said, annoyed at the cop for insulting him and his car as well, but mostly annoyed with himself for falling asleep and blowing his chance. "I'll leave."

Gillian took Kirk to her favorite pizza place. She wondered if she would have had the nerve to come here if Mr. Spock had accompanied them. He was so strange—there was no telling how he would act in a restaurant. Come to think of it, she was not entirely sure how Kirk would act.

"Listen," she said to Kirk. "I like this restaurant, and I want to be able to come back, so you behave yourself. Got it?"

"Got it," he said.

Nevertheless she was relieved when a waiter she did not know took them to their table. She glanced over the menu, though she almost always had the same thing.

"Do you trust me?" she asked Kirk.

"Implicitly," he said without hesitation.

"Good. A large mushroom and pepperoni with extra onions," she said to the waiter. "And a Michelob."

He took it down and turned to Kirk. "And you, sir?"

Kirk frowned over the menu. Gillian had the distinct impression that he had never heard of pizza before. Where was this guy from, anyway? Mars?

"Make it two," Kirk said.

"Big appetite," the waiter said.

"He means two beers," Gillian said.

The waiter nodded, took the menus, and left. Gillian toyed with her water glass, making patterns of damp circles with its base and drawing clear streaks in the condensation on its sides. She glanced at Kirk just as Kirk looked at her, and they saw that they were both doing the same thing.

"So," Kirk said. "How did a nice girl like you get to be a cetacean biologist?"

The slightly condescending comment jolted her. She hoped Kirk meant the lines as a joke. She shrugged unhappily. "Just lucky, I guess."

"You're upset about losing the whales," he said.

"You're very perceptive." She tried to keep the sarcasm down. Just what she needed, Bob Briggs all over again, telling her she shouldn't think about them as if they were human, or even as if they were intelligent. They were animals. Just animals.

And if the whale hunters got to them, they would be dead animals, carcasses, raw meat . . .

"How will you move them, exactly?"

"Haven't you done your homework? It's been in all the papers. There's a 747 fitted out to carry them. We'll fly them to Alaska and release them there."

"And that's the last you'll see of them?"

"See, yes," Gillian said. "But we'll tag them with radio transmitters so we can keep track of them."

The ice in Kirk's water glass rattled.

His hand's trembling! Gillian thought. What's he so damned nervous about?

He drew back before he exploded the glass in his grip. "I could take those whales where they wouldn't be hunted."

Gillian started to laugh. "You? Kirk, you can't even get from Sausalito to San Francisco without a lift."

The waiter reappeared. He put plates and glasses and two bottles of beer in front of them.

"Thanks," Gillian said. She picked up the bottle, raised it in a quick salute, and took a deep swig. "Cheers."

"If you have such a low opinion of me," Kirk said grimly, "how come we're having dinner?"

"I told you," Gillian said, "I'm a sucker for hard-luck cases. Besides, I want to know why you travel around with that ditzy guy who knows that Gracie is pregnant . . . and calls you admiral."

Kirk remained silent, but Gillian was aware of his gaze. She took another swig of her beer and set the bottle down hard.

"Where could you take them?" she said.

"Hmm?"

"My whales! What are you trying to do? Buy them for some marine sideshow where you'd make them jump through hoops—"

"Not at all," he said. "That wouldn't make sense, would it? If I were going to do that, I might as well leave them at the Cetacean Institute."

"The Cetacean Institute isn't a sideshow!"

"Of course not," he said quickly. "That isn't what I meant."

"Then where could you take them where they'd be safe?"

"It isn't so much a matter of a place," Kirk said, "as of a time."

Gillian shook her head. "Sorry. The time would have to be right now."

"What do you mean, *now?*"

Gillian poured beer into her glass. "Gracie's a very young whale. This is her first calf. Whales probably learn about raising baby whales from other whales, like primates learn from primates. If she has her calf here, she won't know what to do. She won't know how to take care of it. But if we let her loose in Alaska, she'll have time to be with other whales. She'll have time to learn parenting. I think. I hope. No humpback born in captivity has ever survived. Did you know that?" She sighed. "The problem is, they won't be a whole lot safer at sea. Because of people who shoot them because they think they eat big fish. Because of the degradation of their environment. Because of the hunting." Her voice grew shaky. "So that, as they say, is that." She cut off her words and dashed the tears from her eyes with her sleeve. "Damn."

Gillian heard a faint beep. "What's that?"

"What's what?" Jim said.

The beep repeated.

"A pocket pager? What are you, a doctor?"

At the third beep, Kirk pulled the pager out and flipped it open angrily.

"What is it?" he snapped. "I thought I told you never to call me—"

"Sorry, admiral," the beeper said. "I just thought ye'd like to know, we're beaming them in now."

"Oh," Kirk said. "I see." He half-turned from Gillian and spoke in a whisper. Gillian could still hear him. "Scotty, tell them, phasers on stun. And good luck. Kirk out." He closed the beeper and put it away.

Gillian stared at him.

"My concierge," Kirk said. "I just can't get it programmed not to call me at the most inconvenient times." He stopped, smiling apologetically.

"I've had it with that disingenuous grin, Kirk," Gillian said. "You *program* your concierge? I'll bet he loves that. And if this is the most inconvenient time anybody ever called you, I don't know whether to envy you or feel sorry for you. Now. You want to try it from the top?"

"Tell me when the whales are going to be released."

"Why's it so important to you? Who *are* you?" she said. "Jeez, I don't even know the rest of your name!"

"It's James," he said. "Who do you think I am?"

She tried to take another swig from her beer bottle, but she had emptied it into her glass. She picked up the glass, drank, and put it down.

"Don't tell me," she said sarcastically. "You're from outer space."

Kirk blew out his breath. "No," he said. "I really am from Iowa. I just work in outer space."

Gillian rolled her eyes toward the ceiling in supplication. "Well, I was close. I *knew* outer space was going to come into it sooner or later."

"All right," he said. "The truth?"

"All right, Kirk James," she said, "I'm all ears."

"That's what you think," he said with a quick grin

that she ignored. "Okay. The truth. I'm from what, on your calendar, would be the late twenty-third century. I've been sent back in time to bring two humpback whales with me in an attempt to repopulate the species."

Gillian began to wish she were drinking something stronger than beer. "Hey, why didn't you *say* so?" she said, going along with him. "Why all the coy disguises?"

"Do you want the details?"

"Are you kidding? I wouldn't miss this for all the tea in China."

"Then tell me when the whales are leaving," Jim said.

"Jesus, you are persistent," Gillian said. She looked down into her beer. "Okay. Your friend is right. Like he said, Gracie is pregnant. Maybe it would be better for her to stay at the Institute till the end of the year. Then we could let her loose in Baja California just before she's ready to calve. But if the news gets out before we release her, we'll be under tremendous pressure to keep her. And maybe we should. But I told you the reasons for freeing her. We're going to let her go. At noon tomorrow."

Kirk looked stunned.

"Noon?" he said. "Tomorrow?"

"Yeah. Why's it so important to you?"

The waiter appeared and placed a large round platter on the table between Jim and Gillian.

"Who gets the bad news?" he said, offering the check to the air between them. Kirk looked up at him blankly.

Gillian took the bill. She had expected to go Dutch, but Kirk could at least offer to pay his share. "Don't tell me," she said. "They don't have money in the twenty-third century."

"Well, we *don't*," he said. He pushed himself to his feet. "Come on. I don't have much time."

He strode out, nearly running into a young man at the door.

Perplexed, Gillian watched Kirk leave. The waiter was staring after him too. Gillian wondered how much of their conversation he had heard. The waiter glanced at her with a confused frown. He could not be more confused than she was, and she had heard the whole thing.

"Uh, can we have this to go?" She gestured to the pizza.

Shaking his head, he went away to get a box, and Gillian wondered if she would ever be able to come back to the restaurant after all.

Uhura re-formed within the cool tingle of the transporter beam. She let out her breath with relief. The beam had placed her in an access corridor that led to the nuclear reactor. The reactor and all its shielding skewed the tricorder readings sufficiently that she had not been absolutely certain where she would appear. She pulled out her communicator and opened it. "I'm in," she whispered. "Send Pavel and the collector."

A moment later Chekov appeared beside her, carrying the photon collector. He started to speak. She gestured for silence. Her tricorder suggested the presence of one human being and a dog on the other side of the door to the access corridor, and many other people in the close to intermediate range. Many were pacing in back-and-forth patterns that suggested guard duty.

The dog's sharp single bark startled her. The door transmitted the sound clearly.

"Oh, come on, Narc, there's nothing in there." On the other side of the door, the guard chuckled. "If

184

anybody *did* stow dope in the reactor room, they deserve whatever they get back out." His voice faded as he continued his patrol along the outer corridor. "That's a good one. Radioactive coke. New street sensation. Snort it and your nose glows. Come *on*, Narc."

Uhura could even hear the tapping of toenails on the deck as the dog trotted away. She wondered what in the world the security officer had been talking to his dog about.

"Let's go," she whispered.

As she and Pavel headed deeper into the reactor area, the tricorder's readings grew more erratic. The only steady information it could give her concerned radiation. The shielding was less efficient than she would have liked. She and Pavel should not have to remain within the reactor's influence long enough to be in danger. But fission reactors had caused earth so many problems, some of which persisted even till her time, that she could not be comfortable around one.

A flashing reddish light reflected rhythmically through the corridor. Uhura rounded a bend. Above the reactor room door, a red warning light blinked on and off, on and off.

A large bright sign reading "DANGER" did not increase Uhura's confidence one bit.

Seeking the highest radiation flux with her tricorder, she found the spot and pointed it out to Pavel. He attached the collector to the wall. The field it created would increase the tunneling coefficient of the reactor shielding, causing the radiation to leak out at an abnormally high rate. It was a sort of vacuum cleaner for high-energy photons, and it could vacuum them up through a wall.

Pavel turned the collector on. It settled; it hummed.

"How long?" Uhura whispered.

Pavel studied the collector's readout. "Depends on amount of shielding, depends on molecular structure of reactor wall."

Uhura hoped the patrol would not come into the reactor looking for coke, whatever that was, radioactive or not.

Gillian parked the Land Rover on a bluff above the sea. The tide was out. The rocky beach gleamed in starlight.

Gillian ate pizza and listened to Kirk James's wild story. He had invented all sorts of details that sounded great. If they had been in a novel, she would have suspended her disbelief willingly.

The only trouble is, she thought, this is reality. He hasn't offered me anything to check the details against. And with this baloney about not leaving anachronistic traces in the past, he has a perfect excuse.

"So, you see," Kirk said at the end of his tale, "Spock doesn't want to take your whales home with him. I want to take your whales home with me."

Gillian handed Kirk a slice of pizza. The corner drooped over his fingers. He bit a chunk from the outer edge. Cheese strings stretched from his mouth to the piece of pizza.

He's never eaten pizza before, that's for sure, Gillian thought. Whoever heard of somebody who doesn't know you eat the point first? Maybe he really is from Iowa. Via Mars.

"Are you familiar with Occam's Razor?" she said.

"Yes," Kirk said. "It's just as true in the twenty-third century as it is now. If two explanations are possible, the simpler is likely to be true."

"Right. Do you know what that means in your case?"

His shoulders slumped. He put down the half-eaten piece of pizza and scrubbed at the cheese on his fingers with a shredding paper napkin.

"I'm afraid so." He raised his head.

Gillian liked his eyes, and his intensity attracted her. The trouble was, he kept offering evidence that it was the intensity of madness.

"Let me tell you a little more," he said.

One of her professors in graduate school preferred another theory over Occam's Razor for sorting out competing hypotheses. "Gillie," she always said, "if you've got two possibilities, go with the beautiful one, the aesthetically pleasing one." The possibility Kirk wanted her to believe was certainly the aesthetically pleasing one. His stories were almost as good as the stories her grandfather used to tell her when she was little, before.

"Do they have Alzheimer's disease in the twenty-third century?" she asked.

"What's Alzheimer's disease?" Kirk said.

"Never mind." She started the Land Rover and headed back into Golden Gate Park. She wished she could believe in his universe. It sounded like a great place to live.

"Tell me about marine biology in the twenty-third century," she said.

"I can't," he said. "I don't know anything about it."

"Why? Because you spend all your time in space?"

"No. Because when I spend time on boats, it's for recreation."

Gillian chuckled. "You're good. You're really good. Smart, too. Most people, when they try to take somebody in, they try to snow you too far and they catch themselves up. If they thought it'd help, they'd claim to *be* a marine biologist."

"I don't even *know* any marine biologists. My mother's a xenobiologist, and so was my brother."

"Was?"

"He . . . died," Kirk said.

"Then there's no immortality in your universe, either."

"No," he said, smiling sadly. "Not for human beings, anyway."

"Let me tell you some more about whales," Gillian said.

"I'd like to hear anything you've got to tell me," he said. "But if you won't help me, then I'm a little pressed for time."

"People have had killer whales in captivity for a couple of decades," she said. "Do you have killer whales in your world? Orcas?"

"No," he said. "I'm sorry, no. All the larger species are extinct."

"Orcas are predators. They swim fifty miles a day, easy. They have an incredible repertoire of sounds they can make. They talk to each other. A lot. That's what it sounds like they're doing, anyway. But when you put them in a tank, they change. They haven't got anywhere to go. They're kept in a deprived environment. After a couple of years, their range of sounds shrinks. Then they become aphasic—they stop talking at all. They get apathetic. And then . . . they die."

Gillian turned in at the parking lot.

"Gillian, that's a shame. But I don't understand—"

She turned off the engine and stared out into the darkness and the silence.

"George didn't sing this spring."

Kirk reached out, touched her shoulder, and gripped it gently.

"Kirk, humpback whales are meant to be wild. They migrate thousands of miles every year. They're part of an incredibly rich, incredibly complex ecosystem. They have the whole ocean, and a thousand other species to interact with. I was up in Alaska last summer, on a research trip observing humpbacks. We were watching a pod, and a sea lion swam right in beside one of them and dived and flipped and wiggled his flippers. The whale rolled over and waved her pectoral fin in the air, and she dove and surfaced and slapped her flukes on the water—she was playing, Kirk. We had a tape deck on the boat, we were listening to some music. When we put on Emmylou Harris, one of the whales swam within twenty feet of the boat—wild humpbacks just don't come that close —and dove underneath us and came up on the other side and put her head out of water, to listen. I swear, she liked it." She shivered, remembering her own wonder and joy and apprehension when the whale glided beneath her, a darkness against darkness, the long white pectoral fins gleaming on either side, their reach nearly spanning the boat's length. "I'm afraid for George and Gracie, Kirk. I'm afraid the same thing will happen to them that happens to orcas. George didn't sing. Maybe soon they'll both stop playing. And then . . ." Her voice was shaking. She fell silent and looked away.

"We'd take good care of them. They'll be safe."

"I want them safe! But I can keep them safe at the Institute. Till they die. It's freedom that they need most. I like you, Kirk, God knows why. And I'd like to believe you. But, you see, if you're going to keep them safe—imprisoned—it doesn't matter whether they're here at the Institute or with you . . . wherever. Whenever."

"Gillian, if their well-being depends on freedom, I swear to you they'll be free. *And* safe. There are no whale hunters in my time, and the ocean isn't polluted. There aren't any great whales anymore, no orcas, but there are still sea lions to play with. I'll even play country-western music to them, if you think it would make them happy."

"Don't make fun of me."

"I'm not. Believe me, I'm not."

He tempted her. Oh, he tempted her. "If you could prove what you've told me—"

"That's impossible."

"I was afraid of that." She reached over him and opened the door. "Admiral," she said, "this has been the strangest dinner of my life. And the biggest cockamamie fish story I ever heard."

"You did ask," he replied. "Now, will you tell me something?"

She waited.

"George and Gracie's transmitters," Kirk said. "What frequencies are you using?"

She sighed. He never gave up. "Sorry," she said. "That's—classified."

"That's a strange thing to hear from somebody who accused me of being in military intelligence."

"I still don't have a clue who you are!" she said angrily. "You wouldn't want to show me around your spaceship, would you?"

"It wouldn't be my first choice, no."

"So. There we are."

"Let me tell you something," Kirk said, his voice suddenly hard. "I'm here to bring two humpback whales into the twenty-third century. If I have to, I'll go to the open sea to get them. But I'd just as soon take yours. It'd be better for me, better for you . . . and better for them."

"I bet you're a damn good poker player," Gillian said.

"Think about it," Kirk said. "But don't take too

long, because we're out of time when they take your whales away. If you change your mind, this is where I'll be."

"Here? In the park?"

"Right."

He kissed her, a quick, light touch of his lips to hers.

"I don't know what else to say to convince you."

"Say good-night, Kirk."

"Good-night." He left the Land Rover and strode through the harsh circle of illumination cast by the street lamp.

Gillian hesitated. She wanted to believe him; she almost wanted to join in his attractive craziness and turn it into a *folie à deux*. Instead, she sensibly shoved the Land Rover into gear and stepped on the gas.

A strange shimmery light reflected from her rearview mirror. She braked and glanced out the back window, wondering what she had seen.

The street lamp must have flickered, for it cast the only illumination over the meadow. Whatever had caused the shimmery effect had disappeared.

And so had Kirk. The meadow was empty.

Chapter Ten

SPOCK WATCHED ADMIRAL Kirk re-form on the transporter platform.

"Did you accomplish your aims in your discussion with Dr. Taylor, admiral?"

"In a manner of speaking," Admiral Kirk said. "I told her the truth, but she doesn't believe me. Maybe you should try to talk to her. Without your disguise."

"Do you think that wise, admiral?"

"It wouldn't make any difference. She'd just explain you away with plastic surgery," he said with an ironic smile. "I wish she'd stop explaining me away. As it is, when we beam the whales on board, all Gillian will ever be sure of is that they've disappeared. She won't know if they lost their transmitters, or if they died, or if the whalers killed them." He blew out his breath in frustration. "What's our status?"

"The tank will be finished by morning."

"That's cutting it closer than you know. What about team two?"

"We have received no word since their beam-in. We can only wait for their call."

"Damn!" Kirk said. "Dammit!"

Spock wondered why Kirk employed two similar words of profanity, rather than repeating the same one twice or using two entirely different ones. No doubt the admiral had been correct in his statement that Spock did not yet know how to hang that part of the language.

"We've been so lucky!" Kirk said. "We have the two perfect whales in our hands, but if we don't move quickly, we'll lose them."

"Admiral," Spock said, "Dr. Taylor's whales understand our plans. I made certain promises to them, and they agreed to help us. But if we cannot locate them, my calculations reveal that neither the tank nor the *Bounty* can withstand the power of a frightened wild whale. In that event, the probability is that our mission will fail."

"Our *mission!*" Admiral Kirk shouted. He swung toward Spock, his shoulders hunched and his fists clenched.

Spock drew back, startled.

"Our *mission!* Goddamn it, Spock, you're talking about the end of life on earth! That includes your father's life! You're half human—haven't you got any goddamn feelings about *that?*" He glared at Spock, then turned, infuriated, and strode down the corridor.

Spock lunged one step after him. "Jim—!" He halted abruptly. The admiral vanished around a corner. He had not heard Spock's protest, and for that Spock felt grateful. He did not understand why he had made it. Spock did not understand the terribly un-Vulcan impulse within him that had led him to make it. He should have repressed it almost before he became aware of it. That was the Vulcan way. James Kirk's anger should have no effect on Spock of Vulcan, for anger was illogical. More than that, it was useless. It led to confusion and misunderstanding and inefficiency.

He knew all that as well as he knew anything. Why, then, did he himself feel anger toward the admiral? How could James Kirk's reaction cause a Vulcan so much pain?

He sought some explanation for Kirk's fury. Worrying about what would happen to earth if the *Bounty* did not return could have no effect on the fate of the planet; nor could worrying about Sarek's fate save the elder Vulcan. What did Kirk expect him to do? Even if he did feel concern and anguish, what possible benefit could be extracted from revealing the emotions to his superior officer, and humiliating himself with his lack of control?

Spock drew a deep breath, trying to calm himself, wrestling with his confusion and the emotions he could not continue to deny. He wanted to return to his quarters; he wanted to meditate and concentrate until he drew himself completely back into control. But he could not. Too much work remained to be done.

Trying to pretend nothing had happened, or at least that Kirk's outburst had not affected him, Spock squared his shoulders, slipped his hands inside the wide sleeves of his robe, and followed the admiral toward the engine room.

Uhura kept her eye on the tricorder readings as Pavel took a readout on the collector's charge for the tenth time in as many minutes. The process was taking far longer than Mr. Scott had estimated. Uhura and

Pavel had been at the reactor for nearly an hour. If their luck held for another ten minutes . . .

In the radar room of the aircraft carrier *Enterprise,* the radar operator started a routine equipment test. The image on the screen broke up. Frowning, he fiddled with the controls. He managed to get a clear screen for a moment, then lost it.

"What the hell—? Say, commander?"

The duty officer joined him. When he saw the screen, he, too, frowned. "I thought you were just running a test program."

"Aye, sir. But we're getting a power drain through the module. It's coming from somewhere in the ship."

The operator kept trying to track down the problem. The duty officer hung over his shoulder until the phone rang and he had to go answer it.

"CIC, Rogerson. . . . Yes, chief, we're tracking it here, too. What do you make of it?" When he spoke again, his voice was tight. "You sure? Check the videoscan. I need a confirm." He put his hand over the mouthpiece. "He thinks there's an intruder in one of the MMRs."

In the reactor access room, the collector's hum rose in pitch and suddenly ceased.

"Hah!" Pavel said. "Finished." He detached the machine from the wall.

Uhura opened her communicator. "Scotty, we're ready to beam out." Static replied to her message. "Scotty? Uhura here, come in please." She waited. "Come in please. Scotty, do you read?"

"Aye, lass." Static blurred the response. "I hear ye. My transporter power's down to minimum. I must bring ye in one at a time. I'll take you first. Stand by."

Pavel shoved the collector into Uhura's hands.

The beam surrounded her. Its frequency sounded wrong. The usual cool tingle felt like thousands of pinpricks. Finally she vanished.

Pavel waited patiently for the *Bounty*'s transporter to recharge and sweep him from this place. Silence, after the constant high-pitched hum of the energy collector, made him nervous. The reactor's flashing red light gave him a headache.

He started at the sudden shrill of a Klaxon alarm. People shouted between its bleats. Pavel snapped open his communicator.

"Mr. Scott," he said, "how soon will transporter be ready? Mr. Scott? Hello?"

"Chekov, can ye hear me?" Scott's voice was all but unintelligible through the static.

"Mr. Scott, now would be good time—"

The hatch clanged open. A large man leaped into the doorway, an equally large weapon held at the ready and pointing at Pavel. He entered the access chamber. Other large men, all in camouflage uniforms, came in after him.

"Freeze!" the leader shouted.

Pavel looked at him curiously. "Precisely what does this mean," he said, "freeze?"

Pavel tried to pretend he did not care about his communicator, while at the same time he tried to stay within reach of it and hoped desperately that they would not take it away to disassemble it. If he could get ten seconds with the communicator in his hands, he might still escape. But if his captors opened it improperly, it would self-destruct.

Unfortunately, the guards did not look like the type to give him the chance to grab his equipment.

He felt foolish. Not only did they have his communicator, but they had his phaser. They even had his identification, because he had neglected to leave it safely on board the *Bounty*. To make matters worse, he had worn his phaser underneath his jacket, out of reach while the guards covered him with weapons— primitive weapons, perhaps, but powerful at close range. Now he was trapped.

A uniformed interrogator asked him again who he was and who he worked for.

"I am Pavel Chekov," he said. "The rest I cannot tell you."

The interrogator swore softly under his breath. A dark-haired man in civilian dress entered the room. He wore dark spectacles that hid his eyes. The interrogator joined him.

"If the FBI knew this was going to happen," he said angrily, "why didn't you warn us?"

"We didn't know! It's a coincidence! The report came from a nut. He spies on his neighbors and anybody else he can think of and then calls my office and tries to tell me about them. It's embarrassing."

"But he knew—"

"It's a coincidence!" the FBI agent said again. "Watch." Looking disgusted, he approached Pavel. "We caught your friend," he said.

Pavel started. "But—that is impossible!"

The FBI agent turned pale under his tan. "Your black South African friend."

"She is not from south of Africa," Pavel said. "Bantu Nation is—" He stopped. "You did not catch her. You are fooling me."

"Then you weren't alone." The FBI agent looked stunned.

"Yes I was," Pavel said.

The agent left him alone with the guards.

Humiliated by having given his captors evidence of Uhura's existence, Pavel wished the interrogators would chop off his head, or shoot him, or whatever they did to prisoners in the twentieth century.

Would serve me right for stupidity, he thought. If twentieth-century people shoot me, then Admiral Kirk will not have to be concerned with me. He can rescue whales, take *Bounty* back home, and stop probe.

He imagined Starfleet's memorial service for Pavel Chekov, fallen hero who had helped save earth. Admiral Kirk delivered his eulogy. He took some comfort from his fantasy.

His communicator beeped. He snatched at it. One of the guards grabbed him and pushed him back. The interrogator and the FBI agent hurried across the room.

"Let's get rid of that thing," the interrogator said. "It might be a bomb."

"It's not a bomb," said the FBI agent, the man who had fooled him.

"How do you know?"

He shrugged. "It just isn't. It doesn't *look* like a bomb. You develop a feel for these things."

"Uh-huh. Like you develop a feel for loony informants who invent Russian agents and black South African spies."

The agent blushed. "Look, if it were a bomb, our terrorist here would either be sweating, or he'd be threatening us with it."

Pavel wished he had thought of that, but it was too late now.

"Maybe."

"Shall I prove it?" He reached for the communicator.

"No. Leave it alone. I've got somebody from demolition and somebody from electronics coming down to check it out."

"Suit yourself."

Pavel knew that somehow he had to get himself and his equipment out of there before anybody had a chance to inspect it and destroy it. Even his I.D. was causing a good bit of comment.

"Can I see that again?" The FBI agent picked up Chekov's I.D., inspected it, and glanced up again.

"Starfleet?" he said. "United Federation of Planets?"

"I am Lieutenant Commander Pavel Andrei'ich Chekov, Starfleet, United Federation of Planets," Pavel said.

"Yes," the dark-haired agent said sarcastically. "And my name is Bond. All right, commander, you want to tell us anything?"

"Like what?" Pavel said.

"Like who you really are and what you're doing here and what this stuff is." He gestured to the phaser and the communicator, lying useless on the table just out of Chekov's reach.

"My name is Pavel Andrei'ich Chekov," he said again. "I am lieutenant commander in Starfleet, United Federation of Planets. Service number 656-5827B."

The interrogator sighed. "Let's take it from the top."

"The top of what?" Pavel asked curiously.

"Name?"

"My name?"

"No," the interrogator said. The sarcasm had returned to his tone. "*My* name."

"Your name is Bond," Pavel said.

"My name is *not* Bond!"

"Then I do not know your name," Pavel said, confused.

"You play games with me, and you're through!"

"I am?" Pavel said, surprised. "May I go now?"

With a scowl of exasperation, the agent who had claimed to be named Bond, then denied it, turned his back on Pavel and joined the interrogator.

"What do you think?"

Pavel edged toward the table on which his phaser lay.

The interrogator glared poisonously at Pavel, who pretended he had never moved.

"I think he's a Russian."

"No *kidding*. He's a Russian, all right, but I think he's . . . developmentally disabled."

"We'd better call Washington."

"Washington?" the agent said. "I don't think there's any need to call Washington. I don't know how this guy got onto your boat—"

"Ship. It's a ship. And there's nothing wrong with the security on the *Enterprise.*"

"—but he's no more a spy than—"

The guards were distracted by the argument. Pavel lunged and grabbed his phaser.

"Don't move!" he shouted.

Everyone turned toward him, startled.

"Freeze!" Pavel said, hoping they would respond better to their own language.

Bond took one step forward. "Okay," he said. "Make nice and give us the raygun."

"I warn you," Pavel said. "If you don't lie on floor, I will have to stun you."

"Go ahead." The agent sounded tired. "Stun me."

"I'm very sorry, but—" He fired the phaser.

The phaser gurgled and died.

"It must be radiation . . ." Pavel murmured.

Before they could draw their primitive weapons, he grabbed his communicator and I.D., bolted for the door, flung it open, and fled.

"Sound the alarm," the agent yelled. "But don't hurt the crazy bastard."

Pavel ran. A patrol clattered after him. He dodged around a corner and kept running. Voices and footsteps closed in on him. He flung open a hatch and dogged it shut. Another hatch opened into darkness below; a ladder led upward. He swarmed up the ladder. If he could just elude them long enough to communicate with Mr. Scott, if he could just stand still long enough for the transporter to lock onto him—

Booted feet clanged on the metal rungs below and behind him. He ran again. He burst out onto the hangar deck. Ranks of sleek jets filled the cavernous space. Even if he could steal a plane, he had no experience with antique aircraft. On the other side of the deck, misty moonlight stretched in a long rectangle. He fled toward it, ducking beneath backswept wings, around awkward landing wheels.

He plunged into the open air and down the gangway. Footsteps clattered behind him; footsteps clattered ahead. He stopped short. A second patrol ran toward him from shore. He was trapped.

A streak of dark water stretched between the dock and the ship. If he could dive in and swim under the pier—

He grabbed the rail. He started to vault, then tried to stop short when he saw what lay below. His boot caught on the decking. He stumbled, bounced into the rail, tumbled over it, flung out his hands to catch himself. The phaser and communicator arced out and splashed into the sea. The wind caught his I.D. and fluttered and spun it away. His fingertips slipped on the wire cable. He cried out.

He fell.

The FBI agent shouldered his way through the shore patrol. They all stood at the edge of the gangway, looking downward, stunned.

"Oh, damn! Get an ambulance!"

The crazy Russian lay sprawled on a barge moored below the gangway. Blood pooled on the deck around his head.

He did not move.

Frightened and frustrated, Uhura hovered at Scott's elbow while he worked frantically over the transporter console.

"His communicator's gone dead," Scott said. "I canna locate him."

"You've got to find him," Uhura said.

"I know that, lass."

Minutes passed without any trace of Chekov.

"I'm going up to the bridge," Uhura said. "I'll try to—"

Admiral Kirk strode into the transporter room. "What's holding things up?" He spoke in this clipped, impatient tone only under conditions of the greatest stress.

"I ha' . . . lost Commander Chekov," Scott said.

"You've *lost* him!"

"You've got to send me back!" Uhura said. "I'll find him, and—"

"Absolutely not!" Admiral Kirk said.

"But, sir—"

"It's out of the question. If he's been taken prisoner, you'd be walking straight into the same trap. And if he's all right, he'll contact us or he'll make his way back on his own."

"I'm responsible—"

"We're all responsible, Uhura! But he voted to take the risk with the rest of us. I need you here, commander." He inspected the photon collector. "This is it?"

"Aye, sir," Scott said, still fiddling with the transporter controls.

"Then get it in place! Uhura, Scotty, I understand your concern for Chekov. But I've got to have full power in the ship, and I've got to have it soon!" He rose and put one hand on Scott's shoulder. "Scotty, I'll stay here and keep trying to reach Pavel. Go on now."

"Aye, sir." Scott picked up the photon collector. Shoulders slumped, despondent, he left the transporter room.

"Uhura," the admiral said, "you listen in on official communications. If he *was* captured, you may be able to find him that way. But I'll bet he turns up knocking on the hatch within the hour."

"I hope so, sir." Uhura hurried to the control chamber.

She set the computer to monitoring the cacophony of this world's radio transmissions. It would signal when it detected key words. She scanned the frequencies by ear, listening for a few seconds at each channel. Uhura missed the computer on the *Enterprise*. She could have asked it to relay anything unusual to her; she could have explained to it what she meant by unusual. But the computer on the *Bounty* considered everything about the Federation of Planets to be unusual. The centuries-long time jump added to the problem.

Time passed.

"Any luck?"

Uhura started. Admiral Kirk stood beside her.

"Nothing," she said. "I should never have left him."

"Uhura, you did what was necessary. You got the collector back. It wouldn't do any of us any good if you were both lost." He tried to smile. "Keep trying. You'll find him."

The admiral sank into the command chair.

At the power chamber, Scott made a minuscule adjustment of the photon collector as it transferred energy to the dilithium crystals. With Spock's help, Scott had managed to improve the cross-channeling rate. He hoped it was enough. Scott glanced through the observation window. He shook his head. He still could see no difference in the crystals, though both his instruments and Mr. Spock claimed they had begun to recrystallize. That was, by a long way, the least that he had hoped for.

The intercom came on. "Mr. Scott," Admiral Kirk said, "you promised me an estimate on the dilithium crystals."

Scott rose wearily to reply. "It's going slow, sir, verra slow. It'll be well into tomorrow."

"Not good enough, Scotty! You've got to do better!"

Now I'm expected to speed up quantum reactions, Scott thought. Perhaps I'll be wanted next to alter the value of Planck's constant. Or the speed of light itself.

"I'll try, sir. Scott out." He squatted down beside Spock again. "Well now, he's got himself in a bit of a snit, don't he."

"He is a man of deep feelings," Spock said thoughtfully.

"So what else is new?" Grimly, Scott buried himself in the cross-channeling connector.

In the control room, Jim Kirk rubbed his face with both hands. Behind him, the voices Uhura monitored buzzed and jumped. For the first time since leaving Vulcan, Jim had nothing to do. Nothing to do but wait.

And that was the hardest thing of all.

Chapter Eleven

LONG PAST MIDNIGHT, Gillian Taylor drove back toward Sausalito. She had a Springsteen tape playing on the tape deck, too loud as usual. More than twelve hours ago, she had left the Institute early to go home and stare at the ceiling. So much for that.

She would rather be with the whales. She envied the people fifteen or twenty years ago who had lived with dolphins in half-flooded houses in order to do research on human-cetacean communication. But no funding existed anymore for that sort of esoteric, Aquarian-age work. Sometimes Gillian felt like she had been born fifteen years too late.

Or maybe, she thought, three hundred years too early.

Then she laughed at herself for taking Kirk's story seriously, even for a second.

She stopped at an intersection. The red light reflected into the Rover. Springsteen was singing "Dancing in the Dark." Gillian turned it up even louder and glanced at her own reflection in the rearview mirror as he got to the line about wanting to change his clothes, his hair, his face.

Yeah, she thought. Sing it to me, Bruce.

She wished she could change herself so she could stay with the whales. She allowed herself a wild fantasy of diving into the cold Alaska water with George and Gracie, to help them adapt to their new life, never to be seen again.

No kidding, Gillian, she thought. Never to be seen again, indeed; you'd die of hypothermia in half an hour. Besides, you know less about whale society than Gracie and George do, even if they did get separated from it as calves. You know as much about them as anybody in the world. But it isn't enough.

And if Mr. Spock knew what he was talking about —which she tried to convince herself she did not believe for a minute—and humpbacks were soon to become extinct, human beings would never know much about the whales.

Her vision blurred. She angrily swiped her forearm across her eyes. The smear of tears glistened beneath the fine, sun-bleached hairs on her arm, changing from red to green with the traffic light. She put the Rover in gear and drove on.

If I could go with them, she thought. Or if I could protect them. If I could tell them, before they leave, to turn and swim away every time they hear the engine of a boat, or the propeller of a plane, or even a human voice.

That was what frightened her most. The two humpbacks had known only friendship from human beings. Unlike wild humpbacks, they might swim right up to a boat. They had no way of distinguishing between relatively benign whale-watchers and the cannon-armed harpoon ships of black market whale hunters.

And yet she felt glad that Gracie and George would experience freedom. She tried to reassure herself about their safety. Public opinion and consumer boycotts and just plain economics continued to push toward the end of all whaling. If Gracie and George could survive for a couple of years, they might be safe for the rest of their lives.

She slowed as she approached the turnoff to her house. She ought to go home. She would need to be rested in the morning if she wanted to withstand the stress of moving the whales, and dealing with the reporters that Briggs planned to let in on the story, and most of all saying good-bye.

Instead, she stayed on the main road that led to the Institute.

What the hell, Gillian thought. So I'll be tired tomorrow. I don't care what Bob Briggs thinks about my feelings for the whales. I'm going to sit on the deck by the tank and wait for sunrise. I'll talk to George and Gracie. And watch them and listen to them. I'll get the boom-box out of my office and let Willie Nelson sing "Blue Skies" to them. It will be the last time, but that's all right. Because whatever happens, they'll be free. And maybe George will sing again.

Gillian parked the Rover, entered the dark museum, and clattered up the spiral staircase to the deck around the tank. She peered into the darkness. The whales ought to be dozing. Every few minutes they would surface, blow gently, and breathe. But she could not find them.

Maybe they caught a case of nerves from me and everybody else. Maybe they don't feel like sleeping any more than I do.

"Hey, you guys!"

She did not hear the blow and huff of their breathing.

Frightened, Gillian clattered down the spiral stairs to the viewing window. Surely nothing could have happened to them. Not now. Not with their freedom in sight. She pressed her hands against the cold glass, shading her eyes to peer into the tank, afraid she might see one whale dead or injured on the floor of the tank, the other nuzzling the body in grief and confusion and trying to help.

She heard footsteps. She turned.

Bob Briggs stood in the entrance to the viewing area.

"They left last night," he said softly.

Gillian stared at him with complete incomprehension.

"We didn't want a mob scene with the press," he said. "It wouldn't have been good for them. Besides, I thought it would be easier on you this way."

"Easier on me!" She took one step toward him. "You sent them away? Without even letting me say good-bye?" Rage and grief and loss concentrated inside her.

The rage burst out and Gillian slapped Briggs as hard as she could. He staggered back.

"You son of a bitch!" she cried. She did not even wait to see if she had hurt him. "You stupid, condescending son of a bitch!" She fled.

In her car, she leaned her forehead against the steering wheel, sobbing uncontrollably. Her palm hurt. She had never punched anybody, but she wished she had struck Bob Briggs with her fist instead of her open hand.

George and Gracie were free. That was what she wanted. But she wanted them safe, too.

She raised her head. She reached the decision she had been approaching, roundabout and slowly, all night long, and she hoped she had not waited too long to make it. She started the Land Rover, threw it into gear, floored it, and peeled out of the parking lot.

Sulu hoisted the battered helicopter into the air. It flew as if it were a bumblebee and believed the old theory that bumblebees should not be able to fly. It reached the end of the harness around the acrylic sheeting.

The cable snapped tight, pitching the huey forward with a jolt and a shudder. Adrenaline rushing, Sulu fought to keep the copter in the air. Gradually, it steadied.

Sulu edged the power up and took the copter higher. The acrylic sheeting rose. A breeze, imperceptible on the ground, caught the flat of it and started it swinging. The oscillation transferred to the huey. Loaded, the copter was far more difficult to fly.

"How the hell did they ever keep these things in the air?" he muttered. He gave it a bit of forward momentum, which helped damp the swing. The sheeting turned edge on to the copter's direction. More steadily now, the huey clattered and chopped toward Golden Gate Park.

The Land Rover screeched to a stop in the parking lot by the meadow. Gillian leaped out, dodged a clump of garbage cans, and ran across the grass. Mist swirled around her, glowing silver in the dawn.

She stopped in the last place she had seen Kirk.

"Kirk!" She could hardly hear her own voice over the clattery racket of an approaching helicopter. "Kirk!" she cried in fury. "Damn you! If you're a fake—if you lied to me—!"

Gillian turned in a complete circle, searching. But Kirk did not answer. There was nothing there, no Kirk, no strange friend, no invisible spaceship. Tears of anger burned her eyes. She did not even care that Kirk had made a fool of her. He had offered her safety for the humpbacks. She had wanted to believe him, she had made herself believe him, and he had lied.

A downward blast of wind turned the tear tracks cold and whipped her hair around her face. The helicopter, closer now, hovered over a landscaped terrace. A huge pane of glass hung from its cargo harness. The copter lowered the glass slowly toward the blossoming rhododendrons. Beneath it, a man gestured instructions.

Gillian gasped.

The man hung unsupported in the air. But from the waist down, he did not even exist. It was as if he were standing within a structure that could not be seen and that could conceal him as well. An invisible structure . . ."

"Kirk!" Gillian cried. "Kirk, listen to me!"

She ran up the bank to the terrace, crashing through the shiny dark green leaves and fluorescent pink and scarlet flowers of the rhododendrons. They flicked back at her, showering her with dew.

Excited and amazed, she clambered headlong over the edge of the terrace. She ran smack into something. She fell, stunned, a metallic *clang* reverberating around her. Still dizzy, she reached out and encountered a strut, cold, hard, solid . . . and invisible. In wonder and joy, she clenched her hands around it and pulled herself to her feet.

The half-visible man above her guided the acrylic sheet, letting it descend into invisibility. He waved off the helicopter. It rose, spun, and clattered away. The propwash and the noise decreased precipitously.

"Where's Kirk?" Gillian shouted. "Kirk!" she shouted. "God, Kirk, I need you!"

The partly invisible man stared down at her, blinked, bent down, and vanished.

Gillian held the strut more tightly. Kirk won't disappear on me now, she thought. I won't let him!

She waited a moment for the invisible man to become half-visible again, but he remained hidden and she saw no sign of Kirk. She reached up, feeling for handholds, wondering if she could climb the invisible framework supporting the invisible ship.

Fluid, insubstantial, the strut dissolved from beneath her hands. Her vision blurred and a tingly, excited feeling swept over her.

The park faded away, to be replaced by a bright chamber lit by fixtures of odd, angular construction. The proportions of the room seemed strange to her, and the quality of the light, and the colors.

Not strange, Gillian thought. Alien. *Alien.*

She was standing on a small platform. The glow and hum of a beam of energy faded. In front of her, Kirk James reached up to the controls of a console built to be operated by someone much larger.

"Hello, Alice," Kirk said. "Welcome to Wonderland."

She pushed her tangled hair from her face.

"It is true," she whispered. "It's all true. Everything you said . . ."

"Yes. And I'm glad you're here. Though I'll admit, you picked a hell of a time to drop in." He took her by the elbow. "Steady now. We need your help."

"Have I flipped out?" Gillian asked. She stepped down from the platform, staring around her in amazement. A script she had never seen labeled the controls of the console, but bits of plastic hand-lettered in English were stuck beside some of them. "Is any of this real?"

"It's all real," Kirk said. He guided her around, led

her through a corridor, and took her to an echoing enclosed space. Sunlight slanted through the hatch above. The half-invisible man, whole now, secured the large sheet of transparent plastic.

"This is my engineer, Mr. Scott," Kirk said.

Scott straightened up and stretched his back. "Aye, how d'ye do." He spoke with a strong Scots burr. "'Tis finished, admiral. An hour or so for the epoxy to cure, and it'll hold slime devils, ne'er mind Dr. Taylor's critters."

"It's a tank for the whales," Kirk said to Gillian. "Good work, Scotty."

"But, Kirk—" Gillian said.

"We'll bring them up just like we brought you. It's called a transporter beam—"

"Kirk, listen to me! They're gone!"

He stared at her. "Gone?" he said.

"Briggs—my boss—sent them away last night. Without telling me. To 'protect' me, damn him! They're in Alaska by now."

"Damn." Kirk pressed his closed fist very firmly and very quietly against the transparent surface of the plastic.

"But they're tagged!" Gillian said. "I told you that. Can't we go find them?"

"At the moment," Kirk said, "we can't go anywhere."

Gillian scowled at him. "What kind of spaceship is this, anyway?"

"A spaceship with a missing man," Kirk said.

Mr. Spock entered the cargo bay. He still wore his white kimono, but he had taken off his headband. Gillian saw his ears and his eyebrows for the first time.

"Admiral, full power is restored."

"Thank you, Spock," Kirk said. "Gillian, you know Mr. Spock."

Gillian stared at him agape.

"Hello, Dr. Taylor," Mr. Spock said with perfect calm. "Welcome aboard."

A woman's voice, tense with strain, came over the intercom. "Admiral—are you there?"

Kirk answered. "Yes, Uhura. What's wrong?"

"I've found Chekov, sir. He's been injured. He's going into emergency surgery right now."

"Uhura, *where?*"

"Mercy Hospital."

"That's in the Mission District," Gillian said.

"Admiral, his condition's critical. They said . . . he isn't expected to survive."

Gillian reached out to Kirk, in sympathy with his distress. Spock, on the other hand, listened impassively to the report. Kirk squeezed Gillian's hand gratefully. Another man hurried into the cargo bay.

"You've got to let me go after him!" he exclaimed without preliminaries, without even noticing Gillian. "Don't leave him in the hands of twentieth-century medicine."

"And this, Gillian, is Dr. McCoy," Kirk said. "Bones—" He stopped and turned to Mr. Spock instead. "What do you think, Spock?"

He raised one eyebrow. Now Gillian understood why she had never met anyone like him. She had a sudden, irrational urge to laugh. She was standing face to face with a being from another planet. An alien.

Probably, she thought, an illegal alien.

"Spock?" Kirk said again.

"As the admiral requested," Spock said, "I am thinking." He continued to think. His face showed no expression. "Commander Chekov is a perfectly normal human being of earth stock. Only the most detailed autopsy imaginable might hint that he is not

214

from this time. His death here would have only the slightest possible chance of affecting the present or the future."

"You think we should find the whales, return home . . . and leave Pavel to die."

"Now just a minute!" Dr. McCoy exclaimed.

"No, admiral," Spock said. "I suggest that Dr. McCoy is correct. We must help Commander Chekov."

"Is that the logical thing to do, Spock?"

"No, admiral," Spock said. "But I believe you would call it the human thing to do."

For a moment it seemed to Gillian that a gentler expression might soften his severe and ascetic face. This was practically the first thing Gillian had heard Mr. Spock say that did not surprise her, yet Kirk looked surprised by his friend's comment. He hesitated. Spock gazed at him, cool, collected.

"Right," Kirk said abruptly. He turned to Gillian. "Will you help us?"

"Sure," she said. "But how?"

"For one thing," Dr. McCoy said, "we'll need to look like physicians."

This time Gillian paid attention to the transporter beam. The sensation of being lifted, stirred around, and placed somewhere else entirely filled her with astonishment and joy.

Maybe it's just an adrenaline reaction, she thought, but early trials suggest it as a sure cure for depression.

When she had completely solidified, darkness surrounded her. She felt her way to the wall, the door, the light switch. She flipped it.

Bingo! she thought. She had asked Mr. Scott to try to place them within a small, deserted cubicle. He had done her proud: not only had they come down in a closet, they had come down in a storage closet of linens, lab coats, and scrub suits.

"Damned Klingon transporter's even worse than ours," Dr. McCoy muttered.

"What does he mean?" Gillian said. She flipped through a stack of scrubs. Did these things have sizes, or were they one size fits all? Stolen hospital scrubs had enjoyed a minor fashion popularity when she was in graduate school, but she had never had much interest in them. Nor had she ever had a medical student boyfriend to steal one for her. All she knew was that you could wear them inside out or outside in.

"Oh—Dr. McCoy doesn't like transporter beams."

"You don't? God, I think they're great. But I meant why isn't it *your* transporter beam?"

"Our ship—and our transporter—are from the Klingon empire," Kirk said. "Not our . . . regular brand, you might say."

"How come you're flying a foreign ship?" Gillian dug through the stack of scrubs. They only came in three sizes, so she did not have to worry much about the fit.

"It's a long story. The short version is, it was the only one available, so we stole it."

"We don't even have time for short versions of stories!" Dr. McCoy snapped. "Let's find Chekov and get out of here." He reached for the doorknob.

"Wait," Gillian said. She handed McCoy the blue scrub suit. "Thought you wanted to look like a doctor."

"I thought *you* said I would, with my bag," he said grumpily. He hefted his medical kit, a leather satchel hardly different externally from the sort of bag doctors carried in the twentieth century.

"You do. But you won't get into surgery in regular clothes." She slipped the scrub on over her head.

"Dr. Gillian Taylor, Ph.D., very recent M.D.," she said.

Suddenly the doorknob turned. Instantly Gillian grabbed both Kirk and McCoy. She drew them toward her, one hand at the back of each man's neck. She kissed Kirk full on the lips. He put his arms around her. Startled, McCoy at first pulled back, then hid his face against her neck.

The door swung open. Gillian pretended to be fully involved. She did not have to pretend too hard. Kirk smelled good. His breath tickled her cheek.

"*Preverts*," a voice said cheerfully, *tsk*ed twice, and chuckled. The door closed again.

Gillian let Kirk and McCoy go.

"Um," she said. "Sorry."

McCoy cleared his throat.

"No apologies necessary," Kirk said, flustered.

A moment later, all attired in surgeons' garb, they opened the door cautiously and peered out into the corridor.

"All clear," Kirk said.

On the way out of the storage closet, Gillian snagged a handful of surgical masks in sterile paper packages.

"We'll check this way, Bones," Kirk said. "You try down there."

McCoy strode down the hallway, doing his best to pretend he knew exactly where he was going and what he was doing. He nodded to the people he passed as if he knew them. They all nodded back as if they knew him.

A frail and elderly patient lay on a gurney just outside a room full of esoteric equipment that looked, to McCoy, like medieval instruments of torture. McCoy stopped beside the gurney, hoping to get his bearings.

"Doctor . . . " the frail patient said. She had poor color and her hands trembled. A large black bruise had spread around a vein cut-down on the back of her left hand.

"What's the matter with you?" McCoy asked.

"Kidney," she said. She stared with resignation into the room beyond. "Dialysis . . ."

"*Dialysis?* What is this," McCoy said without thinking, "the dark ages?" He shook his head. To hell with not leaving traces of anachronistic technology. He took a lozenge from his bag and slipped it into the patient's mouth. "Here. Swallow one of these." He strolled away. "And call me if you have any problems," he said over his shoulder.

McCoy looked for a comm terminal—surely the twentieth century must have comm terminals?—to query about the location of surgery. Instead he saw Jim gesturing to him from down the hall. McCoy hurried to join him and Gillian.

"They're holding Chekov in a security corridor one flight up," Jim said. "His condition's still critical. Skull fracture—they're about to operate."

"Good Lord. Why don't they just bore a hole in his head and let the evil spirits out?" A gurney stood empty nearby. McCoy grabbed it. "Come on."

He pushed the gurney into a vacant room and threw back the sheet.

"Give us a couple of those masks," he said to Gillian, "and jump up here."

She handed him the masks. "Wait a minute," she said. "How come I have to be the patient and you guys get to be the doctors?"

"What?" McCoy said, baffled.

"Good lord, Gillian, what difference does it make?" Jim said.

Gillian saw that he honestly did not understand why

218

his suggestion might irritate her; and that gave her a view of his future that attracted her far more than all his descriptions of wonders and marvels. She jumped onto the gurney and covered herself with the sheet.

A moment later, McCoy and Kirk rolled the gurney onto the elevator. Gillian lay still. The two people already on the elevator, paying them not the least bit of attention, continued their discussion of a patient's course of chemotherapy and the attending side effects.

Twentieth-century technology was so close to the breakthroughs that would spare people this sort of torture, and yet this world continued to expend its resources on weapons. "Unbelievable," McCoy muttered.

Both the other elevator passengers turned toward him. "Do you have a different view, doctor?" one asked.

The elevator doors opened. McCoy scowled. "Sounds like the goddamn Spanish Inquisition," he said. He plunged out of the elevator, leaving startled silence behind him. He had to get Pavel Chekov out of here before these people did too much damage for even the twenty-third century to repair.

Jim followed, pushing the gurney.

Two police officers guarded the operating wing's double doors.

"Out of the way," McCoy said in a peremptory tone.

Neither officer moved. McCoy saw Gillian's eyelids flicker. Suddenly she began to moan.

"Sorry, doctor—" the police officer said.

Gillian moaned again.

"—we have strict orders—" The officer had to raise his voice to be heard above Gillian's groaning. He glanced down at her, distressed.

"Dammit!" McCoy said. "This patient has immediate postprandial upper abdominal distension! Do you want an acute case on your hands?"

The two officers looked at each other uncertainly.

Gillian wailed loudly.

"Orderly!" McCoy nodded curtly to Jim, who pushed the gurney between the two officers.

The doors opened. Safe on the other side, Jim blew out his breath with relief.

"What did you say she was getting?" he asked McCoy.

"Cramps," McCoy said.

Gillian sat up and threw off the sheet. "I beg your pardon!"

Jim tossed her a surgical mask. He pulled his own mask over his face and led his intrepid group into the operating room. Chekov lay unconscious on the operating table.

A young doctor looked up from examining him. He frowned. "Who are you? Dr. Adams is supposed to assist me."

"We're just—observing," McCoy said.

"Nobody said anything to me about observers."

Ignoring him, McCoy went to Chekov's side, took out his tricorder, and passed it over Chekov's still, pale form.

"What the hell do you think you're doing?" the young doctor said.

"Reading the patient's vital signs."

"It's an experimental device, doctor," Jim said quickly.

"Experimental! You're not doing any experiments on my patients—even one who's in custody!"

"Tearing of the middle meningeal artery," McCoy muttered.

"What's your degree in?" the other doctor said angrily. "Dentistry?"

"How do *you* explain slowing pulse, low respiratory rate, and coma?"

"Funduscopic examination—"

"Funduscopic examination is unrevealing in these cases!"

The young doctor gave McCoy a condescending smile. "A simple evacuation of the expanding epidural hematoma will relieve the pressure."

"My God, man!" McCoy exclaimed. "Drilling holes in his head is not the answer. The artery must be repaired, without delay, or he'll die! So put away your butcher knives and let me save the patient!"

Their antagonist glowered. "I don't know who the hell you are, but I'm going to have you removed."

He headed for the door. Jim blocked his path.

"Doctors, doctors, this is highly unprofessional—"

The doctor snarled and tried to get around him.

Jim grabbed him at the juncture of neck and shoulder, and caught him as he collapsed.

"Kirk!" Gillian said.

"That never worked before," Jim said, astonished. "And it probably never will again. Give me a hand, will you?"

Gillian helped him carry the unconscious doctor to the adjoining room. Jim closed the door and slagged the lock with his phaser. He and Gillian rejoined McCoy. McCoy had already induced tissue regeneration. He passed his tricorder over Chekov again.

"Chemotherapy!" McCoy growled. "Funduscopic examination! Medievalism!" He closed the vial of regenerator and shoved it back into his bag. Chekov took a deep, strong breath. He breathed out, moaning softly.

"Wake up, man, wake up!"

"Come on, Pavel," Jim said.

Chekov's eyelids flickered and his hands twitched.

"He's coming around, Jim," McCoy said.

"Pavel, can you hear me? Chekov! Give me your name and rank!"

"Chekov, Pavel A.," he murmured. "Rank . . . " He smiled in his dreams. "Admiral . . ."

Jim grinned.

"Don't you guys have any enlisted types?" Gillian said.

Chekov opened his eyes, sat up with Jim's help, and looked around.

"Dr. McCoy . . . ? *Zdrastvuyte!*"

"And hello to you, too, Chekov," McCoy said.

Jim drew out his communicator. He was about to call Scott and have them beamed out when McCoy elbowed him and gestured toward the slagged door. The groggy doctor appeared at the window.

"Let me out of here!" he yelled.

He could not have seen too much of McCoy's operation, and even if he had it would not have been obvious what he was doing; but beaming out in plain sight would be too much.

"Let's go." Jim helped Chekov onto the gurney, threw a surgical drape over him, and pushed the gurney through the double doors and past the two policemen.

"How's the patient?" one of them asked.

"He's going to make it!" Jim exclaimed, hurrying on without pause. Gillian and McCoy followed. As he rounded the corner, Jim began to think they would get away clean.

"He?" one of the officers said. "They went in with a she!"

"One little mistake!" Jim said with disgust. He started running, pushing the gurney before him.

A moment later the loudspeakers blared with alarms. Jim cursed. At an intersection he turned one way, saw dark uniforms through the windows of a set of doors, slid to a halt, spun the gurney around, and headed in the other direction. Gillian and McCoy dodged and followed him as he pelted down the opposite corridor. At the next set of doors he dragged the gurney to a more normal pace and pushed it through. Gillian and McCoy followed sedately.

Before them, an elderly woman sat smiling in a wheelchair. Two doctors conferred intently just behind her. As Jim passed, one said to the other, "So? How do you explain it?"

"According to the CAT scan," the other replied, "she's growing a new kidney!"

Jim glanced back. The elderly woman saw McCoy, reached out, grasped his hand, and held it.

"Doctor, thank you."

"You're welcome, ma'am."

The doors burst open behind them. Hospital security and police officers crowded the corridor. Jim plunged into a run.

"Freeze! Stop, or I'll—" The voice cut itself off. Jim trusted that nobody would be stupid enough to shoot in a hallway full of people. But then they passed into a deserted corridor. The pursuers began to close on them. Jim kept going. Gillian and McCoy ran alongside. Still confused and a little groggy, Chekov raised his head. McCoy reached out and pushed him back down. They were only twenty meters from the elevator. Its doors opened as if Jim had called to them.

Suddenly a guard stepped out of a cross-corridor

and barred their way. Jim did not even pause. Pushing the gurney like a battering ram before him he flung himself at the guard. The guard backed up fast and stumbled. Jim plunged into the elevator. Gillian and McCoy piled in after him. He slammed his hand on the "up" button and sagged back against the wall, gasping for breath. The doors closed.

The elevator rose.

"If we keep going up, they'll catch us!" Gillian said.

"Calm yourself, Dr. Taylor," Kirk said. He pulled out his communicator and opened it. "Scotty, get us out of here!"

In the corridor outside, the guard hoisted himself off the floor and grabbed at the edges of the elevator doors just as they closed. He heard the elevator cage moving away. Cursing, he kicked the doors. The indicator light flicked to the next floor. Most of hospital security and a dozen uniformed police officers clattered down the corridor.

"Come on! They're in the elevator!" He headed for the stairs and mounted them three at a time. The others followed, a few stopping at each floor to keep the fugitives from escaping. Walkie-talkies began to buzz and rasp: "They didn't get out. The elevator's still going up."

At the top floor, he raced for the elevator. It had not yet reached this floor. It rose without stopping. He drew his gun.

The elevator doors opened.

"All right—" he said. And stopped.

The elevator was empty.

Gillian reappeared on board the *Bounty*. Again the transporter gave her a feeling of exultation. Kirk and McCoy, supporting Chekov, solidified beside her. Another member of the spaceship crew, an Asian man she had not met before, joined McCoy and helped him take Chekov away. Kirk stayed with Gillian. They walked along the oddly proportioned corridor. Before Gillian realized what was happening, the corridor extended into a ramp and Kirk led her onto the terraced bank beneath the ship. The ramp rose and disappeared behind them. Gillian looked back, but nothing remained of the spaceship. It was as if it had never existed.

"Gillian, would the whales be at sea by now?"

"Yes." Gillian turned eagerly toward the spaceship. "If you've got a chart on board, I can show you."

"All I need is the radio frequency to track them."

"What are you talking about? I'm coming with you."

"You can't. Our next stop is the twenty-third century."

"What do I care? I've got nobody but those whales!"

"Maybe the whales here in the twentieth century need you, too. You can work for their preservation. Maybe they don't have to become extinct."

"And what happens then? Does that mean you won't have to come back, and I never will have met you?" She stopped, tangled in the time paradoxes. "Kirk, don't you understand? There are hundreds—thousands—of people working for the preservation of whales! If Mr. Spock is right, nothing they do makes any difference. I can't do anything more. What do you think I'd say? How about, 'I met a man in an invisible alien spaceship from the twenty-third century, and his greenish friend with the pointy ears told me whales were about to become extinct.' Do you think anybody would listen to me? They'd throw me in the loony bin and throw the key into San Francisco Bay!"

"Gillian, I'm sorry. I don't have time to argue. I

don't even have time to tell you how much you've meant to us. To me. Please. The *frequency*."

"All right. The frequency is 401 megahertz."

"Thank you." He hesitated. "For everything." He pulled out his communicator and flipped it open. "Beam me up, Scotty."

The familiar sound whined. A faint glittery haze gathered around Kirk's body. He started to disappear.

Chapter Twelve

NOT KNOWING WHAT would happen, not caring, Gillian flung herself into the beam and grabbed Kirk around the waist. She felt him dissolving in her hands.

She felt herself dissolving.

They reappeared in the transporter room.

"Surprise!" Gillian said.

Kirk glared at her. "Do you know how dangerous— no, how could you? You could have killed both of us. Never mind. Come on, you'll just have to leave again."

"Hai!" She jumped into a karate crouch, both hands raised. "You'll have to fight me to get me out of here."

He put his hands on his hips and appraised her stance. "You don't know the first thing about karate, do you?"

"Maybe not," she said, without backing down. "But you don't know the first thing about whales. I won't let you take George and Gracie and not take me!"

"Gillian, we could all die trying to get home! The whales, my officers, me . . . you."

He made her pause, but he did not change her mind. "So much for your promise to keep my whales safe," she said. "I'm staying."

He sighed, raised his hands above his shoulders, and let them fall to his sides.

"Suit yourself." He strode away.

She followed him through the amazing ship of odd color combinations, odd intersections, odd angles. Finally he reached a room full of controls and computer screens and instruments, all with the same unfamiliar proportions and unusual colors as the transporter room. Here, too, the controls had been relabeled.

Mr. Spock stood nearby.

"Mr. Spock," Kirk said, "where the hell is the power you promised me?"

"Admiral," Mr. Spock said, "you must wait one damn minute."

A Black woman glanced up from her console, saw Gillian, and smiled at her. The Asian man who had helped Chekov entered and took his place at another control console. Gillian stared around in wonder. She was in a spaceship that could travel from star to star, among a group of people who lived and worked together without being concerned about race or gender, among people from earth and a person from another planet. Gillian broke into a grin. Probably a silly grin, she thought, and she did not care.

"I'm ready, Mr. Spock," Mr. Scott said over the intercom. "Let's go find George and Gracie."

"Mr. Sulu?" Kirk said.

Mr. Sulu, the slender, good-looking Asian man, touched the controls. "I'm trying to remember how this works," he said with a smile. "I got used to a huey."

Gillian felt a hint of vibration beneath her feet. Kirk faced her, frowning.

"That was a lousy trick," he said.

"You need me," Gillian replied.

"Ready, sir," Sulu said.

"Go, Mr. Sulu."

The alien ship's vibration increased to a roar. On the viewscreen before Gillian, dust and leaves and fallen blossoms swirled in a cloud.

Javy felt awful. He should have stayed awake all night instead of tossing and turning and finally dropping off and then oversleeping. Ben had been bitching at him all day for being late to work. He did not stop griping till they reached the line of trash cans near the meadow in Golden Gate Park. At the entrance to the parking lot Ben hesitated, cursed, and lurched the truck into the lot. They both got down and started unloading the cans.

Trying to pretend it was still a regular spot, Ben started griping again.

"Jeez, Javy, we've hardly made up any time at all. We're three, four hours behind. We're not gonna get done till I don't know when—"

"I already told you thanks for covering for me," Javy said. "Look, you take off at noon like always, and I'll finish the route myself."

Ben immediately demurred, which was worse than if he had accepted Javy's offer. Javy knew Ben just wanted to be persuaded some more, so he started persuading him. But his gaze kept being drawn to the meadow, to the place where he had seen the man disappear. He replaced the last can.

"Hang on a minute, I'll be right back."

"Javy, dammit—"

Javy found nothing in the meadow, no seared spot on the ground, not even any footprints. Maybe he remembered it wrong. He walked in a spiral around the most likely place.

"Javy, if you don't hurry up—!"

An enormous roar vibrated the ground. A wind from nowhere blew downward. Crumpled paper and leaves and brilliant pink rhododendron blossoms whipped around Javy's feet. He looked up. The roar intensified and a wave of heat blasted past.

A huge birdlike shadow cut off the sunlight, moved slowly over him, accelerated across the meadow, and vanished over the trees.

The shadow had come from the direction of a terraced bank and the wind had ripped blossoms from the bushes planted there. Javy sprinted up the hill, slipping between branches of dense foliage. Ben followed, crashing through the plants and yelling at him.

He reached the terrace, pushing past wilted vegetation. The heat surrounded him with a strange pungent odor. Whatever had been here had vanished into the sky.

"Javy, dammit, I think you've gone straight around the bend—Jeez Louise."

Ben stopped at the edge of the terrace, staring. Javy looked down.

Around his feet lay a circle of scorched ground.

Immersed in time-warp calculations, Spock could spare only a minimum of attention for the operation of the *Bounty* or the sight of the receding earth. He did note that the ship's controls answered Sulu's demands with a slight hesitation. Far below, a green stripe led from the western edge of the city toward its center: Golden Gate Park, its details obscured by distance. San Francisco reached across the water with its tentacles of bridges.

"Cloaking device is stable," Chekov said. "All systems normal."

"Stabilize energy reserve," Admiral Kirk said. "Report, helm."

"Maintaining impulse climb," Sulu said. "Wing five by zero, helm steady."

"Advise reaching ten thousand. Steer three-one-zero."

"Three-one-zero, aye," Sulu replied.

"Uhura, scan for the whales: 401 megahertz."

"Scanning, sir."

"Ten thousand MSL, admiral," Mr. Sulu said.

"Wings to cruise configuration. Full impulse power."

"Aye, sir. Three-one-zero to the Bering Sea. ETA twelve minutes."

The California coast sped beneath them and vanished behind them and they soared over the open sea.

Admiral Kirk opened an intercom channel. "Scotty, are the whale tanks secure?"

"'Twould be better to give the epoxy more time to cure, but there's no help for it. Maybe 'twill hold, but I'd give my eyeteeth for a forcefield. Admiral, I've never beamed up four hundred tons before."

"*Four hundred* tons?" Kirk exclaimed.

"It ain't just the whales, it's the water."

"Oh," Kirk said. "Yes. Of course."

Spock gazed at the unfinished equations, troubled.

"Uhura," Admiral Kirk said, "any contact with the whales yet?"

Spock took note of her negative gesture as he

continued to puzzle out the formulae. The doors of the control chamber slid open. Dr. McCoy entered. He stopped beside Spock and observed him for some moments.

"You . . . er . . . " McCoy hesitated, then continued in a diplomatic tone. "You present the appearance of a man with a problem."

"Your perception is correct, doctor," Spock said. "In order to return us to the exact moment at which we left the twenty-third century, I have used our journey back through time as a referent, calculating the coefficient of elapsed time in relation to the deceleration curve."

"Naturally," McCoy said, with apparent comprehension.

Spock raised one eyebrow. Perhaps the doctor's connection with Vulcan rationality had benefited him after all.

"So . . . " McCoy said, "what *is* your problem?"

"The ship's mass has not remained constant. This will affect our acceleration."

"You're going to have to take your best shot," McCoy said.

"My best shot?"

"*Guess*, Spock. Your best guess."

Spock experienced distress at the idea. "Guessing is not in my nature," he said.

McCoy suddenly grinned. "Well, nobody's perfect."

The speakers produced a noise unfamiliar to Spock.

"That's it!" Gillian Taylor exclaimed.

The sound was more than familiar to Gillian. It was the transponder pattern assigned to Gracie.

"Affirmative," Uhura said. "Contact with the whales."

"Bearing?" Kirk said.

"Bearing three-twenty-seven, range one thousand kilometers."

"Put them on screen."

"On screen!" Gillian said. "How can you do that? It's radio!"

Uhura smiled at her. Gillian blushed. She had a lot to learn. She hoped she had a chance to learn it.

"Image translation on screen," Uhura said.

A faint image appeared and gradually gained resolution. Gillian gasped. George and Gracie swam in the open sea, breaching and playing. Kirk gave an exclamation of triumph.

"Vessyl kit," Chekov whispered.

Under the surface, they swam as eagles flew. Until now, Gillian had seen them only as falcons in hoods and jesses.

"Admiral," Uhura said, "I have a signal closing on the whales. Bearing three-twenty-eight degrees."

"On screen," Kirk said.

A blurrier image appeared. Gillian froze in disbelief.

"What kind of a ship is that?" Dr. McCoy asked.

"It's a whaling ship, doctor," Gillian whispered.

"Estimate range, whaler to whales."

"Range two kilometers, admiral," Uhura said.

"Oh my God," Gillian said, "we're too late!"

"Mr. Sulu! Full-power descent!"

The ship tilted and the acceleration increased for an instant before another force—artificial gravity?—compensated for it. Gillian barely noticed the roller-coaster effect. On the screen, the modern ship roared toward the whales, an explosive-powered harpoon gun looming on its bow. These whalers would hardly ever lose their prey.

George and Gracie had no way of knowing they should turn and flee.

"Dive speed is three hundred kilometers per minute. Five kilometers per second," Mr. Sulu said. "Estimate reaching whales in one point two minutes."

Gillian knew the routine on the whaler all too well. She had seen the films a hundred, a thousand times. The blurry image cleared to a crystalline intensity. The crew sighted their quarry and prepared their weapons. The whale boat collected itself and surged forward on powerful engines. Its deep wake cut the ocean. Gillian stared at the image as if she could communicate with the whales by will.

The image changed: wispy clouds parted before the alien ship's bow. The open ocean stretched out before it. Far ahead, George and Gracie played. The whale boat sped closer.

"Range to whales," Sulu said, "thirty seconds."

The image was so clear that Gillian could see the whalers loading the harpoon gun and preparing to fire. George and Gracie noticed the ship. They stopped playing and floated in the sea. Gillian urged them in her mind to take fright and swim away.

With a languid stroke of his flukes, George propelled himself toward the whale boat.

Laughing, the whalers aimed.

"Ten seconds, sir!"

"Hover on my mark, Mr. Sulu," Kirk said. "Mr. Chekov, stand by decloaking. Scotty, ready for power buildup." He paused. "Mark, Mr. Sulu."

The *Bounty* shot ahead of the whales and dropped between them and the whaling vessel. The harpoon gun emitted a cloud of gunpowder smoke. The harpoon moved too fast to see.

The *Bounty* reverberated with a tremendous *clang!* The spent harpoon tumbled away from the viewscreen and splashed into the ocean. Beyond it, the whale hunters stared in confusion and disbelief.

"Scotty," Kirk said. "Disengage cloaking device."

"Aye, sir."

Gillian felt a shimmery shiver around her. The walls of the ship flickered so quickly she was not sure she had really seen any change. A wash of light flashed over the whalers and they reacted in terror as Kirk's invisible spaceship became visible. The gunner jerked back from the harpoon cannon, flinging up his hands to protect his eyes. The ship lost way, pitching the gunnery crew forward against the rail, then sideways as the pilot spun the wheel and slewed the boat around so sharply that he nearly swamped it. The boat yawed, straightened, fled.

Sulu let out a whoop of triumph, and the others all cheered. Gillian tried to join them. She gasped. She had been holding her breath.

"Mr. Scott," Kirk said. Everyone in the control room fell silent, but the exultation remained. "It's up to you now. Commence buildup for transporter beam."

"I'll give it me best, sir," Scott said. He tried to conceal the concern in his voice. "'Twould be a right mess if we came all this way and got this far, only to lose Dr. Taylor's wee beasties in a weak transporter beam."

"The cloaking device has strained the power system," Spock said. "The dilithium recrystallization may have reversed."

"Mr. Chekov, put everything you can into the transporter charge."

"Aye, sir."

The lights dimmed and the sounds on the bridge faded.

"Any better, Scotty?"

"A bit, sir. I willna let this alien bucket o' bolts gi'

ou' on me now, or I'll see i' in a scrap heap. And never mind that Mr. Sulu likes to fly it."

"Mr. Scott!" Kirk said.

"Stay wi' me, sir," Scott replied. "I need a steeper power curve."

"How long, Scotty?"

"Ten seconds, admiral. Five . . ."

In the control room, as Mr. Scott's voice counted down the last seconds, Gillian clenched her fists and stared at the viewscreen as if her will could force everything to turn out all right.

"Four . . ."

In the sea below the *Bounty*, George and Gracie ceased their playing. They hovered just beneath the surface, watching, waiting, without fear.

"Three . . ."

Gillian wished she could tell the whales that the transporter beam was fun, that they would like it.

"Two . . ."

Perhaps Mr. Spock had told them it was fun. But that did not seem very much in character for Mr. Spock.

"One . . ."

The whales flickered and vanished in the glittery beam of the transporter. The surface of the ocean collapsed and a circular wave burst away as sea water rushed in to fill the space where they had been.

"Admiral," Scott whispered, "there be whales here."

The viewscreen shifted to show the two whales safely in their tank, massively beautiful, lying still in the cramped space. No one spoke. The eerie cry of a humpback's song filled the ship, the first song George had sung in more than a year. Gillian blinked hard. She looked at Jim.

Jim felt the tension in him quivering, about to

break. He wanted to leap up and shout with glee. But he sat motionless, showing no more emotion than Spock—less, perhaps, for the science officer watched the screen with one eyebrow expressively arched.

We're not home free yet, Jim thought. Not by a long shot.

"Well done, Mr. Scott," he said. "How soon can we be ready for warp-speed?"

"I'll have to reenergize."

"Don't take too long. We're sitting ducks for their radar systems. Mr. Sulu, impulse climb."

"Aye, sir."

The *Bounty*'s nose lifted toward the sky and the ship accelerated to the limit of its structural strength. Friction turned air to an ionized plasma. The bow of the ship glowed with heat.

"Unidentified aircraft," Uhura said. "40,000 MSL, range fifty kilometers, bearing zero-one-zero."

Jim swore softly to himself. It would be a fine mess if they returned home after all this, only to find that their presence here had caused the nuclear war that the twentieth century had avoided.

They blasted into the ionosphere. Uhura's instruments showed the earth aircraft still following, straining to catch them. The air grew thin enough for transition to warp speed to be only moderately dangerous, rather than suicidal.

"Mr. Scott—how soon?"

"Stand by, sir. Miracle worker at work."

"Mr. Scott, don't make jokes!" Jim snapped. "We are in danger of—"

"Full power, sir," Scott said, in a slightly chiding tone.

Jim reined in his irritation. "Mr. Sulu, if you please."

"Aye, sir."

The *Bounty* vanished into warp space.

Jim rose from his place, still keeping himself in complete control. "Mr. Sulu, take the conn. Dr. Taylor, would you like to visit your whales?"

Gillian felt shaky with excitement. She did not understand half of what had just happened, but all she really cared about for the moment was that Gracie and George were safe. And she was with them. She grinned at Kirk. He smiled. He looked exhausted and on the brink of exultation. They started for the doors, but Kirk paused at Mr. Spock's station.

"Mr. Spock, are you able to adjust for the changed variables in your time reentry program?"

"Mr. Scott cannot give me exact mass change figures, admiral," Spock said. "So I will . . . " He hesitated. Gillian thought he looked a little embarrassed. "I will make a guess."

"You?" Kirk exclaimed. He gave a quick laugh of astonishment. "Spock, that's extraordinary." He clasped Spock's hand, very briefly.

After Admiral Kirk and Dr. Taylor departed, Spock shook his head, thoroughly puzzled. Through their handshake, he had experienced Admiral Kirk's astonishment and joy. He did not believe that he understood either emotion in the abstract, and he certainly did not comprehend why the admiral should react with joy to being told their survival rested on a guess.

"I do not think he understands," Spock said.

McCoy chuckled. "No, Spock, he understands. He means he feels safer about your guesses than about most other people's facts."

Spock considered McCoy's statement for some moments. "You are saying," he said, offering a tentative conclusion for analysis, "that it is a compliment."

"It is," McCoy said. "It is indeed."

Spock squared his shoulders. "I will, of course, try to make the best guess I can."

Gillian walked with Kirk through the neck of the *Bounty* toward the cargo bay.

"Congratulations, Gillian," he said.

"Shouldn't I be saying that to you, Kirk?"

"No," he said thoughtfully. "I think I've got it right. But I've been meaning to tell you, it's my family name that's Kirk. James is my given name. Most of my friends call me Jim."

"Oh." She wondered why he had not said so before. "Gee. I've kind of got used to calling you Kirk."

"You still can, if you want to. I've kind of got used to you calling me Kirk."

Gillian stopped. The music of the humpback echoed through the *Bounty,* surrounding her with an eerie song of cries and clicks, wails and glissandos.

"If you go sailing around humpbacks, you can hear their song through the hull of your boat," Gillian said. "When you're lying at anchor, late at night, you can imagine how it must have sounded to sailors two or three thousand years ago, before anyone knew what the music was. They thought it was a siren song, calling men to their deaths."

"But this siren song may call a whole planet back to life," Jim said.

The cool salt tang of sea water filled the air. Gillian hurried ahead. She strode past Mr. Scott, who stared fascinated at the whales. Gillian placed her hands flat against the cold, transparent plastic. George and Gracie, cramped but calm in the huge tank that for them was tiny, shifted to look at Gillian. The song filled the cargo bay.

239

Jim joined Gillian beside the tank.

"Ironic," he said. "When human beings killed these creatures, they destroyed their own future."

"The beasties seem happy to see ye, doctor," Scott said to Gillian. "I hope ye like our little aquarium."

"A miracle, Mr. Scott."

Scott sighed and headed off to check the power supply. "The miracle is yet to come," he said.

"What does he mean?" Gillian asked.

"He means our chances of getting home aren't very good," Jim said. "You might have lived a longer life if you'd stayed where you belong."

"I belong here," Gillian said.

Kirk's skeptical glance made Gillian fear that he planned to try again to persuade her to remain in her own time, or even to send her back against her will.

"Listen, Kirk," she said, "suppose you pull off this miracle and get them through. Who in the twenty-third century knows anything about humpback whales?"

He looked at the whales in silence. "I concede your point."

The ship trembled around them. Gillian pressed her hand against the tank, trying to give the whales a confidence she did not entirely feel. Gracie and George flexed their massive bodies and blew bright spray into the air, no more afraid of anything in space than they were of anything in the sea.

Kirk touched Gillian's hand in an equally comforting gesture. The irregular vibration continued.

"Ye'd better get forward, admiral," Scott said. "We're having some power fall-off."

"On my way." Kirk squeezed Gillian's hand, then hurried out.

"Buckle up, lassie," Mr. Scott said. "It gets bumpy from here."

As Jim raced through the neck of the *Bounty,* the vibration increased. The Klingon ship had never been intended for such extreme gravitational stresses. A resonant frequency increased the intensity of the shudder and threatened to rip the *Bounty* apart. The control room doors opened. The ship bucked. Jim lunged for his chair, grabbed the back to steady himself, then sidled around to take his place.

On the viewscreen, the sun blazed in silent violence. The screen damped out the brightest central light, but left the corona brilliantly flaming.

Scott announced their increasing velocity. "Warp seven point five . . . seven point nine . . . Mr. Sulu, that's all I can gi' ye!"

"Shields at maximum," Chekov said.

Jim made his way to Spock's station. "Can we make breakaway speed?"

"Hardly, admiral, with such limited power. I cannot even guarantee we will escape the sun's gravity. I will attempt to compensate by altering our trajectory. This will, however, place the ship at considerable risk."

Jim essayed a smile. "A calculated one, I trust, Mr. Spock."

"No, admiral," Spock said without expression.

"Warp eight," Sulu said. "Eight point one . . . " He waited, then glanced at Jim. "Maximum speed, sir."

Spock straightened from his computer. "Admiral, I need thruster control."

"Acceleration thrusters at Spock's command," Jim said without hesitation.

Spock gazed into the sensor. Its light rippled across his face and hands. He could hear the nearly imperceptible wash of the solar wind that penetrated the *Bounty*'s shields; he could feel the beginnings of the

241

increase in temperature. The human beings would soon perceive the heat. If he made an error, they would succumb to it sooner than a Vulcan. If he made an error, he would live only a few more moments than they. The moments would not be pleasant.

The gravitational whirlpool around the sun pummeled the fragile starship. Spock gripped the console tightly to keep himself from shifting.

Spock could smell tension. He raised his head for an instant. Everyone on the bridge watched him intently.

He realized they were frightened. And he understood their fear.

"Steady," he said. He bent over the console again. "Steady."

His decision now meant the lives of all these people, his friends; and the future of all life on earth.

"Now."

Sulu blasted the thrusters on full.

Spock felt the jolt of additional acceleration. The sun's face touched the edges of the viewscreen, then filled it completely. A sunspot expanded rapidly as the *Bounty* plunged downward.

The viewscreen flickered and died, its receptors burned dead by the radiation of Sol. Spock's eyes adapted to the change in the light level. Around him, the human beings blinked and squinted, trying to see. Gravity and acceleration buffeted the ship, brutally wrenching its structure. The sun's heat and radiation penetrated the *Bounty*'s shields.

Spock recalled an earlier, similar death, heat and radiation blasting around him as he struggled to save the *Enterprise*. That time he had succeeded. This time he feared he must have failed. He glanced for an instant at each of the people in the control room, at each of his friends.

Only Leonard McCoy returned his gaze. The doctor looked at him for a long moment. Sweat glistened on his face. The ship plunged obliquely and McCoy had to snatch at the railing to keep his feet. He straightened again. He was frightened, but he showed no evidence of terror or panic.

To Spock's astonishment, he smiled.

Spock had no idea how to respond.

Abruptly, impossibly, the *Bounty*'s torture ceased. Silence gripped the starship, a silence of such intensity that even a breath would seem an intrusion.

The viewscreen remained dark and Spock's sensor readings hummed in useless monotone.

"Spock . . . " James Kirk's voice broke the hypnotic stasis. "Did braking thrusters fire?"

Spock collected himself quickly. "They did, admiral."

"Then where the hell are we?"

Spock had no answer.

In the silence, the humpback's song whispered through the ship.

The quiet threat of the probe's wail answered.

Chapter Thirteen

THE TRAVELER'S JOY overcame the distress of losing contact with the beings on this little world. The planet lay enshrouded in an impenetrable cloud. Soon the insignificant life that remained would perish from the cold.

Until then, the traveler need only wait.

Turbulence blasted through the silence. The *Bounty* trembled and shook. Only the wail of the probe seemed real and solid.

"Spock! Condition report."

"No data, admiral. Computers are nonfunctional."

"Mr. Sulu, switch to manual control."

"I have no control, sir."

"Picture, Uhura?"

"I can't, sir, there's nothing!"

Jim cursed softly. "Out of control, and blind as a bat!"

"For God's sake, Jim," McCoy said, "where are we?"

In all his years on Vulcan, on earth, and on many worlds in between, Sarek had never observed such weather.

James Kirk is coming to earth, Sarek thought. All ships have been ordered away. But instead of obeying, he will come. He has been ordered to earth. But instead of disobeying, he will come.

James Kirk was incapable of standing by while his home world died. But Sarek also knew that there was no logical way to save earth. The Klingon ship would face the probe and be destroyed. So, too, Kirk and all his companions would die.

"Analysis." Kirk's voice rose and faded in the static and the resonance. A strange cry whistled and moaned in the background. "Probe call . . . Captain Spock's opinion . . . extinct species . . . humpback whale . . . proper response . . ."

Kirk's voice and image both failed, but Sarek had already gleaned Spock's explanation of the probe's intent and desire. A bright stroke of pride touched the elder Vulcan's equanimity.

"Stabilize!" Cartwright exclaimed. "Emergency reserve!"

"Do you read me?" Kirk said clearly. His image snapped into focus, then deteriorated. "Starfleet, if you read, we are going to attempt time travel. We are computing our trajectory . . ."

"What in heaven's name?" the fleet commander said.

The power failed utterly.

"Emergency reserve!" Cartwright said again, his voice hoarse.

"There *is* no emergency reserve," the comm officer said.

The groan of tortured glass and metal cut through the scream of the wind and the pounding of rain and waves. Sarek understood what Kirk proposed to do. Somehow, in the madness of its desperation, the plan possessed an element of rationality.

"Good luck, Kirk," Sarek said. "To you, and to all who go with you."

The shoring struts on the window failed. The glass imploded. Sarek heard cries of pain and fear. Cold, sharp shards of glass spattered around him, and freezing needles of sleet and wind impaled him.

Sarek dragged himself up, trying to protect his face from wind and debris. Fleet Commander Cartwright held himself steady against the railing of the observation deck. Sarek detected a strange motion beyond the blasted window and the howling wind. Shielding his eyes as best he could, he peered out.

"Look!" he said.

Cartwright exclaimed in horror.

Sarek and Cartwright watched in disbelief as the Klingon fighter ship streaked across the sky. It plunged downward in an unpowered glide, its engines dead, held aloft only by the structure of its wings.

Kirk's plan failed, Sarek thought.

The Golden Gate Bridge lay directly in the ship's path. Sarek thought, Better to die quickly than to perish in endless cold. But another thought kept coming to his mind, with bitterness: Kirk, after all your successes, this time you have failed.

Sarek steeled himself for the explosion and the flames. The Klingon starship reached the bridge—and skimmed beneath it and safely out the other side.

246

Sarek remembered something Amanda once had said.
Something about blind luck.

Sulu gritted his teeth and clenched his hands on the
Bounty's controls. Suddenly he felt a response.
Though he did not know where they were or what lay
ahead, atmospheric turbulence buffeted the ship. It
was plunging toward a planetary surface at terminal
velocity.

"Sir—I've got some back pressure on manual!"
Sulu wrestled *Bounty*'s nose up.

"Ground cushion! Keep the nose up if you
can!"

The flight characteristics deteriorated as the ship
disintegrated beneath the force of friction, vibration,
and wind shear. He knew he had lost the ship already.
After this voyage, it would never fly. The only question to be answered was whether he could keep the
passengers—human, Vulcan, and cetacean—alive
when it crashed. The *Bounty* struggled to respond to
his commands. When the bow crept up, the aerody-
namics changed. Destructive forces increased. The
airspeed decreased, but stressed metal shrieked and
groaned. Sulu eased some power into the retro-
thrusters, but did not dare take too much from the
ground cushion. The probe wailed.

The *Bounty* hit with a tremendous, wrenching
crash. The impact flung Sulu from the console. He
staggered up, aware of his ship dying around him and
his shipmates in distress.

Then, to his astonishment, all the sounds of destruction ceased. A few interminable seconds passed
as he and the others struggled back into position and
clung there.

A second blow struck. The ship screamed in agony.
Again, the battering stopped. For another long mo-

ment Sulu could not understand how they still survived.

We came in almost flat! he thought. We came in horizontal, and we came in over the sea! Now we're skipping across the water like a stone—

He grabbed for the controls, fighting to raise the bow so the ship would skim instead of bounce. The *Bounty* crashed again. The third time, it did not regain the air. It plunged forward and down, pitching Sulu over the control console. He struck the bulkhead and fell back, stunned.

Jim Kirk flinched at the horrible high-frequency squeal of rending metal. He struggled to his feet. A wave of frigid sea water crashed through the broken bulkheads, washed past Jim, and slapped Sulu down. Gasping and coughing, Sulu tried to rise.

Jim grabbed his arm and helped him up. The deck tilted beneath them as the tail section of the *Bounty* began to sink.

"Blow the hatch!" Jim shouted.

Against the sound of the wind and the sea and the dying ship, against the omnipresent crying of the probe, the explosive bolts made a restrained thudding noise. The force flung the hatch open. Rain pounded through it. Waves beat against the *Bounty*. Torrents rushed through its stove-in sides. The water shorted systems, adding a pall of ozone-tinged smoke to the crashing rain and sea.

Jim glanced at Sulu.

"I'm all right now, sir," Sulu said. "Thanks." He looked dazed but coherent.

Jim flung his dripping hair back off his forehead. He and Sulu struggled toward the hatch against the steepening grade of the deck. Uhura and Chekov and McCoy clung to a console near Spock. Somehow, everyone on the bridge had survived. "Get topside!"

Jim shouted at Sulu. "Help the others out!" High above, clouds roiled and vibrated with the calling of the probe. Jim boosted Sulu through the hatch and turned to Spock. "Spock, you got us to the right place!" His voice nearly disappeared in the violence of the storm. "Mr. Spock, see to the safety of all hands."

"I will, admiral."

While Spock helped the others out of the dying starship, Jim struggled back to the comm. "Mr. Scott, come in. Gillian? Scotty?" He waited, but received no reply. "Damn!"

Jim waded through knee-deep water to the exit. He had to force the doors apart. They crashed open and he ran into the neck of the *Bounty*. The water deepened, slowing his headlong plunge. By the time he reached the cargo bay the water rose to his waist. Leaks sprang through the seals of the cargo bay doors. On the other side, someone fought desperately to get the doors open.

Jim grabbed the emergency release and pulled it. Nothing happened. He pulled again. For an awful moment he thought he would not budge it. If he failed, Gillian and Scotty and the whales would drown without his ever reaching them. Odd to think that two marine creatures could drown, but without air Gracie and George would perish along with the human people, only a little more slowly.

With the whole force of his body, he wrenched the release. The jolt blew it open. The doors parted as smoothly as if the ship were cruising the gentlest region of space. Water gushed through, carrying Gillian and Scotty into the corridor and sweeping Jim off his feet. He splashed up, coughing, and dragged Scott out of the current. Gillian waded against the rush of water, trying to return to the cargo bay. The doors opened to their limits, more than far enough for a person to pass. A human person. Not a whale.

"The whales?" Jim shouted.

The juncture between the *Bounty*'s neck and body ripped apart. Water sprayed in all around. Wind whistled, blowing sea foam through the openings.

"They're alive!" Gillian cried. "But they're trapped!"

"No power to the bay doors," Scott said.

"What about the explosive override?"

"'Tis underwater! There isna any way to reach it!"

"Go on ahead!" Jim shouted.

"Admiral, you'll be trapped!"

"Kirk, I won't—!"

Jim plunged between the doors and closed and secured them so Gillian could not follow. The doors muffled the sound of wind and rain, giving an eerie illusion of peace. Gillian shouted for him to open the door and Scott pounded on the metal. He ignored their pleas. Though he could hear them, though he was perfectly aware of them, they were a step removed from the reality of what he had to do.

Breathing deeply to build up his reserves of oxygen, Jim waded deeper. Water crept to his thighs, to his waist. The pressure of the sea forced spray through sprung seals above him. Luminous wall panels glowed with the eerie blue of emergency light. In the far end of the cargo bay, the water nearly reached the top of the acrylic tank. Gracie raised her flukes and slapped them down into the tank, splashing water into the flooding compartment. Soon both whales would be able to swim out. But if Jim could not open the bay doors, they would be freed into a larger coffin. He kicked off his boots, took one last deep breath, and dove.

The freezing water clamped around his chest like a jolt of electricity. He clenched his teeth to keep from gasping. He kicked himself forward, groping for the override. It ought to be—he wondered if he had lost his sense of direction in the dimness and the cold, with the screaming gibberish of the probe whipping through him. His breath burned in his lungs.

Outside the cargo bay, Gillian leaned her head against the locked doors and cried.

"Kirk, let me in," she whispered. The wind dragged her hair across her face.

"Come along, lassie," Mr. Scott shouted above the pelting of the rain. "If anyone can get your beasties free, the admiral can. Ye canna help him now." He took her arm and guided her around and led her up the steep slope toward the control room. The rain and her tears blinded her.

Fighting the instinct to breathe, Jim kicked through the deep water. He broke the surface and flung up his arm to fend off the ceiling. The sprung seals had allowed most of the air to escape. Only a hands-breadth of airspace remained between the water and the top of the cargo bay. Gasping, treading water, he tilted his head back so his nose and mouth remained in the air. He took a long, deep breath, and dove again.

The series of crashes had buckled panels and knocked the bay into wreckage. He swam through a drowned dark junkyard forest, searching through a directionless melange for a single panel. His heart pounded in counterpoint with the cruel music of the probe.

He took the risk of a pause. He hung suspended in the water and reached with all his senses to get his bearings.

Jim stroked around and swam directly to a tangle of

251

wreckage. He pushed it aside. The panel lay beneath. He dragged it open with his fingernails and yanked the override.

A pressure wave flung him against the bulkhead. The impact drove half the air from his lungs. His ears rang. Unconsciousness drew him. Another, deeper darkness opened beneath him as the cargo bay doors slowly parted.

Every instinct pulled him upward into the airless trap of the water-filled cargo hold. Instead, he dove deeper. He passed from the protection of the *Bounty* into the open sea. Following the outer hull, he kicked and pulled himself along its curve. He broke the surface, gasping. A powerful wave smacked him in the face, blinding him, filling his nose and mouth. Water burned in his throat and his lungs. He coughed and choked and finally drew breath.

Jim struggled to see over the waves and through the pounding sleet, willing the whales to fling themselves upward in a joyous leap of freedom, willing them to swim into the sea and sing their song. But he saw nothing, nothing but the ocean and the slowly sinking ship. Through the ringing in his ears he heard nothing but the storm, and the unremitting, piercing, amelodic probe.

With an intake of breath like a sob, he dove again, following the curve of the *Bounty*'s side. He passed the open cargo bay doors and gazed up into the ship's belly. He used some of his precious breath to power one inarticulate shout.

Slowly, gracefully, with perfect ease and composure, the two humpback whales glided from the ship. Joy and wonder rushed through Jim's spirit. He wished he could swim away with them to explore the mysteries that still remained in the sea.

But suddenly a current slammed the crippled *Boun-*

ty around, catching Jim and pushing him inexorably toward the angle between the cargo bay door and the hull. He swam hard, but could make no headway against the strength of the sea. His air was nearly exhausted. Cold and exertion had drained his strength.

Gracie eased through the water, balancing on her pectoral fins like a massive bird. She slid beneath Jim on the powerful stroke of her tail. Her flukes brushed past him. In desperation he grabbed and held on. The whale drew him easily from the grasp of the current and pulled him free of the ship. She glided upward, then curved her body so she barely broke the rough interface between air and water. She gathered herself, arched her back, and lifted her flukes. The vertical flip pulled Jim to the surface. Gracie sounded and disappeared.

"Kirk!"

Jim turned. A wave slapped the back of his head, but raised him high enough to see the floating control sphere of the *Bounty*. All his shipmates clung to the smooth surface. Gillian reached toward him. He floundered through the chop to the pitching solidity of the sphere. Gillian and Spock helped him clamber up its side.

Unabated, the probe continued its cry.

Jim looked for the whales, but they had vanished.

"Why don't they answer?" he shouted. "Dammit, why don't they sing?"

Gillian touched her fingertips to his. He could not tell if rain or tears streaked her face, or if the tears were of joy or despair.

Shivering violently, he pressed himself against the cold, slick metal. Sleet spat needles against his face and hands. The cargo bay had broken off and vanished, and soon, inevitably, the control sphere would sink. No one could be spared to come and rescue him and his shipmates; perhaps no one was left to do so. If he was to fail anyway, he wished the *Bounty* had perished in the fire of the sun. He preferred a quick and blazing failure to watching his friends die a slow death of cold and exposure.

A whale song whispered to him. A second song answered. Both whales, male and female, began to sing.

The sea transmitted it to the control sphere and the control sphere focused and amplified it. Jim pressed his ear, his hands, his whole body against the hull, taking the music into himself. It soared above the range of his hearing, then fell, groaning to a level that he could not hear, only feel. He looked up at Gillian. He wanted to laugh, to cry. She was doing both.

The probe's call paused. The humpbacks' song expanded into the hesitation, rising above the crashing wind and water.

Basking in the bright, unfiltered radiation of deep space, the traveler paused in the midst of turning the blue world white with snow and ice and sterility. Something was occurring that had never occurred before in the myriad of millennia of the traveler's existence. From a silent planet, a song replied.

The information spiraled inward. Even at the speed of light, seconds passed before the song reached the most central point of the traveler's intelligence. Even in the superconductive state in which that intelligence operated, it required long moments to recover from the shock of a unique event.

Tentatively, with some suspicion, it responded to the song of the beings on the world below.

Why did you remain silent for so long?

They tried to explain, but it reacted in surprise and disbelief.

Where were you? it asked.

We were not here, they replied, but now we have returned. We cannot explain, traveler, because we do not yet understand all that has happened to us.

By "us," the traveler understood them to mean themselves as individuals and all their kind for millions of years in the past. By their song it recognized them as youths.

Who are you? it asked. Where are the others? Where are the elders?

They are gone, the whales sang, with sadness. They have passed into the deep, they have vanished upon white shores. We alone survive.

Your song is simple, the traveler said, chiding. It was not above petulance. Where are the tales you have invented in all this time, and where are the stories of your families?

They are lost, replied the whale song. All lost. We must begin again. We must evolve our civilization again. We have no other answer.

The traveler hesitated. It wondered if perhaps it should sterilize the planet anyway despite the presence of the untaught singing youths. But if it began a new evolution here, the planet would be silent at least as long as it would take the traveler to circumscribe the galaxy. The traveler would have to endure the pain of the world's silence. Organic evolution required so much time. Besides, the traveler possessed very little cruelty. It could consider destroying the young singers, but the conception caused great distress. It abandoned the idea.

Very well, it said. I shall anticipate young stories. Fare thee well.

The traveler fell silent. The whales bid it farewell.

The traveler collected its energy. It ended its interference with the patterns of the blue-white planet. It ceased to power the violent storms ravaging the surface. It sought its usual course, oriented itself properly, and sailed on a tail of flame into the brilliant blackness of the galaxy.

The whale song, attenuated by distance, faded below the limits of Jim's hearing.

Only wilderness existed in this kind of utter silence. Jim recalled such moments of quiet, when he stood on a hilltop and heard the sunlight fall upon the ground, heard its heat melting the pine pitch from the trees to fill the air with a heavy pungency.

He looked up. The rain stopped. The sea calmed. The control chamber moved as gently as a soap bubble in still air. The clouds roiled, then broke, and a brilliant streak of blue cut through them. Sunlight poured onto the sea. Speechless, Jim clambered to the upper curve of the control sphere. He and his shipmates gazed at the world and at each other, in wonder.

Sarek and Cartwright lost sight of the Klingon fighter when it crashed into the sea. Sarek feared that Spock must be dead, lost. That he did not outwardly show his grief helped in no way to attenuate it. Sleet battered him.

Only when the probe's cry hesitated did he feel, against his will and judgment, a blossom of hope.

When the searing wail ended and did not return, when the sun broke through the clouds, he hurried to the edge of the shattered window and strained to see what lay on the surface of the sea.

"Mr. President!" Fleet Commander Cartwright exclaimed. "We have power!"

Reviving electronic machines chattered to each other. New light glowed in Sarek's peripheral vision. But he could spare none of it his attention. Far distant, metal caught and reflected the new sunlight.

"Look." His voice was quiet.

The council president joined him. "By God!" he exclaimed. "Do we have a working shuttle left?"

Cartwright saw what they had found on the surface of the sea.

"I'll find one," he said. "I'll find one somewhere."

The sky had almost cleared. Jim turned toward the sun, letting its heat steam the cold out of his exhausted body and his bedraggled clothes. He glanced at his shipmates with a smile.

"We look like we've been out here a week," he said.

"I want to grow a beard if I'm going to be a castaway," McCoy said. He perched precariously on the control sphere, his knees drawn up and his forearms resting on them, his hands dangling relaxed. He grinned. "Congratulations, Jim. I think you've saved the earth."

Jim glanced at Gillian, squeezed her hand, and searched the sea. Gillian nudged him and pointed.

"Not me, Bones," Jim said. "*They* did it."

In the distance, one of the humpbacks leaped. It cleared the water completely. Jim recognized which one it was, but human names meant nothing to the humpbacks anymore. The whale made a leisurely spiral in the air and landed back first and pectoral fins extended with a tremendous splash. Beside the first whale, the second humpback leaped and breached.

257

Gillian laughed. *"Vessyl kit,"* she said. "Merry whale."

A great double rainbow glowed against the sky. The inner arc began with violet and ended with red; its shadow, as intense as any ordinary rainbow, began with red and ended with violet.

"Oh, jeez," Gillian said, and burst into tears.

Epilogue

LEONARD McCOY STRODE through the gateway, across the manicured lawn, and up the steps of the Vulcan embassy. He pounded on the carved wooden door. When it did not open in a few seconds, he pounded again.

"Let me in!" He was in no mood to be polite. He had been trying to reach Spock for days. "Spock, dammit, if you won't take my calls, I'm staying on your front porch till you talk to me!" He raised his fist to hit the heavy polished wood for a third time.

The door swung open. "Proceed."

Alone except for the disembodied voice, McCoy entered the elegant old mansion. The Vulcans had changed the house very little, or they had furnished it in the style of its world and its time. Oriental carpets covered golden hardwood floors; heavy velvet-covered furniture hunkered in the rooms he passed. The voice directed him down a long hallway to a set of wide glass doors. They swung open as he approached, admitting a hot, dry breeze. He might have expected the house's atrium to contain a gazebo, a topiary, even a maze. Instead it held a sere expanse of swept sand and wind-polished granite blocks, reddened light and thin air, concentrated heat. The microclimate and the illusion of a great scarlet sun banished the morning's fog.

Spock stood in full sunlight in the center of the atrium, robed but bare-headed. McCoy started toward him without waiting for Spock to acknowledge his presence. The sand scraped beneath his boots.

"Spock!"

"Yes, Dr. McCoy," Spock said.

"Why didn't you answer my call?"

"I was helping Dr. Taylor ensure the safety and well-being and the freedom of the whales. Afterward, I found it necessary to meditate. If you had been patient—" He stopped and gazed at McCoy; he smiled very slightly. "But of course you are a doctor, not a patient."

"I—what?" He really had heard Spock say what he thought he heard him say.

"It is of no consequence, Dr. McCoy," Spock said. "Did you come to take me to task?"

"No. Why do you think I've come to take you to task? Take you to task for what?"

"For occupying myself elsewhere while you and Admiral Kirk and my other shipmates await the judgment of the tribunal."

"No. I—" McCoy realized he had not even considered berating Spock for his absence. "I understand why you didn't stay. You testified, you did all you could. It wasn't logical . . ." Groaning, he buried his face in his hands. "It's driving me crazy, Spock!" he cried. "To understand you so well. T'Lar said you were whole again. She swore she'd freed us of each other!"

"Dr. McCoy, sit down. Please."

McCoy collapsed on one of the polished granite boulders. Spock sat nearby.

"Is it so terrible," the Vulcan said, "to understand me?"

"I—" McCoy managed to smile. "It isn't something I'm used to." He rubbed his hands down the smooth, stippled sides of the sun-warmed boulder. Between him and the mansion, the deep line of his footprints began to blur and vanish. "No, Spock, the understanding isn't so terrible. It isn't terrible at all— though I'm not sure I believe I'm admitting that. But it shouldn't be happening! I feel like I'm losing myself again. Spock . . . I'm afraid."

Spock leaned toward him, elbows on knees. "Doctor, you are not alone in this experience."

McCoy rubbed his temples. The facilitation sessions horrified him. He had thought he would do anything, even conceal the madness he feared, to avoid enduring another one. Only the sensation of having another entity taking over his mind could be worse.

"It depends on the tribunal's verdict," McCoy said, staring into the sand. "The terms may not permit me the freedom to return to Vulcan. Maybe, if you aren't yet healed, if your sanity requires my presence—"

"But the facilitation sessions are complete. We need not return to Vulcan."

McCoy glanced up.

"Dr. McCoy," Spock said, "T'Lar spoke the truth. To the degree that is possible to achieve, we are free, each of the other. But we have our own true memories. We retain resonances of each other. I understand you better, too. Can you accept what has occurred? If you cannot, you will suffer. But it will be your own

261

suffering, not mine. If you can take yourself beyond your fear, you will take yourself beyond danger as well."

"Is it true?" McCoy whispered.

Spock nodded.

The Vulcan spoke of resonances: the truth of what he said resonated within McCoy.

He rose. "Thank you, Mr. Spock. You've eased my mind considerably. I'll leave you to your meditation. I have to return to Starfleet headquarters. To wait with Jim and the others."

"Spock."

Spock rose. "Yes, father."

McCoy glanced back. Sarek crossed the sand toward them. The desert garden began to obliterate his footprints.

"The tribunal has signaled its intention to deliver a verdict."

"I've got to hurry," McCoy said.

"We will accompany you," Spock said.

In a pleasant room with a wall of windows, Admiral James T. Kirk stared into San Francisco Bay and pretended a calm that he did not feel. The water glittered in the sunlight. Somewhere out there, a hundred fathoms deep, lay the battered remains of the *Bounty*. Somewhere more distant, out in the Pacific, two whales swam free. Jim was imprisoned, bound by his word of honor to stay.

I can't believe this is happening, he thought angrily. After all we've been through—I can't believe Starfleet still insists on a court-martial.

Earth was recovering from the effects of the probe. Because of the evacuation of the coasts, few lives had been lost on earth. Most of the neutralized Starfleet ships had been crippled, not killed; they had sustained few casualties. Jim was glad of that. He had seen too much death, too recently. He touched the narrow black mourning band on his cuff. His grief over David's death returned suddenly, as it often did at unexpected times, and struck him with its full force. If Carol would only speak to him, if they could offer each other both sorrow and comfort . . . but she remained on Delta, refusing his attempts to contact her. Jim looked down, blinking rapidly, forcing his vision to clear.

He tried to take comfort in the resurrection of his friend, in the survival of his home world, and in the recovery of an extinct species of sentient being. Spock had made promises to the whales. The work that would carry out those promises had kept Spock and Gillian away from the trial.

Samples of whale cells, preserved in the twentieth century, would add to the species' genetic diversity through cloning. Legends and myths to the contrary, two individuals—even three, when Gracie's calf was born—were not sufficient to reestablish any species. The whales would never again be hunted, and their freedom would never again be curtailed.

Gracie and George, youths trying to rebuild their species' civilization, seemed undaunted by the scope of the task. It would take far longer than rebuilding their minuscule population. But, according to Spock, humpbacks thought in terms of generations and centuries, not in minutes or seasons or years.

Jim smoothed the mourning band and the sleeve of his uniform jacket.

Will I still have the right to wear my uniform or my insignia after the next few hours? he wondered. He could not answer the question. He could not even be certain how he would react when the tribunal delivered its judgment.

He wondered how the others were holding up. His officers, lacking McCoy, had gathered here this morning to wait through another day. No one spoke much. Scott sat nearby, fidgeting, glowering, hating the wait. Every so often Chekov tried to make a joke, and Uhura tried to laugh.

Sulu stood alone, staring out the far window. Perhaps he was gazing at the spot where the *Bounty* had gone down. It might be the last starship he ever flew, if Jim's attempt to shield his shipmates failed. Jim rose and crossed the room to stand with Sulu.

"It was a good little ship," Jim said.

The young captain did not reply. Of all his shipmates, Jim worried most about him. Outrage lit Sulu from within.

"Captain Sulu, whatever happens, you aren't to make any foolish gestures."

"I have no idea what you're talking about, admiral," Sulu said stonily.

"A protest. An outburst, or resignation. The sacrifice of your career, to make a point. I think you do know what I mean."

Sulu faced him, his dark eyes intense. "And do you also think nobody noticed what you were doing during the testimony? Taking everything as your own responsibility? If you want to convince somebody not to make a sacrifice, you haven't got much moral ground to stand on! I'll tell you what I think. I think this court-martial stinks, and I don't intend to keep my mouth shut on the subject no matter what you order!"

Jim frowned. "Be careful how you speak to me, captain. It *was* my responsibility—"

"No, admiral, it wasn't. We all made our own choices. If you try to stand alone, if you deny our accountability for what we did, where does that leave

264

us? As mindless puppets, following blindly without any sense of our own ethics."

"Now wait one minute!" Jim started to protest, then cut himself off. He could see Sulu's point. By trying to draw all the blame to himself, Jim had, in a strange way, behaved thoughtlessly and selfishly. "No. You're right. What we did, none of us could have done alone. Captain Sulu, I won't discount the participation—or the responsibility—of my officers again."

He offered his hand. After a moment, Sulu grasped it hard.

The door opened. Everyone in the room fell silent. The chancellor appeared in the entryway.

"The council has returned," she said.

The shipmates gathered together. Jim led them from the anteroom. McCoy joined them in the corridor, hurrying, out of breath.

As Jim entered the council chamber, whispers brushed his hearing. Spectators filled the observation seats and the spaces around the walls. Gillian Taylor sat with Christine Chapel and Janice Rand, and, to Jim's surprise, with Sarek and Spock. Though grateful for their support, Jim did not acknowledge their presence. Eyes front, he strode to the center of the council chamber. His shipmates lined up beside him. On the floor, the seal of the United Federation of Planets formed an inlaid circle around them.

Behind the wide bench, the members of the council gazed down at Jim and his shipmates. Their expressions revealed no hint of their decision.

A louder murmur, a collective whisper of astonishment, rippled across the audience. Someone walked across the chamber with long, quiet strides.

Spock stopped beside Jim and came to attention like the others. He, too, wore a Starfleet uniform.

"Captain Spock," the council president said, "you do not stand accused."

"I stand with my shipmates," Spock replied. "Their fate shall be mine."

"As you wish." The president touched each of them with his intent gaze. "The charges and specifications are conspiracy; assault on Federation officers; theft of the starship *Enterprise,* Federation property; sabotage of the starship *Excelsior,* Federation property; willful destruction of the aforementioned U.S.S. *Enterprise,* Federation property; and, finally, disobeying direct orders of Commander, Starfleet. How do you plead?"

Admiral James Kirk formally repeated his plea. "On behalf of all of us, Mr. President, I am authorized to plead guilty."

"So entered. Hear now the sentence of the Federation Council." He glanced down at his papers, cleared his throat, and looked up again. "Mitigating circumstances impel the tribunal to dismiss all charges except one."

The spectators reacted. A glance from the president quieted them.

"I direct the final charge, disobeying the orders of a superior officer, at Admiral Kirk alone." He gazed at Jim, his expression somber. "I am sure the admiral will recognize the necessity of discipline in any chain of command."

"I do, sir," Kirk replied. It was too late to argue about self-reliance and initiative.

"James T. Kirk, it is the verdict of this tribunal that you are guilty of the charge against you."

Jim stared ahead, stony-faced, but inside he flinched.

"Furthermore, it is the judgment of this tribunal that you be reduced in rank. You are relieved of the rank, duties, and privileges of flag officer. The tribunal decrees that Captain James T. Kirk return to the duties for which he has repeatedly demonstrated unswerving ability: the command of a starship."

The reaction of the crowd washed over him. Jim forced himself not to react. But a shout of astonishment and relief, a shout of pure happiness, trembled beside his heart.

"Silence!" the president exclaimed. Slowly, the audience obeyed. "Captain Kirk, your new command awaits you. You and your officers have saved this planet from its own shortsightedness, and we are forever in your debt."

"Bravo!"

Jim recognized Gillian's voice, but a hundred other voices drowned her out. In another moment he was surrounded by well-wishers, acquaintances, strangers, all wanting to congratulate him, to shake his hand. He complied, but he hardly heard or saw them. He was searching for his shipmates. He saw McCoy, reached out, grabbed him, and drew him into a bear hug. McCoy returned it, then grasped Jim by the shoulders and looked him straight in the eye.

"You can always appeal, you know," he said.

Jim stared at him for a moment, speechless, his fear for the doctor renewed. And then he noticed the smile McCoy tried to hide. Jim started to laugh. McCoy gave up trying to keep a straight face. He laughed, too—finally, after too long, back to his old self.

They eased their way between spectators till they reached Chekov and Scott and Uhura, hugging each other and shaking hands. Sulu stood nearby, perhaps more stunned by a positive verdict than by the negative one for which he had prepared himself.

"Congratulations, Admi—I mean, Captain Kirk," he said.

"The congratulations are for all of us, Captain Sulu," Jim said. He wanted to tell him something more, but the onlookers pushed between them.

In San Francisco, in the twentieth century, Javy and Ben climbed down the terraced bank and headed for their dieseling truck. Despite everything, the rest of their day's work remained.

"I'm really sorry, Javy," Ben said. "I should of believed you right off. Maybe if I had we would of seen what made that burn."

"I saw it," Javy said. "I saw its shadow, anyway."

"But, I mean, we would of seen it and we would of been able to show it to other people. To a reporter, maybe, and they'd write us up in a book and maybe we'd get on Johnny Carson." He brightened. "Maybe if we show them the burned place—"

"Maybe if we show them the burned place, they'll arrest us for arson. Or they'll write us up as a couple of nut cases," Javy said. "And maybe they'd be right. We don't have any proof. A burned place and a shadow."

"I'm really sorry," Ben said again, downcast.

"Don't be, Ben, it's okay, honest."

"I'd be mad, if I were you."

"Maybe I ought to be," Javy said. "Except . . ." He hesitated, not sure he wanted to say it out loud before he was certain it was true.

"What?"

What the hell. Telling Ben the story had always worked before. Javy grinned. "I figured out how to end my novel," he said.

The FBI agent put all the reports together and looked at them and wished the lights were brighter so he could put on his sunglasses.

I might as well be named Bond, he thought. No-body outside a spy novel would believe this stuff. My boss sure won't, and my partner will say I've been talking to Gamma too much.

"*I* don't even believe it," he muttered. "I don't even believe the parts I saw with my own eyes." The radar reports from San Francisco and Nome did nothing to improve his mood.

Maybe the report will get lost when it's filed, he thought. Stuff sometimes does. Before anybody has a chance to read it. With any luck . . .

But he trusted Murphy's Law more than he trusted luck. He decided to file the report himself.

He picked it up, took it to the proper place, and filed it.

In the circular file.

Finally the crowd in the Federation Council chamber dispersed. Jim felt wrung out. He glanced around, looking for an escape, and found himself face to face with Gillian Taylor.

"My own exonerated Kirk!" she exclaimed. "I'm so juiced, I can't tell you!" She gave him a quick kiss. "I have to hurry. So long, Kirk. And thanks." She headed for the arched exit.

"Hey!" Jim cried. "Where are you going?"

"You're going to your ship, I'm going to mine. Science vessel, bound for Mer to recruit some divers to help the whales. Why, the next time you see me, I may have learned to breathe underwater!" She grinned, honestly and completely happy for the first time since Jim had met her. "I've got three hundred years of catchup learning to do," she said.

Though glad for her happiness, he could not help feeling disappointment as well.

"You mean this is—good-bye?" he said.

"Why does it have to be good-bye?" she asked, mystified.

"I . . . as they say in your century, I don't even have your phone number. How will I find you?"

"Don't worry," she said. "I'll find you." She raised her hand in farewell. "See you 'round the galaxy!" She strode away.

Just farewell, Jim told himself. Not good-bye. He shook his head fondly as she vanished through the wide, arched doorway of the council hall.

In a secluded corner, Spock waited for the last spectators to disperse. He wished to leave, but he did not want to go anywhere on this planet. Spock knew now—he had learned again, or he had remembered; it did not matter which—that he had never felt at home on earth or on Vulcan, or indeed on any planet. He felt at home in space.

Sarek, tall and dignified, his face expressionless, approached him.

"Father," Spock said.

"I will take passage to Vulcan within the hour," Sarek said. "I wanted to take my leave of you."

"It is kind of you to make this effort."

"It is not an effort. You are my son." He stopped abruptly, controlling his instant's lapse. "Besides," he said, "I wished to tell you that I am most impressed with your performance in this crisis."

"Most kind, father," Spock said, and again Sarek had no suitable response for the charge of kindness.

"I opposed your enlistment in Starfleet," Sarek said. "It is possible that my judgment was incorrect."

Spock raised his eyebrow. He could not recall his father's ever having confessed to an error before, or, indeed, ever having committed an error.

"Your associates are people of good character," Sarek said.

"They are my friends," Spock said.

"Yes," Sarek said. "Yes, of course." He spoke in a tone of acceptance and the beginnings of understanding. "Spock, do you have any message for your mother?"

Spock considered. "Yes," he said. "Please tell her . . . I feel fine."

Spock took his leave of his bemused father and crossed the council chamber to join James Kirk and his other shipmates.

"Are you coming with us, Mr. Spock?" the captain asked.

"Of course, captain," Spock said. "Did you believe otherwise?"

"I haven't been quite sure what to believe, the last few days."

"Sarek offered you a compliment," Spock said.

"Oh, really? What might that be?"

"He said you were of good character."

Kirk stopped, nonplussed, then recovered himself.

"Sarek is getting effusive in his retirement," Kirk said. "I wonder what I did after all these years to make him come to that conclusion?"

Spock felt astonished that Captain Kirk did not understand. "Captain—Jim—!" he said in protest. Then he noted James Kirk's smile. Solemnly he replied, "I am sure that I do not know."

Jim Kirk began to laugh.

Inside Spacedock, a shuttlecraft dove through the great cavern of a docking bay. The *Enterprise* shipmates searched among ships and tenders and repair scows, curious to discover their destination.

They passed the *Saratoga,* being towed in for inspection. Its captain—Alexander, isn't it? Jim thought—had saved her officers and crew in stasis before the life-support systems gave out entirely.

"The bureaucratic mentality is the only constant in the universe," McCoy said. "We're gonna get a freighter."

Jim remained silent, but he tightened his hand around the envelope of thick, textured paper that he carried. The envelope held written orders, not a computer memory chip, and by that alone Jim knew that the orders were something very special. But he was forbidden to break the holographic epoxy of the Starfleet seal until he had accepted his new command and taken it beyond the solar system.

He turned the envelope over and over, then pulled his attention back to the conversation.

"—I'm counting on *Excelsior,*" Sulu was saying to McCoy.

"*Excelsior!*" Scott exclaimed. "Why in God's name would you want that bucket of bolts?"

Before Sulu could retort and the two men could embark on one of their interminable arguments about the merits of *Excelsior,* Jim cut in.

"Scotty, don't be judgmental. A ship is a ship." At the same time he had to wonder how Sulu would handle being subordinate to James Kirk on a ship that should have been Sulu's own.

It appeared that they were indeed heading for *Excelsior.* The massive ship filled the wide shuttlecraft windows. Scott watched it apprehensively.

"Whatever you say, sir," he said, resigned. Under his breath he added, "Thy will be done."

To Jim's surprise the shuttlecraft sped past *Excelsior.*

Jim blinked. In the next slip, a constellation-class

starship echoed the lines of his own *Enterprise*. And this time the shuttlecraft did not duck around it. On the saucer section of the ship, Jim made out the name and the registration number.

U.S.S. *Enterprise*. NCC 1701-A.

A suited-up space tech put the finishing touches on the "A," turned, saw the shuttlecraft, waved jauntily, and powered away on travel jets.

Everyone in the shuttlecraft gazed in wonder at the ship. Spock, silent, stood at Jim's right and McCoy, chuckling, at his left. Scotty leaned forward with his nose practically pressed against the port. Sulu and Chekov clapped each other on the shoulder, and Uhura smiled her quiet smile.

"My friends," Jim said softly, "we've come home."

When he took his place on the bridge of the *Enterprise,* Jim Kirk gripped the sealed envelope so tightly he crumpled it. "Clear all moorings. Reverse thrust."

Jim unclenched his hands, still trying to keep them from trembling with excitement. He settled into the difference of the ship, and the sameness.

"Rotate and hold."

Below, Scotty would be mother-henning the engines. Sulu and Chekov held their places at navigation and helm. Uhura conferred with Spacedock control, and Spock bent over his computer console.

The *Enterprise* spun slowly and hovered as Spacedock's doors slid open.

McCoy lounged easily against the arm of the captain's chair.

"Well, captain?" he said. "Are we just going to sit here?"

Deep space stretched out before them.

"Thrusters ahead one-quarter," Captain Kirk said.

"Course, captain?" Chekov said.

Beside Jim, McCoy grinned. "Thataway, Mr. Chekov," the doctor said.

Spock glanced up from the science station. "That is, I trust, a technical term."

The impulse engines pressed them beyond Spacedock.

Jim wanted to laugh with joy. "Let's see what she's got, Mr. Sulu." He rubbed his fingertips across the glimmering Starfleet seal. "Warp-speed."

"Aye, sir!"

The *Enterprise* plunged into the radiant spectrum of warp space, heading toward strange new worlds, new life, and new civilizations.

THE EXPLOSIVE NEW
STAR TREK:®
HARDCOVER
PROBE
by
Margaret Wander Bonanno

Pocket Books Hardcovers is proud to present PROBE, an epic length novel that continues the story of the movie STAR TREK IV.

PROBE reveals the secrets behind the mysterious probe that almost destroyed Earth—and whose reappearance now sends Captain Kirk, Mr. Spock, and their shipmates hurtling into unparalleled danger...and unsurpassed discovery.

The Romulan Praetor is dead, and with his passing, the Empire he ruled is in chaos. Now on a small planet in the heart of the Neutral Zone, representatives of the United Federation of Planets and the Empire have gathered to discuss initiating an era of true peace. But the talks are disrupted by a sudden defection—and as accusations of betrayal and treachery swirl around the conference table, news of the probe's reappearance in Romulan space arrives. And the *Enterprise* crew find themselves headed for a final confrontation with not only the probe—but the Romulan Empire.

Now Available In Hardcover
from Pocket Books

POCKET
BOOKS

106-01

THE STAR TREK PHENOMENON

ABODE OF LIFE
70596/$4.50

BATTLESTATIONS!
70183/$4.50

BLACK FIRE
70548/$4.50

BLOODTHIRST
70876/$4.50

CORONA
70798/$4.50

CHAIN OF ATTACK
66658/$4.95

THE COVENANT OF
THE CROWN
70078/$4.50

CRISIS ON CENTAURUS
70799/$4.50

CRY OF THE ONLIES
740789/$4.95

DEEP DOMAIN
70549/$4.50

DEMONS
70877/$4.50

DOCTOR'S ORDERS
66189/$4.50

DOUBLE, DOUBLE
66130/$3.95

DREADNOUGHT
72567/$4.50

DREAMS OF THE RAVEN
70281/$4.50

DWELLERS IN THE
CRUCIBLE
74147/$4.95

ENEMY UNSEEN
68403/$4.50

ENTERPRISE
73032/$4.95

ENTROPY EFFECT
72416/$4.50

FINAL FRONTIER
69655/$4.95

THE FINAL NEXUS
74148/$4.95

THE FINAL REFLECTION
70764/$4.50

A FLAG FULL OF STARS
64398/$4.95

HOME IS THE HUNTER
66662/$4.50

HOW MUCH FOR JUST
THE PLANET?
72214/$4.50

IDIC EPIDEMIC
70768/$4.50

ISHMAEL
73587/$4.50

KILLING TIME
70597/$4.50

KLINGON GAMBIT
70767/$4.50

THE KOBAYASHI MARU
65817/$4.50

LOST YEARS
70795/$4.95

MEMORY PRIME
70550/$4.50

MINDSHADOW
70420/$4.50

MUTINY ON
THE ENTERPRISE
70800/$4.50

MY ENEMY, MY ALLY
70421/$4.50

PAWNS AND SYMBOLS
66497/$3.95

PROMETHEUS DESIGN
72366/$4.50

RENEGADE
65814/$4.95

ROMULAN WAY
70169/$4.50

RULES OF ENGAGEMENT
66129/$4.50

SHADOW LORD
73746/$4.95

SPOCK'S WORLD
66773/$4.95

more on next page...

THE
STAR TREK
PHENOMENON

Follow the adventures of the Starship *Enterprise* by beaming aboard Paramount Pictures' Official *STAR TREK* Fan Club. When you join, you receive a one year subscription to the full-color Official *STAR TREK* Fan Club Magazine filled with exclusive interviews, articles, and photos on both the original *STAR TREK* and *STAR TREK: THE NEXT GENERATION.* Plus special columns on *STAR TREK* collecting, novels and special events as well as a convention listing and readers' comments. Members also receive with each issue our special merchandise insert filled with all the latest *STAR TREK* memorabilia.

Join now and receive an exclusive membership kit including an 8 x 10 full-color photo, embroidered jacket patch, membership card and more!

Don't miss out on another issue of The Official *STAR TREK* Fan Club Magazine. Join now! It's the logical thing to do.

Membership for one year — $9.95-US, $12.00-Canada, $21.95-Foreign for one year (US dollars only!)

Send check, money order or MasterCard/Visa order to:

STAR TREK: THE OFFICIAL FAN CLUB
P.O. Box 111000
Aurora, Colorado 80011 USA